'We are dazzled by the nightmare-like luxuriance of Mr O'Neill's imagination'   *New York Times*

'It belongs to the ancient school of fiction which includes *The Pilgrim's Progress* and *The Water Babies* . . . A piece of compelling imagination'   *Harper's Bazaar*

'Superlatively exciting'   Sir Compton Mackenzie

'*Land Under England* is historically significant, eminently readable and belongs in any reasonably complete collection'
                                                    Science Fiction and Fantasy Review

'Attains the heights of literary excellence'   *Publishers Weekly*

SF MASTERWORKS

Land Under England

JOSEPH O'NEILL

This edition first published in Great Britain in 2018 by Gollancz
an imprint of the Orion Publishing Group Ltd
Carmelite House, 50 Victoria Embankment
London EC4Y 0DZ

An Hachette UK Company

The authorised representative in the EEA is Hachette Ireland,
8 Castlecourt Centre, Dublin 15, D15 XTP3, Ireland (email: info@hbgi.ie)

5 7 9 10 8 6

A CIP catalogue record for this book is
available from the British Library.

ISBN 978 1 473 22406 3

Printed and bound by Clays Ltd , Elcograf S.p.A.

www.gollancz.co.uk
www.sfgateway.com

CONTENTS

There are literal underground spaces and there are metaphorical underground spaces. World literature is full of stories about the latter masquerading as stories about the former. The attentive reader needs to be clear about the difference.

Returning to the earliest stories of fantastical underground worlds takes us back to ancient Rome – something particularly relevant to Joseph O'Neill's *Land Under England* (1935), as we'll see. At the heart of Vergil's *Aeneid* – the central epic of Latin literature, the greatest expression of imperial Roman self-identity – is a lengthy episode in which Aeneas descends into the underworld through the cave-mouth at the lake of Avernus, near Cumae. He passes through a nightmarish landscape of torture and punishment of evil-doers before coming into the bright-lit pastures of Elysium where the virtuous dwell in bliss. Here he meets his own father and hears a prophesy of the coming greatness of Rome, the city he himself is destined to found.

This sixth book of the *Aeneid* is one of the most influential works in all classical literature. Dante and Milton drew on it to portray their own epic subterranean underworlds, and it fed through into popular imagination. This is where we derive our notion that Hell is somehow underground (it's not in the Bible, for instance). Serious theological enquiry about the interior of our world fed into more fanciful hollow-earth theories, and from the eighteenth-century onwards there developed a lively sub-genre of subterranean fantasy, often comic or satiric in aim. These sorts of stories enjoyed remarkable success, from Holberg's *Journey of Niels Klim* (1741), through Jules Verne's *Journey to the Centre of the Earth* (1864), Wells's Morlocks in *The Time Machine* (1895) and Edgar Rice Burroughs's *At the Earth's Core* (1914) into a whole spread of twentieth-century science fiction and fantasy. *Land Under England* must be understood as part of this longstanding tradition, although one of the distinctive things about O'Neill's novel is the way it returns, as it were, to the source – the prototype of the subterranean fantasy as such. The *Aeneid*.

The father of O'Neill's protagonist, Anthony Julian, is obsessed with Ancient Rome, convinced he himself is descended from Julius Caesar and given to exploring by the ruins of Hadrian's Wall. When he disappears Anthony believes he has passed through a portal into an under-realm, and when he eventually follows his old man under the earth he discovers a cavernous realm under England – a *terra sub Anglia* – where Rome still thrives. It is, though, an oppressive, twisted version of the imperium, a place where telepathy has bound most of the population into a single hive-mind enslaved to certain 'Masters of Knowledge'. There is no such thing as individuality. Every citizen dedicates his or her whole life to the good of the state, and even after death their bodies are used as fuel in the empire's blast furnaces.

Anthony finds his portal to this strange world below in Cumbria not Cumae, at the Julian, rather than the Avernan, pond; but O'Neill is playing a fairly obvious intertextual game in this novel, and for a purpose. Aeneas descends into the underworld to locate his father, just as O'Neill's Anthony does. Like the Roman hero, Anthony passes through a nightmarish place of precipitous cliffs and waterfalls, of strange vegetation and predatory monsters, before finally arriving at Roma Nova, new Rome. This, though, is where O'Neill's novel swerves. Aeneas is happily reunited with his *pater* and sees the glory that his ancestors are fated to inherit. Anthony looks in vain for his father for most of the novel, exploring a totalitarian state where citizens are so intimately controlled, telepathically, that they have been reduced to the level of automata.

The country is a deep valley that lies between mountains which support the roof of the land on all sides. In the middle of the valley the Central Sea runs along its whole length, until at this end of the valley it narrows into a great river that flows under the mountains behind the city. This Central Sea is salt water, and the main source of their food, since in it live most of the creatures from which they get meat and fish, and almost most of the edible plants.

This, clearly, an underground version of the Mediterranean, a body of water which the Romans called, significantly for this novel, 'the internal sea' (*mare internum*) – but rotated through ninety-degrees, so that (like Britain above it) it runs south-north rather than west-east.

O'Neill's New Romans are similarly twisted around a satirical axis. As O'Neill was writing Mussolini's fascists were bolstering their totalitarian control of Italy with reference to the glories of Rome's past, and Hitler's Nazis had recently seized power in Germany. Fascism drew heavily on the history and iconography of the Roman empire. The movement's very name derives from the *fasces*, bundles of sticks tied together around an axe blade that were symbols of Roman judicial authority. The idea is simple: one stick is easy to snap, but the bundle is too strong to break. If the 1930s teach us nothing else it is how easily this common sense apprehension – we are stronger together than alone – can be perverted into totalitarian dictatorship and oppression.

This, at any rate, is the satirical force of O'Neill's fantasy.

What began for the first settlers of these underground spaces as a means of defence against 'the deep fear of the darkness and the forces of destruction and death that they dreaded in the darkness' has calcified over time into a nightmarish elimination of individuality as such. The novel's portrait of its twisted neo-Roman underworld is also O'Neill's diagnosis of how civilisations like Italy and Germany can fall under the sway of figures like Mussolini and Hitler. 'The driving force behind it,' Anthony tells us, 'was the throb of dread, the mass-hysteria of the race, that kept welling up through the everpresent darkness.' Nor is he entirely immune to its appeal: the society he discovers, even in its tyranny and annihilation of self, calls 'to the dread and the hysteria that lay deep in the abysses of my subconscious mind,' he confesses, 'urging, compelling me to come into this shelter they had built, away from the storms and agonies of individuality'.

There are actual subterranean spaces in the world; and *Land Under England* does a vividly memorable job of evoking its gloomy, dimly phosphorescent milieu whilst staying, just, on the side of believability. But the underground in this novel is metaphorical rather than literal. What do they mean, then, these subterranean spaces illuminated by flickering sheets of uncertain ionization? These dream-haunting swamps thronged by predatory giant toads and spiders the size of bears, lit by the glow of giant phosphorescent mushrooms? They are the Id of conscious political life: the dark and monstrous subconscious of ideological authoritarianism. O'Neill's is a novel that understands that European civilisation itself is built over the abyss, an abyss that threatens once again to rise up and reclaim it. It would be nice to say, three-quarters of a century after *Land Under England* was first published, that his warning has lost relevance. But it seems to me, re-reading this darkly compelling, claustrophobic novel, that it is more relevant now than ever.

CHAPTER ONE

My Father

THE STORY that I have to tell is a strange one—so strange indeed that many people may not believe it, and the fact that the events related in it happened in Great Britain itself will, probably, make it less credible than if it had happened in Central Africa or the wilds of Tibet or the lands round the sources of the Amazon, now so much favoured by travellers. Perhaps it is better that it should be so, since if people realised the truth of my story some men would certainly be tempted to try to discover the roads by which my father and I went, and, if they did find the road, would either meet the fate that my father met and that I escaped by mere chance, or bring upon us a conflict of which the results would be incalculable.

The beginning of the story and its ending have little connection except the most superficial one. It begins as a family legend that is mostly a fairy-tale, but the results of this romantic beginning had little of romance in them for me at least. What they held for my father I shall never fully discover.

We are the Julians of Julian's Pond. We might indeed be described as the Julians of the Roman Wall, for Julian's Pond is only a section of the fosse of that great rampart, and, though we are now an unknown and almost extinct family, we belong to an ancient order of things, of which the Wall and its Ponds are the most evident remnants left on the surface of Britain to-day. Our name and our family traditions point back to a Roman origin. These were the sources from which the dreams

9

of my father came, and the disaster that came to him from his dreams.

If our family had been able to hold their lands, it is probable that my father would not have fed so much on his fancies, but before the end of the nineteenth century we had lost all our landed property, and the family was so scattered that, when the twentieth century began, my father was the only Julian left in the northern country.

As my mother often pointed out to him, there was no real reason for his remaining there either, for he had been forced to sell everything except the house, and the house also might have been sold, with advantage to our purses, since it was much too big and too expensive for us.

The fact that my mother kept pointing out this obvious fact to my father, and that her suggestions were, from his point of view, so irrelevant as not to be worth discussing, will give some idea of the atmosphere of my home life. Not that it was an atmosphere of discord. There was not even sufficient contact between my father and mother to produce discord. He looked upon her as a kind, gentle woman who had no understanding, and could not have any understanding, of the big matters with which he was concerned, and he would have no more thought of talking to her about them than he would have thought of discussing them with his dog.

Their marriage had been one of those love marriages that bring two people together in a sudden glamorous fusion, and then, if their natures and interests are incompatible, finish up in a swift or slow falling asunder.

When she was a girl of nineteen or twenty, my mother must have been very beautiful, for, as a woman, she was most attractive to look at. She was certainly lovely, when I first remember her, with her broad face with the cat-like curves and the deep-blue eyes, set very widely apart, and the delicate, fair skin and auburn hair.

It was a face full of gentleness, and, though a superficial glance might discover little subtlety in it, it was full of a charming delicacy and sweetness that most people found very attractive—all, indeed, except those who looked chiefly for explicit intelligence in a face. Later on, I discovered that her expression concealed a depth of feeling that gave her far more wisdom than mere intelligence can ever give.

Even in the beginning I found her very attractive, but her influence on my life from the earliest days was overshadowed by that of my father, who was of a type that could hardly fail to dominate the imagination of most boys. To begin with, his appearance was most striking in a romantic sort of way. He was over six feet in height, and had a very handsome, rather aquiline face, with eyes of a brown that was almost black, and curly black hair that fell crisply over a fine forehead with very delicate modelling. When his eyes were dreamy, they were full of soft depths, and when he was in one of his merry humours, which was often, they sparkled and glanced with a most delightful malice that made him extraordinarily good company.

It was no wonder that my mother fell in love with him. Women found him at all times most attractive, and, for the matter of that, so did men. If he had been a social man, he would certainly never have lacked company, and it would probably have been better for him and for all of us, in the end, if he had been so, even though social life would have depleted still more our slender resources. If he had been constantly surrounded by people, he could not have fed so much on his dreams.

If, again, my mother had been as obviously powerful and deep in her emotion during their life together as she showed herself after his disappearance, she would probably have been able to exercise some restraining influence over him, but as long as he was with her she never did herself justice and she had no influence over him, though he always treated her with the utmost courtesy and even tenderness, in so far as his nature allowed him to occupy himself with the details of outer attitudes towards people. That was not a very great deal, for, like many attractive men, he was incapable of thinking of others.

The fundamental interest in the man's life was in fact his dream, and it was this obsession and not an ordinary selfishness that made him act afterwards in such a way as to wreck our family life, without considering what the effect of his acts would be on my mother and myself.

Indeed, if he had been an ordinarily vain and selfish man, we might have been saved much suffering, since he would have occupied himself with slighter matters. He belonged rather to the category of artists and scientists and other dreamers whose life is shaped by the urge of their dreams, and who cannot allow the lives of others to interfere with their course.

If he had had to work for his living, his dreams could not have occupied so great a part of his waking life, but the money that he had got from the sale of the last portion of the Julian lands was just enough, when invested, to allow us to live in decency, and so he was able to spend his time reading and re-reading the classical writers, and doing what he called archæological work along the Roman Wall, to the great worry of my mother and the disgust of our neighbours, who found society scanty enough in that lonely region and could ill afford to do without a man who could be such delightful company.

I shared none of these feelings of the community about his actions. I was an only child, and I was the sharer of his dreams. He was my hero, and, during my early days, I must have been one of the happiest as well as one of the most learned of children—in so far as knowledge of the classics can be considered learning. Latin was a second native language for me; archery, javelin-throwing, and other ancient exercises were my pastime, and, as for archæology, there is hardly a foot of the Roman Wall, of all its seventy odd miles, from Wallsend to Bowness, that I have not worked over with my father, examining the Vallum and the Murus, the dyke and the ditches, and the military stations.

The George Inn at Chollerford is a delightful centre for such wanderings, and so are Burgh, with its clay houses, "the largest village in Cumberland," where Edward I died, and Bruff, where the 6th Legion put up its altar in memory "of things prosperously performed along the Wall." This was the part of the Wall that I loved most, but, indeed, all things connected with the Wall were almost equally delightful to me: the duck-ponds that are the remnants of the Wall-ditch; the altar "dedicated by the hunters of Barra to the holy god Silvanus"; the names of the Roman quarrymen cut in a rock to amuse an idle moment — "Securus" and "Justus" and "Mathrianus"; the goose-flocks that made friends with us, after they had thought over us for a while; the sound of the "beetles" of the farmers' wives on washing-days; the "out-by" farms with their lovely names—"Back-o'-Beyond" and "Hope Alone" and "Seldom-Seen"; the lonely goats that came along to us for company, when we sat down near them, and with little cries tried to prevent us leaving them; the rabbits that scudded away first, showing their white scuts and then stopping suddenly to look back at us; the Nine Nicks of Thirlwall; the Roman water-mill on the Haltwhistle Burn.

In some places the Wall is ten feet high and ten feet thick, and in these spots we would camp for days, as at Cilurnum, which is called Chesters to-day, for my father always held that, somewhere in the still existing chambers of the forts he would find secret passages to the world below.

To the ordinary traveller, I daresay, there would seem to be little evidence of that past world in those remote landscapes of beauty or desolation, but for me they were populous with legionaries and centurions, and consuls and emperors.

Carvoran and Caw Gap and Birdoswald were lovely for themselves, but, when my father began to talk in the evenings, they passed from sight, and in their place I saw Magna and Aesica and Amboglanna populous with their legions. Their names were a fair litany: at Amboglanna the 1st Cohort of the Dacians, "Hadrian's Own"; at Vindolanda the 4th Cohort of the Gauls; at Procolitra the 1st Cohort of the Batavians; at Cilurnum the 2nd Ala of the Asturians; and so on through all the famous names of great legions.

In this way I also passed through the doors by which my father escaped from an upper world of dreary twentieth-century realities into kingdoms that were lit by the suns of other days, but not darkened by their clouds.

It was all a very idyllic and romantic setting for the beginning of an adventure as ghastly as any man has gone through—an adventure so profound and so deadly that it has left a mark on my life that can never be effaced.

However, the Great War, which was not at all a romantic matter, intervened between those early days of which I am speaking and the convulsion that swept aside my father's individual life and nearly shattered mine, and I may as well take events in their order.

I remember the time on the precipitous ground between Dewingshields and Thirlwall when our antiquarian work of those early days came abruptly to an end.

We were eating our lunch, perched on a crag under a hot August sun, when John Codling, a farmer who knew us well, appeared below us, shouting and waving a newspaper. We got off our perch and went down to find out what was the matter. The matter was that Germany had invaded Belgium, and the papers said that England must defend Belgium and France against the Teutonic attack on Latin civilisation.

I shall never forget the look on my father's face. It was the look of a man who wakens from a dream to find that it is a reality. There he stood, like his forbears 1,500 years before, listening to the cry that penetrated up to the Roman Wall for help for Gaul against the tribes beyond the Rhine.

A week afterwards he had answered the call and joined up, to save, as he thought, the remnant of Roman civilisation from the onrush of the barbarians.

I will not trouble the reader with the details of my life during the years when my father was away at the war. While he was in training in the south of England, my mother and I stayed with relations of hers outside London so as to be near him, and when, after eight months, he left for the front, my mother volunteered as a nurse and sent me to a boarding-school in Brighton.

I cannot say that the years at school had much effect on my life, except in so far as it was a better thing for me, at that stage of my life, to have had to live with boys of my own age than with a dreaming father in a twilight life mixed of past and present.

The work was easy for me, since my knowledge of classics was far beyond that of any of the masters. I was pretty fluent at French, which my father had made me learn owing to its connection with Latin, and I was so advanced in history and literature that I could spend all my study hours at mathematics and science, for both of which I unexpectedly showed an aptitude far above the average.

For the rest, I cannot remember that I learned anything at that school, except some valuable information as to the hard edges of present-day facts and the need to turn aside frequently from pleasant imaginings in order to come to terms with realities. I learned this somewhat painfully, during the first years, at the hands of the bigger boys. At the time the experience made my life rather miserable, but I am naturally a sturdy type of creature, and, looking back now on that period, I can see that the impact of tough realities was necessary as an antidote to the dream-life that I had lived before the war. It certainly did me no harm to have to face the world of living people during my most impressionable years.

The vacations I spent in part with my mother's people, and here my keenness for the sciences got a practical turn, for they were manufacturers of motors and munitions, and my connection with them had important results in my life at a later stage.

During all the war years I never saw my father, for he had been sent to the East in 1915, and later, when he was on his way home on furlough, the Italian front gave way and he asked to be transferred to the British force that was rushed to restore it. The news that came from him, and about him, was, however, very satisfactory, for not only was he not seriously wounded at any time, but he showed such a combination of zeal and capacity that he went from rank to rank rapidly. He had joined up as a private, but he was a colonel when the war ended. My mother's people, the Sacketts, who had never thought much of him, changed their opinion as the war went on, and began to express a hope that, when he came back, he would give up his idle dreaming. They even spoke of getting him to come into the munitions business.

My mother was full of the same hope, and, when she spoke to me about it, I had no great difficulty in agreeing with her, since my science work at the school and my vacations at the Sacketts' had wakened in me a new interest in practical work that had largely displaced the old romantic dreams about the Wall and its legions. At the same time my father had remained my hero—a hero now who had proved his worth on the most terrible battlefields of history, and, unlike the others, I felt that whatever he chose to do would be the right thing, which I would accept gladly if only I could get him back into my life.

CHAPTER TWO

He Hears the Julian Call

I SHALL not easily forget the first time I met my father after the war. It was on Dover Quay, when he disembarked from the boat. I was looking round for him when I saw my mother dart away from me towards a tall harsh-faced soldier who was standing on the quay looking round him with a cold detached look. My mother threw her arms round him. It was my father. I came up to them timidly. I was watching him embracing my mother, and it struck me that he was going through it automatically, as a man does whose mind is far away. When I came up to him, he stared at me. "You have grown a good deal, Anthony," he said, with a cold stare, and gave me his hand. I pressed it, but there was no answering pressure. I felt a rush of tears coming to my eyes, and turned away. Through the mist that seemed to envelop me, I heard my mother's voice explaining to my father that she had found a lovely house in Hove, and they were holding it for her until he could come to see it. Then his voice came back chill and insensitive: "You needn't hold it any longer. I am going back to live at Julian's Pond."

That evening when I went back to school I knew that everything was changed. The father I had known and the life I had known were gone, and there was something very different in their place.

A few months afterwards my father was demobbed and, when the school term ended, I went back to the Pond House.

During my father's stay in the south, my mother and I had gone to see him twice, but I had made as little contact with him during these two visits as when I met him at Dover, and I could see that, whatever little contact my mother had had with him before the war, it was completely broken. He had become a stranger.

It may be thought that this change in my father's manner and attitude to us was a natural result of his war experience, which would wear off, at least partly, in the course of time. My mother tried to console herself with this explanation in the beginning, and, in my desolation over the loss that I was suffering, I was only too glad to grasp at it too.

On my way home at the end of term I was buoying myself up with this hope and imagining that the life in the old familiar surroundings and the sight of the Wall would bring back the father that I knew.

If I expected the change to have begun already, and I believe that I did expect this, I soon discovered my mistake. My father was not at the station to meet me, and the first sight of my mother's face showed me that things were unchanged.

That summer vacation of 1919 at Julian's Pond stands out, even now, very clearly in my memory, in spite of all the experiences that have intervened between this and then, for over it all the figure of my father seems to hang like a menacing cloud.

In the old days one of the most charming things about him had been his swift transitions from one mood to another—from a state of romantic dream to outbursts of mocking brilliance or fantastic humorous laughter, and then perhaps to fascinating talk about history or literature. Above all things, there was his gift of laughter. When he was in one of his merry moods he would laugh at me, at my mother, at everybody and everything in the most attractive way, and his fantastic humour was all the more enjoyable for that touch of charming malice that gave it spice and flavour. Now he never laughed, and rarely talked. If we tried to talk to him about any subject but one, he answered abstractedly. That subject was not the war, but the Wall and the chances of finding a descent through it to a world below. Even about this he did not want to speak to my mother, and, when I tried to get into touch with him through it, he showed little desire to talk much about it with me. Whatever he did say, however, was real, not mere abstract answering, such as he was apt to give us if we talked about other matters.

Most of his time he spent alone, either on the Wall or poring over our family records, and the attempts of outsiders to draw him out about his war experience, or, indeed, to get into touch with him in any way, were received with such frigid indifference that we soon found ourselves isolated in a way we had never been before.

After some time, rumours began to be put about that my father's war experience had unhinged his mind.

Whether there was any truth in this or not, it is certain that, whereas his old fantastic humour and joyous mirth had vanished, his fantastic romance had not only remained, but had engulfed everything else, so that the visions that before the war had merely lured him away a good deal from the world of men now began to take a shape that, though it was bred out of a dream, seemed likely, unless it was checked, to prove as stern a reality to us as the war itself.

In order to make clear the danger that now threatened us, it is necessary to mention that amongst the family documents there were some very curious ones that purported to give accounts of the adventures of Julians who had gone down through the Pond or the Roman Wall to an underground world peopled by a kindred race.

There was, for instance, a circumstantial story of a Julian who had gone down in the reign of Edward II and had come back, after a year, with extraordinary tales. If he had gone, he had certainly returned, for he was killed at the Battle of Bannockburn.

There was another Julian who was supposed to have gone down in the reign of Henry VIII, and who fought at Flodden afterwards and died at home some months after the battle from wounds received there. He also had left a curious, and, indeed, incredible, account of his adventures in the underworld.

Then there was Anthony Julian, who disappeared in 1765 and returned the following year with still stranger tales about a world of curious lights and strange darkness, and a people that he could not communicate with who tried to make him a slave.

According to the family records, indeed, it seemed to be almost a custom of the Julian race from generation to generation to send adventurers into the underworld, just as other families sent them to the Crusade or, in later centuries, to Africa or America. With the exception of the three men mentioned above, however, the Julians who took that road did not come back, and when, after the Napoleonic wars, Lucius Julian went down and did not return, there were no more descents recorded.

One reason may have been that the old map, showing the part of the Wall that held the door of descent, had disappeared, and with it the detailed descriptions of the land given by the three Julians who had been supposed to have made the journey and returned from it. Lucius Julian was said to have taken these documents with him, and the loss of them would have lessened the chances of other Julians being able to follow him.

The more probable cause of the loss of interest in the old romance was, however, the fact that, during the nineteenth century, the fortunes of the Julians were crashing, and they had much more serious matters to occupy them than dreams of descents into underground lands.

Although, however, all detailed plans and accounts of descents had been lost in the scattering of the family, there was sufficient matter left to feed the mind of a dreamer, and this was the stuff that my father's mind was now brooding over intensely.

Mostly these "records" were obviously romances that could not be accepted as having any relation to fact, but there were some of them that had a more convincing ring and there was in particular one rhyme, written in ancient and only half intelligible words, that seemed to have come from a real experience. It went something this way when translated into modern speech:

> *He that hears the Julian call*
> *He shall pass beneath the Wall.*
> *When the Pond makes dry its bed*
> *He shall count amongst the dead,*
> *If he can find the rocking-stone*
> *And stand its Eastward end upon.*
> *And if he reach the Fungus Lands,*
> *And if he pass the Spider Bands,*
> *And if he 'scape the Serpent Doom*
> *He then may find the Lords of Rome.*
> *But if he find, he'll long in vain*
> *To feel the sun and hear the rain*
> *And see green grass in fields again*
> *Since Julian's Pond is Julian's bane.*

However, to come back to my father. This was, as I have said, the stuff his mind was now feeding on, and, whatever the neighbours might think of his mental condition, neither my mother nor I had any doubt as to what would be the upshot of it. My father would discover the way of descent, and, when he had found it, he would follow the same road, that so many Julians had followed, to whatever fate awaited him below.

It may seem strange that my mother and I believed sufficiently in the existence of such a descent to cause us to worry
seriously about him. But the fact was that we did both believe
it, although she would not have acknowledged her belief.

The dreadful thing was that there was no way out of our
trouble. No one looking into my father's eyes now could have
any hope of deflecting him from the purpose that made them
burn so fiercely.

Even if my mother were the type of woman who would
normally have an influence over him, it is certain that she
could not have done anything at that stage, and neither could
anybody else, short of physical seizure and detention, which
would not have been feasible without a doctor's certificate of
mental disorder. The idea of getting this never occurred to us,
for, whatever the neighbours might say, it was quite clear to
both of us that, though the man was in the grip of a terrible
obsession, he had grounds for his imaginings that even we
could not deny. Since both my mother and I believed in the
stories of those other Julians who had gone down below, we
could no more ascribe insanity to my father than we could
ascribe it to explorers who look for the North or South Poles
or try to gain the summits of Everest or Kangchenjunga.

It was not that either my mother or I was superstitious or
credulous. I was certainly neither one nor the other, and she
was, for all her gentleness, as hard-headed and courageous as
any daughter of the industrial Midlands, but, before we were
back at the Pond House for a month, she knew as well as I
did that calamity was hanging over us.

She had always had an instinctive horror of the Wall, as of
something uncanny and unclean and inexplicable. It and the
Pond had been from the beginning a hateful part of the family
into which she had married—a part that she could not assimilate, and that, even before the war, displaced her and put her
aside—but now they began to loom up as something monstrous

that filled the horizon and drew darkness from the very brilliance of the sun.

That was the dreadful part of it—that the brighter and hotter the sun grew, the closer came darkness to our home, for, as the heat mounted up, the Pond shrank, and all the legends told that it was when the Pond emptied that the secret trapdoor in the Wall stood revealed. As the heat grew and the Pond sank lower, my father's obsession waxed steadily greater.

At any other time my mother would have made an attempt to get him to go to the seaside for the month of August—as we had frequently done when the weather was hot—but she made no effort now. It was perfectly obvious that he would not listen to any suggestion, and she made none. She seemed, indeed, to fold her hands and resign herself fatalistically to the coming fate. That it was not far off, she knew, for my father now lived only for the Pond and the Wall.

The Pond sank lower and lower. Towards the end of the month it had already got so low that he camped by its banks at night to keep watch over it. More ominous still, he refused to allow me to stay out with him, and he showed signs of resentment if I came near the Pond during the day, as if he objected to my keeping a watch over him.

In the olden days a man of the Julians had always kept watch over the Pond, and on its northern bank, between it and the Wall, there was still an ancient-looking little house—the guard-house of the watchers of the Pond. Here old Josiah Carshaw lived, the last survivor of the Julian retainers, and, though he was said to be over eighty years of age, I believed that he would keep a watch on my father's doings and let us know if anything was happening.

Such was the position of things on the evening of my nineteenth birthday—the evening on which the drought broke. For three days my father had not come near the house—the first time that he had ever failed to celebrate my birthday, except during the war years.

As evening fell, we were standing silently looking out through the window that faced in the direction of the Pond, but not daring to go towards it, when the gate clanged and I saw the Rector coming up the path to the house. He was not the sort of man who would be likely to come for an afternoon call without some pressing reason, and I knew at once that he had some news about my father. My mother knew it also, for, after a glance at his face as he came into the drawing-room, she sent me off to the study. I had no choice but to go, though, when I got to the study, I couldn't even make a pretence of opening a book.

I kept walking uneasily round the room, opening the door into the dining-room and shutting it, opening the door into the east-room and peering in, in the hope of seeing some sign of the return of my father, as this was the room in which we kept our family documents.

At last the study-room door opened. It was only Anne, the maid, but her face showed me that she was the bearer of bad news.

"Yah poor faitherless bairn," she said, looking at me with eyes full of pity.

"What—what is it, Anne?" I cried. "Is he gone?"

"Ize never wunder but he's waur nor deid," she said slowly. "Josiah see'd t' Pond empty two neets agone—but, when t' call cum for Julian, Julian mun go——"

"Who told you that?" I cried.

"Meenister be telling missus all aboot it—an' I put an ear t' key-hold an' heerd it all—and he sed it's fair flaysome she let maister go on that gait, but he be a strainger, he doan't unnerstan'—when Julian be called Julian mun go."

I didn't wait to hear any more, but rushed out of the house and along the road that led northward to the Wall. "He's

waur nor deid! Waur nor deid!" The words kept burning
my ears. I had no idea as to what had happened, but I
felt that I must get to the Pond and the Wall as quickly as
I could.

The Pond lay almost due north under the Great Wall. It
was two miles, or thereabouts, to it, but a by-road ran almost
up to it from our house, and was, indeed, the nearest way to
it. I covered the distance with such speed that I reached a
point of the road that gave me a view of the Pond in less than
a quarter of an hour.

I hardly know what I expected, but there was nothing
unusual to be seen. The Pond looked much the same as ever,
except that its waters were low. Anne was wrong. It had not
emptied yet.

"A hundherd year, Maisther Tony, sin' it emptied afore,"
said a voice behind me.

I turned. Old Josiah had hobbled out of his hut and come
up behind me.

"A hundherd year," he repeated. "Me faither niver sit eyes
on it, tho' he lived four score and nine year—on the Pond—
and I niver seed it, till now—but ma grandfather seed it—the
day Maister Lucius wint—hundherd years agone."

"But what did you see, Josiah?" I interrupted.

"T' bottom o' t' Pond—I seed it—t' bottom stone—last
nicht afore thunner—t' bottom o' t' Pond."

"But did you see my father?" I cried.

"Tha faither? Naw—he wad na be theer. I seed t' bottom o'
t' Pond—ah tell ee—t' call have come——"

"But," I cried, "the Pond isn't empty——"

"Last nicht it war empty afore t' thunner—half t' nicht—
Pond were bare to t' bone—crackin' with t' drouth—then t'
thunner came an' t' wather cum back with a rush."

"But did you see my father?" I asked.

"Tha faither? Naw, I didn't see tha faither—but he be

gone—baint he? T' Pond have emptied, an' Squire be gone——"

"Then you don't really know anything about his being gone?" said my mother's voice.

I turned round. She had come up behind us unnoticed, and was looking at the old man with hard eyes. He looked back steadily at her under his bushy brows.

"I know t' call be cum," he said sturdily. "When Julian calls Julian mun go."

"But you haven't seen the Squire since you came to the house last Saturday?" she said.

"Naw," he admitted. "I haven't seen t' Squire."

"And this is the rubbish the Vicar builds his information on, and comes to me with," she said to me. "This poor old man's dodderings about the Pond being empty."

"They baint no dotherins," said Josiah angrily. "I seed t' bottom o' t' Pond—as sure as I see you ditherin' there afore me—and Squire seed it—he be gone. When t' call cum, Julian mun go—and I wud hev yah to look out, ma'am, an' not draw t' wrath o' t' Pond—if ye do, I'm mista'an if ye don't do it long," and with that he turned and hobbled back, with dignity, to the house.

I put my arm through my mother's, and tried to lead her home. She resisted, and began to walk towards the Wall. It was the first time for many years that she had taken that direction.

We walked in silence, arm in arm. We knew each other's minds, and each knew that the other was clear that my father was gone. He had found the trapdoor and had gone down into the darkness.

When we reached the Wall the dusk was falling.

There was a worn flight of steps leading from the path up the Wall and we mounted this. Then we stood staring, in the dusk, silently along the Wall.

It was no use looking for the trapdoor in the gathering darkness. If there was one, perhaps it was in the Pond. Perhaps it was in another part of the Wall. We had not come here to look for it. We had come here to bid goodbye to my father—to attend his funeral.

CHAPTER THREE

The World Below

WHOEVER wishes to see the Roman Wall along its course from sea to sea, should see it in the month of May, when the cuckoo is crying over the barren heights, on which the Wall still stands most completely, and over the softer lowlands where men have destroyed its traces.

Carrowburg of the Batavian Cohort, and Rudchester of the Frisians, and Halton Chesters and Walwick Chesters of the Savinians and the Asturians, and Carvoran and Birdoswald of the Dalmatians: they are all at their greatest beauty in May when the Wall ditch is carpeted with primroses and marsh marigolds.

There apple-blossom and the lilac and laburnum linger long after they have disappeared from the more southerly lands. On the higher lands the whistling song of the curlew is always with you, and the air is full of the scent of almonds from the gorse. Yet it was in all the glory of a May of ravishing colour and brightness that I turned my back on the world of sunlight and went down into the darkness.

On that May day, when I accidentally discovered the secret of the Wall, my father had already been gone for seven years. I had left school the year after his disappearance, and, instead of going up to Oxford, as I probably would have done if my father had been with us, I went into the motor business with John Sackett.

Everybody thought that, when I took up work there, my

mother would come down to the Midlands to be near me and her relations. She did not do so, however, nor did she do any of the other things that were expected of her.

If the neighbours had thought that she would supply them with a series of dramatic sensations and scenes after my father's death, they must have been grievously disappointed, for she acted in all respects as he would have wished her to act.

Indeed, from the day of his disappearance, she seemed to have regained the concord and contact with him that she had not had since the first years of their marriage.

Not only did she refuse to discuss his disappearance or to authorise any of the attempts at a search that were planned by well-meaning or curious people, but she gave up all thought of leaving Julian's Pond, in spite of the urgent desire of her brothers that she should turn her back forever on a house and a countryside whose associations were nearly all of anxiety and trouble.

Nor did she stay near the Wall in order to search for traces of my father. She went to the Wall often now, but it was not to search for the trapdoor. It was to keep in touch with him.

Often of an evening, when the sun was setting, I have found her there, with her hands folded on her lap, looking along the Wall, as it ran away to the west, or staring down at the Pond in the gathering dusk. We never mentioned him, but, when I put my arm through hers and led her home, I often felt a soft pressure that told me that she knew my thoughts.

I was not able to accept the situation as calmly as my mother did. As long as the sensation caused by my father's disappearance drew the attention of people to us and to the Wall, I avoided all appearance of looking for him; but, when it died down, I spent all my spare time, vacations, and week-ends looking for the trapdoor, and trying to discover, from our records, where it was likely to be.

I discovered nothing. The records that remained gave no

information; during all those years the Wall kept its secret, and the only result of my searches was that the Sacketts began to press my mother very strongly to come to live with them, not merely because they disliked the idea of her living alone near the scene of her trouble during the week-days when I was down with them, but also because they wanted to get me away from the Wall. I know that they urged the latter reason most strongly on my mother, but they had as little effect on her as they would have had on my father. In this, as in other things, it was indeed remarkable how she took up his outlook and made it her own, as if it was her only sure way of keeping in touch with him.

To their arguments that it was most desirable that I should break all connection with the Wall, she answered that neither she nor my father had any desire that I should do so.

It is probable that what happened was that the disappearance of the real man enabled her to reconstruct in her mind the image that she had fashioned of my father in the early days of her life with him, and that she was now living with a dream-lover and trying to carry out his wishes as far as she could divine them.

As far as my safety was concerned, she was not only under the influence of her dreams, but she was too sure of her own beliefs, too secure in her faith and trust in God, to think it necessary to divorce me from the place where I had been born and that was now consecrated for her in all her memories. This at least is my reading of her stubborn refusal to leave the neighbourhood of the Wall, and her ignoring of the possibility that I too would discover the trapdoor and go to look for my father in the world that had swallowed him up.

When my mother's family had failed to move her, they tried to work on me to get her to leave Julian's Pond, and, when I refused to do that, they tried by every method they could think of to keep me away from the North Country. One of their plans for doing this was trying to arrange a marriage for me with Hilda Meadowes, a wealthy girl of their own set, who was keen on my company.

They might as well have tried to marry her to one of their machines. My working-life was given to them and their interests, but my real life was lived apart from them—in the same world in which my mother lived hers. Like her, I had been most profoundly moved by my father's disappearance, and, as in her case, my dream-life was lived in the atmosphere of the Wall. It had been the source of my earliest and dearest associations with my father, and, now that it had deprived me of him, it had given me in his place an obsession that possessed my mind as strongly as it had possessed his, and, indeed, justified itself as a continuance of my life with him. There was, in my case, the additional incentive that I could not settle down to live the normal life of humanity without making a final effort to find him, as well as solve the mystery of the world that had taken him from me.

Therefore I spent all my spare time searching the Wall for its secret, as he had done.

The countryside thought that I was mad, and prophesied for me the same tragic fate that had befallen my father. The Sacketts agreed, although they acknowledged that I was not mad in any other respect, since, in their works, I had proved to be not merely a competent scientific worker and a good business man, but an inventor. I had in fact transformed the motor business of John Sackett into a thoroughly progressive concern, and even in the munitions work of Edward Sackett, in which I took less interest, I had introduced not merely improvements, but some new inventions of my own that had greatly impressed both the brothers.

I was, indeed, well on the way to making my fortune as well as greatly increasing their income, and they could not understand how, when the week-ends came, particularly in summer,

I turned my back on all their hopes and dreams and went back to the Wall.

The truth was that, while I had sufficient of their breed in me to make me share their interest in industry and finance, I was fundamentally a man of an entirely different type. At bottom, I, like my father, am a romantic dreamer, to whom external things matter comparatively little, and my imagination was not concerned with their life and projects, but deeply engrossed with the problem of my father's fate and the discovery of the secret path by which he had disappeared from my world.

Whether the entrance to the world of my dreams lay through the floor of the Pond, or through a secret passage under the Wall, or both, was the question that I was determined to solve.

There was one time when I toyed with the idea of having the Pond drained, but I finally rejected it, as I could not have it done privately, and, if once the story got abroad, it would immediately draw on us the glare of publicity that had disgusted me at the time of my father's disappearance. Besides, owing to the wording of the legends, I did not believe that the trapdoor was in the Pond. I was certainly determined to be present, if by any chance it ran dry, partly in order to examine its bottom thoroughly, but more because the legends seemed to indicate that the emptying of the Pond in some way freed or revealed a trapdoor in the Wall. Meantime I spent my time searching every inch of the Wall and the ground near it, and the fosse.

It was during one of these searches that I suddenly discovered the trapdoor in the floor of the Wall; and like many another discovery that is eagerly sought, this one came by accident more than through the actual search.

It was, as I have said, a most colourful May. The weather was at its brightest and the North Country along the Wall was beautiful, as only it can be in the first days of summer.

I had come up to the Wall on that Saturday as heavily equipped with food and camping outfit as the most austere hiker, and suddenly I found myself on the strangest road that ever a hiker has followed.

I will not say in what section I discovered the trapdoor lest others may be tempted to search for the road I entered on so unexpectedly. The time was the late afternoon. Away below me the country stretched for miles in all the quiet summer beauty of our English landscape: the scattered homesteads; the little fields; the winding streamlets; the joy and happiness and cosiness of rural England on a summer's day.

I stood on a flagstone beside the Wall, looking at it with delight. Then suddenly I was falling through darkness. My body struck a soft heap of something, my eyes and mouth were choked with dust, and I was rolling, sliding, rushing down a steep slope in a heap of moving sand or dust. I made frantic efforts to grasp something. My struggles only increased the movement of the sliding mass. I realised this, and let myself go with it, keeping my eyes and mouth tightly closed. I remember thinking in a flash that I had searched the Wall, troubled it, intruded on it, and now it had seized me. Then I felt something more solid under the dust that was carrying me along. The avalanche was slowing down, settling.

My lungs were bursting. I could stand it no longer. I was being smothered—drowned. I made a great effort, and sat up through the heap of dust that was on top of me. My head came clear. I drew a deep breath, and struggled to rise.

I was up to my breast in a heap of something like ashes, but I could see nothing. I was in complete darkness. I felt for my kit. It was intact. I groped for my electric torch, got it and flashed it round. I was standing up to my waist in a heap of ashes on a rocky floor that showed from under the ashes some distance farther down. Behind me the slope, down which the avalanche had carried me, ran up into the darkness out of my sight. I could not see the underpart of the ground above me, through which I had fallen. It was too far up to be visible.

I could see no roof or sides to the space in which I was standing, nothing but the ash-heap that surrounded me, and the flat rock floor beyond it. I moved down towards the clear space.

I could see nothing in front of me but empty space, into which the floor sloped very gradually downward. Where I was standing there was a slight cover of ashes, but a little farther down the rock floor stood out clearly.

I went forward slowly, listening for any sound or sign of movement. There was none. When I reached the clear rock, I stooped down and examined it. It was a fairly smooth floor, and I had a feeling that its smoothness was due to the work of men. Then, as I went forward, I realised with a start that this was certainly the case. On the rock on my right-hand side there were figures carved in the stone. I went over and examined them. They were the forms of three women, one of whom had a torch in her hand, another a pitcher, and a third something else that I could not make out, but that looked like a loaf of bread. They were drawn in attitudes of flight, and behind them was a blurred mass of something that looked like men in pursuit.

The direction towards which the women were flying was the downward slope. I followed in this direction, and, after a few feet, came upon a square raised stone with some sort of carving on it. I flashed the torch over it. The top of the stone had a large six-cornered star cut in it, and under this the lettering DIBVS VITERIBVS—soldiers' Latin, "To the old Gods." It was obviously an altar made by somebody who, in despair, had given up the Christian faith. I walked round it. The far side was also carved. On top there was the word DEO, with a wreath round it, and under it a carving of a man holding a bull by the horns.

As I moved nearer, to get a better look at it, my foot struck something. I looked down, and saw a little boat-shaped vessel. I took it up. It seemed to be of bronze. I looked round me, almost expecting to see the men who made the altar coming towards me. There was nothing, however, to be seen, except the walls and floors of solid rock. The stillness was unbroken. I was in a state of extreme excitement, but at the same time cool and collected.

It might be imagined that it would now have occurred to me to get back to the surface of the earth, in order to make proper preparations for a search of this subterranean world, or at least to discover how I could make my exit from it, if I were in danger. No such thought, however, entered my mind. The moment that I had been waiting for so long had come, and the idea of turning back, even for a little, would have seemed impossible to me, especially as there seemed to be no obstacle in my way. In my knapsack I had a certain amount of provision for a journey—plenty of food for two days at least. The air of the place was chilly but pure, and, as far as I could judge, free from noxious gases. If there were still living men in this world, they would be somewhere at the bottom of that slope, and I was determined to find them. The figures and inscriptions showed that they had once been there at any rate.

I began to move forward slowly. The place was extremely dark, so that I could not do without my torch, although it made me conspicuous, and I knew that I should be an easy target for any hostile thing that lurked in the darkness round me. I stopped and listened intently.

There was a slight sound coming from the right-hand side— a little, murmuring, sliding sound. I put my torch out, and stood rigid, staring in the direction of the sound. It was a soft, bubbling noise, quite unmistakable, and it came from the one source. It was continuous—too evenly continuous to proceed from the voice or movements of any living thing.

My attitude of tension relaxed. It was probably running water, for there must be some running water in the neighbourhood, since human beings had lived there.

I moved in the direction of the sound.

My foot struck something. I flashed my torch, and looked down. I had walked into a heap of broken pottery, bits of metal fittings, and other debris that looked like shells. Beyond this heap of stuff there was a stone structure like an altar, and, beyond that again, shallow hollows like stone couches cut into the floor.

I went forward, cautiously, towards the altar. It had an upright front slab, and on this there was a bold drawing of a stork standing over a little stork in a protecting attitude, and over this the letters I.O.M. On the top was a Latin inscription, something about Aurelius Petronius Urbicus of the Julian tribe. I examined the pottery that lay round it. Some of it was lovely work, obviously Samian ware, and mixed with it were some fragments of thick green glass. The pieces of metal were covered with rust, and seemed to be mostly bits of buckles, but there were two small rusty knives with wooden handles, and a broken sword. Evidently nobody had lived in the place for centuries, for all the debris was of ancient make.

As I was examining it, I could hear the murmuring sound quite distinctly. I had no doubt now that it was the sound of running water. I walked on towards it. The floor beyond the altar was cut into a series of stone couches, fifty or sixty at least, showing that all this space had been a living-place for men and women. Beyond the couches I came upon the water—a well that bubbled up from a circular opening in the rock and ran down the slope, in a channel that it had made for itself in the rocky floor. I now realised that I was parched with thirst, owing to the dust that had got into my mouth and throat. I tasted the water. It was quite sweet. I took a long drink, and felt much refreshed. I followed the stream downwards, walking very slowly, watching on all sides.

After about twenty minutes, I saw what I thought at first was a jutting rock in front of me, but, when I came to it, I found that it was not a rock but another altar made of roughly hewn stones, kept together by some sort of cement. There was an inscription on the top of it, and a figure of a flying woman, with her hands stretched towards the slope in front. I looked in the direction in which the hands pointed, and saw a sharp break in the slope, as if it stopped abruptly not far from the foot of the altar. I went towards this break, and found a very steep incline, with a series of uneven ledges either cut into it by human hands or made by water. To right and left the slope was still steeper, and there were no ledges. The fact that they were in that one place seemed to indicate that they were artificial, and that I was following the road by which the early men had gone down. If they had been made by man, they were the first definite indication of direction I had got since I entered the darkness. In any case they seemed to be the only way of descent.

I fixed my kit tightly, and began to clamber down the ledges. They were rather difficult to negotiate as they were very deep and roughly hewn.

The steps proved to be, in the main, adaptations of natural ledges in the rock, and they were so high in some places that I had to climb down them with my face to the rock. As they went down, they became more difficult, and I began to fear that they were only natural ledges leading to a cliff shelf. After nearly an hour, however, I found, to my delight, that they were getting broader and shallower. Then suddenly they ceased.

I looked round me. I was at the bottom of a cliff wall, and from my feet a rough rocky slope ran down with a rather steep incline. There was no sign of a path anywhere, nor any indication of direction. The slope, as far as my torch showed, was no longer smooth, but rough and stony, but it seemed passable, provided I went carefully.

I had lost touch with the stream, and this troubled me some-what, but, as there was no sound of running water anywhere, I had no choice but to go straight downwards. I began to move forward, picking my way between big boulders that looked as if they had been dropped from the earth roof above me. The ground between them was a mixture of dry earth and stones, very rough, but not impassable.

From time to time I stopped to listen, but I heard nothing, not even the echo of my own steps, so that I assumed that there was a large empty space in front of the mountain I was de-scending. My torch showed me nothing but blackness outside the little circle of its light.

I cannot tell exactly how long I was going down this slope when the first flash of light came from above. I was looking down, trying to pick my way by the light of my torch, when, suddenly, the whole ground grew clear for a moment. The next moment it was dark again. I stopped and stared. The light had come from above—a vivid gleam, like a flash of lightning. I hadn't seen it, only its reflection on the ground, but it had certainly come from above. I stood staring upwards. What could it be? Then it came again—a flash across the upper darkness. It was only for a moment, but, when it was gone, I still stared upwards. My heart was beating wildly. What was going to happen? There it was again—longer now—some electric or magnetic emanation from the upper dome of earth above. It was light and I could see the world into which I had come. Now it was coming in a series of flashes.

I looked round me. A tumble of mountains was being re-vealed—a mass of dark slopes, sullen bare sheets of rock, like the one on which I was standing, running up into a pall of darkness that was split by these coruscating flashes. Between the mountain slopes, valleys, as savage as themselves, made

black gulfs. Nowhere was there any sign of life, any movement, any vegetation; but the air seemed full of electricity.

I should have been appalled by the landscapes revealed by
the light: a land of utter desolation—a blasted, empty world
that spread as far as my eyes could see, below me, above me,
in peaks, valleys, whorls of black rock—a hideous jumble of
depths and heights and deadly looking ravines without a vestige of life to be seen anywhere. What could there be in this
jumble of hellish peaks but death! And yet I was not appalled.
Having looked long at that world of chaos and night, I
went on.

The lights died away. It didn't matter. My way lay downwards——

Though I was walking in darkness, it wasn't a total darkness, for the coruscations above had left something behind
them—some sort of very dim gleams that flitted back and forward through the darkness. And I had my torch. I had got it
recharged that morning, and it should be good for some time
yet. When it was gone, I should be done for, if I hadn't
reached some sort of light.

The most ordinary prudence should have made me try to
get back while there was still time, but this my mind refused
to consider. It hung on to the one thing that it had to do—to
get down the mountain to where humanity might be found.
For the moment even the search for my father, which had
brought me to the pass in which I found myself, sank into
unimportance compared with my need to get to men and know
that I wasn't alone under the blind surface of the earth. I
might have tried to get back, but my instinct refused to accept
this possibility. It drove me downwards, clinging to its one
idea, dogged and limpet-like. I went on in this night, moving
cautiously, steadily, feeling with every sense for pitfalls and
obstacles. The light above died away completely, but I paid
no heed to that. I went on, by the light of my torch, ever

downwards, step by step and mile by mile, through a darkness so palpable that I seemed to be wading through it.

The lights above began again, first in single flashes, then in a series of beams that lit up the ground almost continuously, like constant flashes of sheet lightning. The landscape was the same. No change in that ghastly desolation. I turned my eyes away from it, and fixed them on the ground. What was that in front of me—a stick? I rushed to it. It was only a long splinter of rock. I took it up, but could not throw off the idea that it was artificial. It might possibly have been made by men, from the length and the shape of it. I didn't really believe that it was anything but a natural splinter of rock, but there was the possibility that it was a sort of stone sword dropped by a man. The mere thought of the possibility came between me and isolation. I held the sword in front of me, stabbing the ground with it for chasms or pitfalls.

I must have gone on for a good while in this way, but I kept no count of time. I thought only of one thing—grass, water, and life waiting for me below. I tried to keep my eyes averted from the wild defiles, the bleak shoulders of rock, the ghastly valleys of blackness, that rose and fell, as the flashes from above revealed the bowels of the earth to me. At the same time my mind kept going over calculations of space, reckoning the amount of time I had been travelling. I could see my wristlet-watch, but it had stopped. It couldn't be possible that I was more than seven or eight hours in this underworld, yet it seemed to me to be several days since I had left the sunlight. At the thought I began the calculation all over again, counting steps, trying to calculate the height of the mountain, but always going forward, my head and my sword stuck out, my body drawn back.

It was in the middle of one of these calculations that I heard the wail. I had been going on blindly, calculating, stumbling, crouching, stabbing with my sword, all in a thick silence, and then it came to me, far away from the left, out of the darkness. I straightened myself and listened. Yes, there was a sound like a distant wail. It died away. I began to think that I had imagined it. Then I heard it again, very faint, but quite clear. Now it was dying away in a series of gurgling sobs that rang back at me like faint laughter. I stood rigid, listening. The first sound that had come to me in the world of blackness! Silence fell again. I strained my ears, but there was nothing more. There was a slight stir in the air—the beginning of a very faint breeze coming up from below, and on it a faint smell that I couldn't analyse.

For a while I stood rigid, peering into the depths of darkness that lay downwards, but I saw nothing and heard nothing. I resumed my descent. I noticed that the movement of wind from below was getting somewhat stronger, and that the air was getting warmer. It was charged with some electric quality too.

As I descended, my mind became full of wild imaginings. My torch must make me as conspicuous as a glowworm on a dark night. Anything might at any moment leap on me out of the darkness, but the gleams from above had died out completely, and I could not do without the light. I could not keep from imagining that I saw forms moving in the darkness. At every step I stopped to peer and to listen, but I saw and heard nothing.

The descent stopped. I was on level ground. I flashed the torch round. I had reached a rough plateau of bare rock, which seemed to stretch away level in front of me. The ground near me was even—slabs of smooth rock—but to the left there was a sort of channel, like a dry stream-bed. I went over to it. It was certainly an old stream-bed. I followed it. There had been water there once. Perhaps men had camped by it.

Suddenly, out of the darkness, I came on a round hummock

of stone. The whole of the circular top was covered with the figure of a man treading on the prostrate form of a strange-looking animal which seemed to have two bodies, divided by a narrow waist-line, and several spindly legs. I stared at it. Once again I was in touch with the world of men. They had passed by this way. I was on the right road. Immediately my mood changed. From a despairing determination it swung round to confidence and hope. I repeated to myself that I was certainly on the track of men.

And these sounds—they had come from the left hand—it was in that direction that life lay—whatever sort of life it was —I must go in that direction. The dry stream-bed ran over an almost even surface, in that direction also, with a slight downward slope.

I followed it. I was intensely excited. The slight wind had died away, and with it the peculiar smell had ceased, but I felt sure that I was coming, at last, near some form of life.

The channel had now turned more definitely to the left. The gleams of light from above had not returned. The darkness was complete, yet I had a feeling that on my right-hand side a mass of land rose up. The light had shown me that I was descending into a valley between two mountains—the mountain down which I had come, and another that barred the way over against it. It was probable that this channel that I was following was the bed of the valley.

I must have been descending along this sloping valley floor for at least an hour, when, suddenly, in the middle of the channel, I saw the plant right under my feet. It was of a sort I had never seen before—almost like red frog-spawn—but it must be a plant, for it was anchored to the sand by thin trailing tubes. I seized it. It came away with me easily. Then, as I pressed it, it burst, squirting a red juice.

I straightened myself, threw back my head, and laughed. They were right all the time—the legends, and the people who believed in them! There *was* a world here below—a world of life—and I was coming to it!

Yes, there was another of the plants! Two of them!

Then again there came to me the light rustle of wind, and with it a sound like the sound of falling water.

I waited for no more, but hurried along the river-bed.

Undoubtedly the valley was getting narrower. The sides of a gorge were closing on me; now the channel was merely a narrow passage between cliff walls, curving sharply—ah! I very nearly walked over the brink of a rock, so abrupt was the curve and the ending of the path. I pulled myself back, just at the brink, and stood staring in amazement at the view that opened up in front of me.

I say "view," but it was not a view. I was looking at a confused blur of darkness that was visible, because, through it, as through a mist, a strange glimmer made itself felt rather than seen. I was in the presence of light that was not the light from above—a light that was so confused that it was hardly light, yet undoubtedly a brightness.

I stood staring at this strange world that I had reached. I had come to the end of the emptiness, of the vacant spaces. I had reached something different. I felt a sudden check in my confidence—a feeling almost of dismay—I had been expecting real life, real light. Could this be it? This the world I was seeking? This mass of indistinctness that was neither light nor darkness!

I tried to grasp it, to perceive it. Yes, the darkness was the thing that was there—the essential thing—but, below the darkness, as if on the ground, there was a flickering surface of greenish-bluish glimmering, on which the darkness seemed to rest. And above, in the darkness itself, there was here and there a suggestion of whitish blurs, as if of extremely dim light at a distance seen through a black fog. What was I looking at? It could not be a town or any collection of human dwellings, since there was complete silence, except for a slight swishing sound that seemed to fill the air. Yet what were the flickering glimmers of light below, and the suggestion of lights here and there above?

Gradually, as I stood staring at it, my eyes grew accustomed to the strange visual conditions, and I began to pick out points in the confused glimmer of lower lights.

There seemed to be a dim carpet of feeble spots of light mixed with darkness on the ground—if that was ground, but perhaps it was water, though it seemed to be sloping gradually downwards. No, it must be ground. There were lights both above and below; or rather, the darkness was sprinkled here and there, in the distance, with some sort of pale blurs that might be extremely faint lights lifted a little above the other lights upon the slope. What were they?

I listened intently. The slight swishing sound was like a gentle wind waving through soft leaves. I felt the wind on my face, exhilarating, as if it held some quality full of life; yet the smell that was coming to me on it was a smell of sweet decay.

I knelt down on the rock on which I was standing and peered down. I could see nothing at the foot of the rock, but, farther down, there seemed to be some sort of growths that gave out a dim luminosity. I had no choice but to use my torch if I were to try to discover what was at the bottom of the rock on which I was standing. I flashed its light over the brink. Yes, it was ground; a stony slope that began at the bottom of the rock, not more than three or four feet below me, and ran down gradually from it into the glimmering darkness. A few trailing things grew on it near me, but farther down they seemed to get thicker. I had certainly come to a world of life.

I put my legs over the edge, dropped to the ground, and stood with my back to the rock. I felt my heart beating wildly.

Up above, on the barren mountains, I had been alone, in a dead, empty world, but a safe one, as far as attack was concerned—a world, also, that reached to the upper earth and the wall through which I had come. I was now leaving that security.

I could see little. I was still trembling with excitement, but there was a foreboding mixed with the excitement—a presentiment arising from the heavy odour of decay, the strange confusion of light and darkness. I had reached life at last, but I began to feel the barren rock-slopes that I had descended safe and familiar compared to it.

For the first time since my fall through the trapdoor, it occurred to me that it might be advisable to go back and get help in my search. Only for a moment, however. The next moment I knew that I could not go back. Whatever I was to meet in this strange world, I would meet it. This strange confusion of smells, with decay at the heart of them, was not the only thing that was coming to me from the dimness. There was also vitality and the sharpness of life.

There was no sign of any moving thing, and no sound except the slight rustling.

I was coming to the ground-lights. I stared at them eagerly. Then I saw that they were only plants—small round plants like little greenish lamps. I went down to them, and looked at them more closely. They were little, upright growths like fungi, with caps which gave out a phosphorescent glow. One of them, in front of me, threw out such a bright green light that I could have read by it. I went over and plucked it. It was like a big mushroom, but, when I plucked it, I got a strong smell of garlic. At the same time a peculiar mixture of smells came to me from the plants that I was standing on. I thought I could distinguish a smell of fresh meal, mixed with a perfume of violets and one that I had never met before, rather pungent and unpleasant.

It was amazing, this dark garden with its phosphorescent

gleams and strange odours. I stood spellbound, looking down
at it and over it at the dimness beyond. This, then, was the
secret of the lights that I had seen below the darkness. But
what were the pale blurs that I saw up in the air? I could see
them now more clearly, some distance in front of me; and
some of them seemed to be moving. I pulled myself together,
and looked more closely.

They were growing clearer.

I relaxed, and drew deep breaths of relief and disappoint-
ment. They were flitting through the air, hovering. They were
only will-o'-the-wisps, or some similar form of phosphorescence.

I kept on. Underneath, the ground had got quite spongy, as
if there were abundance of water near the surface.

I kept a sharp watch for any sign of an animal or a man,
and a sharp ear for any movement, but there was no sign of
anything, nor any sound, except the one like a soft wind among
leaves. At my feet, the torch showed me masses of clinging
stuff, that gave an extraordinary impression of a red meadow
lying there under the darkness.

But what was that? A gleam of light on the ground!

I stopped. The landscape was beginning to show—lit with
a dim light.

I looked up. There were gleams of light coming out again,
in the vault above me, not sheet lightning, but something like
an Aurora Borealis. I stared. They were brightening, enlarging,
sending spears of light in all directions. As I watched, they
came together and flung out a broad banner of pale light that
swung back and forward, as if it were being tossed by a high
wind, yet there was no stirring of the air nor sound of wind
either below or in the heights where it was waving. Round me,
the air seemed to get more electric, as if the rays were vitalis-
ing it.

I felt my breath coming in gasps, not because the atmosphere was difficult to breathe, but through sheer wonder. After

the world of darkness that I had come through, the sudden wonder of this splendid light took away my breath.

As I stared, it gathered its folds of flame, and seemed to draw away from me into the vaults of darkness. Rapidly it grew dimmer, and I felt afraid that it might die out before I had seen the world that lay before me. I stared, fascinated, down at the weird land that stretched away on all sides. It was dark, except for the light of the rays that swept over it from above, but, as they raced over it, I could see first, tall, scattered growths that might be trees, and, below them, a black mass that looked like a wood. There seemed to be blurs of light high up in the dark mass—dim, scattered lights, in spots, like globes.

As I went on over the clinging ground in the dim light, I got a curious feeling that I was moving under water, that this was a tropical under-sea prairie.

Suddenly the silence was rent by a piercing scream from the lower ground, some distance in front of me. It rang out high and shrill for a moment, then it stopped as abruptly as it had begun. I listened, every nerve torn by the sudden shock. I hadn't realised how much my nerves had been on edge. I forced myself to relax. Whatever was there, I had to face it.

It stopped, but a chattering noise broke out on my left, and was answered by a series of cacklings and chatterings. I stood, staring round me, but nothing appeared, and gradually the sounds died away.

For several minutes I stood there, watching and listening. There were living creatures all round me. At any moment one of them might appear in my path. I began to move forward again—very slowly. Whatever creatures produced the sounds were in front, but I had no choice but to go forward. There was no cover. I might lie down and work along the ground, but I did not know what creatures the ground growths might hold —perhaps poisonous reptiles. It was safer to go forward, upright, ready for action, watching every movement of light and shadow.

I could see the higher growths clearly now. They were certainly trees of some sort—mostly dark, but some with luminous tops. These were the fixed lights that had made the pale blurs high up in the darkness.

As I came near, I began to make out two different kinds—huge seaweedy things, and fungoid growths. The latter threw out a light from their crowns that lit up the ground so that things were much clearer in the wood than on the open land.

I approached the wood, watching it narrowly for any sign of life. I could see none, and, after a halt at the verge, I went in under the trees.

I began to advance slowly through the wood. The ground underfoot was difficult for travelling, and the trailing growths clung to the feet. A warm steam seemed to come up from the earth, and the ground-growths sent up a heavy smell that oppressed me.

I tried to shake off the drowsiness that was falling on me. The excitement that had been produced in me by the strange quality of the air and the sight of the new world, with its curious light and vegetation, was now struggling with a desire to sleep.

I had eaten nothing since I left home, but I didn't feel hungry so much as tired and sleepy. The light that had shone from the dome above me was disappearing, and, with its fading, the electric quality seemed to have gone from the air.

I think that I would have lain down and slept, only for an insistent fear.

The fungoid globes above seemed to be winking and quivering. As I stumbled on, I began to nod and wake by starts. I pulled myself together resolutely, trying to keep my senses alert. Once, in the distance, I thought I saw something that looked much more definite than the other shadows and lights

—something like a vast toad—but it had disappeared among the trees before I could see clearly what it was.

There was one good thing about the situation, and that was that the wood, instead of growing thicker, as I had feared, was remaining quite sparse, so that it was possible, under the light of the fungoid trees, to see some distance on each side.

To my right a stream ran with a sliding noise.

The land was evidently narrowing to a gorge. The fungoid trees were becoming rare, so that the forest was much darker. After flaring up, the light in the sky had faded away rapidly.

I began to hurry as quickly as my heavy senses allowed. I suddenly felt a most intense craving for home and shelter. Somewhere below there might be lights, hearth-fires—something that would save me from the darkness.

I went on, half expecting to see human forms coming through the trees. I stopped, and pulled myself together with a great effort. My mind mustn't wander through this drugged fatigue. I must get somewhere where I could rest—but where? One of the dark seaweedy trees—a high one—would give me some sort of protection, perhaps, if I could climb into a good secure place in a fork and settle myself there.

What was that moving through the trees? I stood stock still —staring.

A monstrous-looking creature, with a pair of bulging bag-like bodies, was galloping down the gorge at a great speed. For a moment I saw it, then it had vanished. I stood staring incredulously. I had seen a creature, about the size of a tiger, with a double body joined by a neck in the middle, and supported by several stilt-like legs. But had I seen aright? I had been heavy and sleepy, and in the dimness I might have been deceived by some curious shaping of the branches of the trees as some animal hurried through. Then I remembered the drawing of the strange animal, on which the man was standing, cut in the stone monument that I had met at the head of the valley. That was the creature!—exactly the thing that I had seen! Then, I reflected, the memory of it in my tired condition might have made my mind produce the illusion.

I stood and listened. I thought I could hear distant noises, and once a far cry, like wailing, but I could make out nothing distinctly.

I went forward slowly. What should I do?

The sight of the monstrous galloping thing, the dimness of the gorge, the failing light! I could not afford to let myself get drowsy; yet the drowsiness was creeping on me again.

Down in the gorge it seemed dark—a pool of darkness—anything might be lurking there. I couldn't go through it. I stood still. All round me a rustling and a stirring were beginning, and, in the dimness under the farthest trees, it seemed to me that stealthy shapes were gliding towards me.

Suddenly I felt that the ground was unsafe. I ran to a large tree that stood near me, and clambered up.

In a moment I was in the first fork. I settled myself in it, and looked down. There was nothing in sight—no animals, nor any movement.

I felt safer now. The fork was roomy, but it might be safer, perhaps, to go up to the second fork, which would have plenty of room for me. Then I realised that I was very thirsty again. I had had a good drink when I fell into the spring in the soft ground, but I had sweated so much, and I felt that I could not sleep without another drink. I looked down, but could see no moving shapes below. It was dim and dark, however, and there might be anything quite near me. I cursed my stupidity in not having thought of a drink before I climbed the tree. Now I couldn't sleep, my mouth was so parched.

The little stream was only a few yards away. I cast one more cautious glance round me, then climbed down the tree, ran to the stream, and lay face downwards to drink. As I drank, a sound struck my ears, so low and deep that at first I only realised it as part of the silence. I raised my head from the water and listened. I could hear nothing. I decided that my ears must have deceived me, and stooped and drank again. In a few moments I heard it again—a low vibrant sound that seemed to be coming up-stream from below, and with it a chuckling and slobbering. I jumped up. The sound ceased, but in the night air a faint stench struck my nostrils. I ran for the tree. Just as I reached it, something like a long cord whizzed past my ear. I ducked and sprang for the branch. My nerves were all awry, but I kept my head, and I swarmed up the tree. As I reached the fork, I heard another whiz, and the end of a second cord struck the branch that ran out on the stream-side from the fork, and stuck to it, coiling round.

I looked down, but could not see who or what had thrown the cord, so I clambered farther up the tree. The higher I got, the more protected I should be against a lasso, by the thick cluster of branches.

When I reached the second fork I was still somewhat over-exposed, but I halted to draw my knife. I looked down.

Almost under the tree there was a large beast with a body that seemed to be in two parts, like a sack divided in the middle. There was the whiz again.

Ah! I felt the cut of a whip across my left shoulder and a downward tug. I was being drawn to the ground by a leash that had fastened round my shoulder. With a backward movement of the knife, I cut the leash in two. The pull on my shoulder loosened, the portion that remained on my clothes fell, and the rest of the cord disappeared.

I must get higher up. I had to put my knife back lest I should lose it, but I must get out of range of that leash.

I swarmed up the tree; my neck felt sore—an irritated weal where the cord had touched me. The thought that it was poisonous came to me, but I could do nothing about it. I must get out of range of the lasso.

Already it might be coiling for another throw, or was it a sucker, like the arm of a polyp?

I was at the third fork. Every moment I expected to hear the whiz again. The third fork was at least thirty-five or forty feet over the ground. The leash could hardly reach me here.

I could hear distinctly sounds of glidings, sobbings, and shufflings coming closer, as if something were climbing the tree.

The sounds stopped. Either the creature was lying quiet, watching, or it had dropped to the ground. I stared down along the trunk, but there was no light now of any sort, and I could not see the boughs below me. I held my knife in readiness to strike downwards at the slightest sign of movement under me, but there was none.

Gradually my tension relaxed and I settled back in my seat. I was well ensconced between the boughs that sprang from the fork.

There was now almost complete silence.

I began to feel more normal; I even realised that I was hungry. I felt in my knapsack for the sandwiches, and began to eat heartily.

As I ate, I thought of my position, but I could not think clearly. I was beyond all thought or calculation. Strange to say this very fact made it easier for me. I had done things wrongly, but I could not mend matters now. This was not the way in which I should have come to this world—entirely un-armed, except for a short knife. Even if I had had a large-bore rifle, I should be in very great danger. What chance of survival had I now that I was almost completely defenceless?

Such were the thoughts that passed through my mind as I ate my sandwiches in the high fork of the tree in the sub-terranean darkness. They should have appalled me. I was alone, and almost defenceless in face of unimaginable things.

If I tried to go back for help, I should have almost as little chance as if I went forward, since, even if I could reach the

exact spot on the top of the slope on which I had fallen, I
knew of no way by which I could get from it to the trapdoor.

On the other hand, if I went forward, without weapons of
any sort, my chances in a struggle for existence must be ex-
ceedingly small.

Yet, as I sat eating my first meal in that underworld, the
chief feeling in my mind was one of unreasoning exultation.
An insatiable curiosity and expectation drowned my fears,
and made my mind a whirlwind of fantastic visions.

When I had eaten a quarter of my sandwiches, I put the
rest back into the knapsack, for, though I still felt hungry,
I could not guess what opportunity of getting food lay in front
of me. I felt better. This world was as strange in one sense
as before, but it had become less strange since I had eaten a
meal in it.

I shut my eyes. Was it fancy, or did I feel a slow deep pulsating movement, like a pulsation from a heavy animal?

I sat up. It stopped. Was there something in the tree? I
listened. There was nothing. I shut my eyes and relaxed. It
came again. Then I knew . . . it was the beating of my own
heart—slow, heavy now—the excitement gone down into a
ground-swell of feeling.

Suddenly I thought of my mother. All the time I hadn't
thought of her. She wouldn't know yet that I was gone—not
yet. I wasn't to be back until Sunday night at earliest—perhaps Monday morning—to catch the early train back to the
factory. I hadn't thought of her, or troubled about her—just
like my father. I had left her alone to bear the brunt of it—
without troubling—blind in my own excitement. She had nobody now—nobody except the Sacketts.

I sat up, and stared into the darkness. What a brute I had
been!

Then I lay back again. I had had no choice. If I had found
the trapdoor in the ordinary way, I would have gone back and

told her. The two of us together would have arranged for my journey. Would it have been any better that way? It would have come to the same thing in the end. We should have had no choice. I could not have avoided coming down to look for my father. There would have been the same suspense, only it would have come before my descent as well as after it. Perhaps this was better. Perhaps by the time she discovered that I was gone I should have found my father. Already I might be quite near human settlements. Perhaps before I slept again I should see him putting his hand up through his thick hair, as he used to do in the old days before the war.

What was that sound below—that heavy brushing sound?

I sat up—the darkness was too thick to see anything—now it was passing—like a bear or a bullock pushing through the undergrowth.

It seemed incredible that a few days ago I had been working in the factory with Ned Carter, the works foreman—talking of stream-lining.

I stared into the darkness, absorbed. John Sackett's face was staring back at me for a moment—then it was my mother's—so like John, except for the blunt look he had in the eyes.

CHAPTER FOUR

Monsters

I WAS AWAKENED by a noise like a very loud braying. I lifted my head drowsily. I had been dreaming of homely things—the broken trash of everyday life that makes most dreams—and for a moment I didn't realise where I was, but listened sleepily to the sound. Then remembrance came to me.

I sprang into a sitting posture and looked about. There was some light coming from above and I could see dimly through the branches. The braying sound was tearing the air. It rose and fell, rose again, then began to die away in a series of chuckles, but, as I listened to it, another sound broke out—a scream of agony. I thought of the brute that had treed me on the preceding night. Had it got a victim, or had it met another creature in the forest, even more fearsome than itself? That scream was the cry of a large animal. It was dying away.

I listened intently. The panic that had seized me before my sleep was gone. I felt quite cool and collected. I was in danger —great danger—but men had come through greater on the upper earth. If the light stayed, I could face it. I was growing stronger. Things were becoming visible again.

The lights were tossing back and forward in a dome of darkness that, over the gleams, looked like an inverted black bowl. As I watched, a crown of light began to take shape, with a rim of rose carmine and a centre of brilliant yellow light that began to contract and dilate like a great heart, so that the fantastic idea came to me that I was watching the heart of the earth.

I sat for a while in the tree-top, staring up at it with a sort of awed wonder, until it shook itself out like a great banner, so that the forest and the cliffs were lit as brightly as if it were full, brilliant moonlight.

I decided that I must take advantage of the light while it lasted. I looked down, searching the tree forks and the ground for signs of any beasts. There were none, nor any sound. Still I sat intently watching.

Then I began to climb down cautiously. After a long examination from the lowest fork, I slid to the ground, and stood with my back to the tree, looking all round me.

The trees were fairly sparse here, with spaces covered by ground growths between them. I began to move warily, examining the ground. The sward had been trampled in a curious way, and in a damp spot there were marks of something resembling big claws. Already the seaweedy trees were becoming familiar to me, so that, under the brilliant light, they almost seemed homely. Nor was there anything fearsome to be seen. Near me, a thing like an enormous slug was dragging itself down to the stream. Farther up, some small creatures that looked like large lizards were watching me from the trunks of trees. None of them seemed to be sufficiently big to be at all dangerous. The slug was about the size of a rabbit; the lizards considerably smaller. Apart from these there was nothing moving on the landscape.

I was thirsty and pushed cautiously through the undergrowth to the stream. When I got to it, there was nothing living in view, so I lay down on the bank and took a plentiful draught. Then I stood with my back to a tree, and ate some more sandwiches and examined the gorge through which I should have to pass if I were to follow the stream that had been my guide up to now. I could see little of it, except a narrow pass between the cliffs.

As I stood by the tree, one of the slug-like creatures dragged itself over the ground towards me, eating the ground growths. I watched for a while. It seemed unaware of my presence. The thought struck me that its flesh might be eatable. As I moved towards it, my knife in my hand, it stopped eating and re-mained perfectly quiet. Then, as I came nearer still, it began to drag itself rapidly away. I ran and drove my knife into the middle of its back. A squirt of blood splashed over my boots. The creature quivered, wriggled a little, then lay still, with blood oozing from it. I stared at it with discomfort, feeling suddenly that I had no right to kill in the underworld.

The creature *was* evidently some sort of enormous slug, for the skin and body were those of a slug. I cut a slice off the back—a pale sort of flesh. But it looked edible, and I might be very glad of it later. I cut off as much of the meat as I could conveniently carry and packed it in my knapsack. Then I started cautiously on my journey through the gorge.

I had a fear that if the brute that had attacked me before I slept were a gigantic spider, or any sort of preying beast, it would probably have its home in caves and dens along the walls of the gorge. I therefore kept a sharp look-out for any signs of movement as I came to the mouth of the ravine.

I was on the point of entering the ravine when I sensed rather than saw a movement. I swung round. One of the double-bodied creatures was coming slowly towards me. I halted abruptly, and stood staring at it, frozen into immobility. There was no tree near me. I had no weapon but the short knife. If it came at me, I should be, I felt, as futile in resistance as a man with no weapon would be before a tiger. I watched, fascinated. When I had stopped, it had stopped also. Now it was standing examining me—a head that was a slobbering leathern bag, with vast eyes that seemed to have countless facets, was contemplating me.

I felt paralysed. What was behind that ghastly face? I couldn't imagine. It seemed to be examining me through curiosity. At least there was no gathering of itself together for an attack.

Behind the face was that vast, unbelievably hideous body stuck up on legs like stilts nearly three feet high. The head seemed to be almost as big as the body. Trailing cords hung from a mouth like the mouth of a huge gurnard. As I stared, the enormous size of the head bag gave me the absurd impression that the creature had a tightly laced waist rather than a neck. I noted every detail as clearly as if I were going to draw it. The time seemed an eternity.

It was moving. Then, with a sort of whistling sound, it was off down the ravine, making its curious din.

Immediately the hooting was taken up farther down the ravine, and in a moment the air was full of noise like shrill fog-horns.

I stood staring after it with a feeling of relief that was almost collapse. My knees were trembling. I had difficulty in keeping myself standing.

It had been merely curious about me—indifferently curious. If it had been hunting or hungry, I should now be lying under it, dying or dead. At any moment I might meet another. They would not all be merely indifferent. Should I try to go back to the shelter of the trees?

I stood irresolute. I could see dim forms moving in front. If I went forward, I couldn't avoid them—yet, if I went backwards, would I be any safer? They were probably behind me as well as in front.

I kept turning round, watching all sides. There was no movement except those of the creatures in front. In a few moments they too disappeared. The ravine was empty, as far as I could see.

Still I stood staring round me. It was only now that the hopelessness of my position was becoming clear to me.

The streamers of light were still as bright as very bright

moonlight. The walls of the cliff now and again, when the gleaming was vivid, stood out so that I could see every detail. This at least gave me a slightly better chance of escaping, since it was certain that these brutes could see as well in the darkness as in the light. I should be seen whether there was light or darkness. As long as the light lasted, *I* also could see. I must get forward to the shelter of trees while the light lasted, take advantage of the periods of light for travelling, and hide in trees during the darkness—if I could afford to stay in the trees so long. It might last for long periods. In my ignorance, I must make my choice blindly, but at the moment there was only one thing to be done—to get forward. These brutes were hunting beasts, and at any moment I might encounter one of them in quest of a meal.

The cliff walls that formed the ravine had turned sharply, leaving open ground in front of me and on both sides. There were scattered groups of trees of the seaweedy type. The stream did not turn to the right or left, but kept straight forward. I followed it, glad to get away from the cliff walls. I wondered if I was again entering a forest, but, instead of thickening, the trees thinned in front of me, so that I began to be afraid that they were going to stop. They were now my only security.

I hurried forward, then came to a halt. I seemed to be standing on the ramparts of a world. Under my feet a cliff fell so steeply that I could see only the brink of it. A great distance below me, a dim land stretched as far as I could see, and I could see quite a good distance, for the streamers of light were flashing like swords of moonlight and lighting the whole country quite vividly. Not far from the cliff foot I saw a very wide river that flowed from the left and kept a course almost parallel with the cliff on which I was standing. Black patches of forest grew here and there over the plain, but I could see no sign of human life, no clouds of smoke, no group of buildings, nothing in all its expanse but the river and the dark vegetation.

From the right came the thunder of cataracts that I had heard in the darkness before I slept. I looked along the edge of the cliff. The stream that I had followed had turned about one hundred yards from the cliff barrier and curved to the right. On this side the cliff curved in and out in a series of bays and wooded headlands. It was from this side, also, that the thunder of the cataracts now came, as if a big river were hurling itself from gulf to gulf over precipices. On the left, the cliff seemed to turn at right angles and curl round backwards.

I stood perplexed, wondering which course to take. At length I turned to the right, and went slowly along the cliff edge.

I was following the outer rim of a narrow band of land that ran between the rocky spurs of the range of mountains through which I had come, and the great cliffs that separated these mountains from the plain. There were no signs of any slugs or tree-lizards, and I thought it likely that this might mean that the rocky spurs along this plateau were the haunts of hunting-beasts. But I had a good light to watch their approach, and they could only come at me from one side or from the rear, so that I had less area to watch.

Round me, all sorts of vegetation was growing—plants like fleshy docks; tall spiked things like thistles; creeping mats of clinging stuff; luminous fungi. I strode over and through them, watching the rocky spurs on my right and the land that stretched out under the cliffs on my left. Under the Aurora, it looked like descriptions I had read of a Canadian or Siberian landscape during the winter nights, but without the cold, for a warm air kept blowing up over the cliff edge.

The waterfall had seemed quite near when I emerged on the cliff face, yet, as I tramped round bays in the cliff and made short cuts across the headlands, it seemed no nearer.

For about three-quarters of an hour the cliff top remained

level, then the land began to drop rapidly, and soon I was hurrying down a steep descent. From below, the roar of the waterfall now came up clear and direct.

In my hurry to get down I had left the line of the cliff, and was rushing through some trees when I felt a large form moving towards me from the right.

I glanced round. It was almost upon me. I sprang for the nearest tree. As I jumped behind the tree, the creature rose from the ground with so great a bound that it was carried past the tree. I sprang for the nearest branch, swung myself on to it and up the tree. When I got to the second fork I looked down. The brute had turned, and was crouching to spring again. I swarmed up to the third fork. Then I saw that the creature had halted. It was squatting on the ground below, watching me through the branches. I stared down at it. It was not one of the great spiders, but one of the toad things. As it watched, it lifted its gaping mouth towards me, and I thought I saw the warty skin of its neck working, but it evidently knew that it could not get me, for it made no further movement. I wondered if it was going to sit there, besieging me. If it did, I should have to come down and try to kill it with my knife, but it was as big as a sheep, and it seemed to me that, unless it was much less powerful than it looked, I should have little chance against it. And I could have little hope of rescue, since it was unlikely that a human civilisation would permit of the existence of such a creature in its neighbourhood.

As I watched the creature, I saw something coming steadily towards me. From the shadow of the trees one of the gigantic spiders was moving softly, watching the great toad. As it came stealthily nearer, I wondered whether it was possible that this was the intelligent creature that dominated this world. There could be no hope of conciliating or getting into touch with such a thing—no possibility of connection of mind, such as there is between a man and an animal. As it moved into the foreground, it seemed more like a demon than an earthly creature. Its leathery face, with the slobbering mouth, the middle flaps instead of a nose, the high bony forehead, and the many-sided eyes, was dreadful to look at, and the more I looked the more horrible it seemed. Yet it appeared so intelligent compared to the toad-like brute that I felt almost as if it were a rational thing coming to my rescue. It was coiling some sort of lasso now, which it seemed to be drawing out of itself, like the arms of a polyp.

I remained perfectly still. If I myself was the object of its pursuit, the fork might not be sufficiently high to be safe against the lasso, but it seemed to be watching the great toad, and, if this was so, it would be wiser not to attract its attention by any movement.

With a whizzing sound, the lasso flew through the air and struck the toad, curling round its neck. The brute spun round with a sort of bark, saw the lassoer, and made a terrific bound to the left, snapping the cord that held it. Another bound carried it out of sight behind the trees. The lassoer galloped after it at a great pace and disappeared.

I watched the place where they vanished from my sight, wondering whether the chase would bring them back again towards me, but nothing further appeared. I came down slowly from the tree. At any moment another of the toad-like brutes or some other hunting creature might attack me.

CHAPTER FIVE

On the River

I HAD GONE DOWN about half a mile beyond the place where the toad had attacked me, when a white wall seemed to start up beyond the trees. I hurried on, and in a few minutes was looking at an immense waterfall. My eyes followed the white mass upwards into the darkness, then downwards to the gulf into which it fell, at least a thousand feet below. I could see that from the gulf a river started and flowed towards the other river that came from the left.

If I could only get down the cliff to the plain, I might be able to find a stranded tree that I could push into the stream. I might even be able to put together some sort of raft—something that would take me out on to the stream of the great water.

If I could not get down, it was clear that I could not go any farther in this direction. I had come to the end of the space on the cliff-wall. It formed a sort of semi-circle round the gulf into which the cataract fell, and then stopped at the foot of the wall of rock down which the water was coming.

I went round it a little, examining the brink of the gulf at my feet, but I could see no break. I came back along the edge of the cliff, searching the ground.

At first there was nothing; then, as I was beginning to lose hope, my eye caught a trail, a confused trail that had obviously been made by many different creatures. It wound through the trees, turned away from the cliff, then came out through the wood to a series of broad shallow steps that led down the cliff.

I examined the top steps. They had been hewn by human hands. There could be no doubt of that.

My heart sprang up. It was hardly credible that I was again in touch with the work of men. If I were, I still had a good chance—some chance, at any rate.

I began to go down the steps. They turned, forming a gallery that had been hewn out in such a way as to connect natural ledges that occurred in the cliff face and make them into a continuous stairway. There was no question that they had been shaped by men.

I was now once again in a state of extreme excitement. The steps seemed to be old ones, and did not give the impression of having been used of late by human beings, but I had no hope now of meeting men soon. It was enough for me that I had struck again their paths. I had got back to the road, or at least to one of the roads, by which human beings had once got down from the surface of the earth to the lands beneath it.

Before I went down the cliff, I decided to take a good view from the top, so as to get the lie of the land.

I came back to the top of the steps, and looked round. As I did so, I caught sight of a heap of dead branches, piled up in an angle of the rock in such a way that it looked as if it had been done deliberately. I went over and examined it. The sticks might certainly have been placed there by human hands, but, on the other hand, they might also have been piled up by a current of air that had whirled the dry branches into a corner. The idea came to me that if I lit a beacon fire on the cliff-top I should be likely to attract the attention of any human beings who might be in the neighbourhood. I could also cook the meat that I had killed. I thought of the great toad and the lassoing creatures. It would attract their attention also, yet I felt impelled to do it. Suddenly I had been seized by an imperative need to do something human, something that would satisfy the hunger for human associations that was beginning to gnaw me. No matter what resulted, I knew now that I must light the fire.

I set a match to the heap of branches. The flame caught at once and blazed up. I began to pile the fire with the juicy branches that were lying about. They burnt like chunks of fat. I looked round me. There was no sign yet of anything moving. I gathered more branches, and threw them on the fire, delighted with the familiar sound of crackling flames. Still there was no sign of any creature being attracted by the unusual sight and sound. I stuck one of the pieces of slug meat on the end of a long stick, and began to roast it, keeping an eye on the stairways behind me as I did so.

If any creature came upon me by the cliff steps from below, I had a weapon ready to my hand in the burning branches. I had little doubt that no animal of that lower world, any more than any animal of the upper earth, would face a blazing torch.

No creature, however, came along to disturb me at my meal. Either they had little sense of smell, or the odour of cooked meat meant nothing to them. As I ate my first bit of cooked food in the underworld, I felt a confidence that I had not felt before. The sight of the fire was at once so homely and comforting. It made the underworld so different, as it sent its smoky banner and its tongues of flames upward, like a challenge from the world of men. I almost felt as if I had found a comrade, that I was no longer alone.

Then came an answer to the challenge. From the forest behind the fire there rose a hooting sound such as I had heard in the gorge. It was answered farther back, and then from everywhere behind the trees, until the woodland seemed alive with the sound. Were they coming to attack me? If so, I had the burning faggots now for a defence. I stared into the woodland. I thought I could make out, in the distance, moving shapes, but I could not make out anything clearly. Near me nothing was visible. I stood on the other side of the fire and chewed my cooked meat, watching the woodland.

While I fed, I cooked some more of the meat. As I was doing this, I saw one of the lassoing brutes quite clearly, coming towards me in the distance. Behind, the shapes of the others grew clearer. If they attacked in a body, I might not be able to scare them away with the burning faggots, but if one came alone, in advance of the others, I would teach it a lesson, if it came near enough. Yes, it was coming nearer; slowly, carefully, watching the smoke and the flames. Behind, the others were coming in a bunch. If I let the first come too near, they might all rush me. I seized a bunch of blazing branches and ran at it. It stood staring. I yelled wildly. I was almost upon it when, with a squeal, it whirled round and galloped away.

I hurled the blazing faggots. The others had turned and were galloping away also. Evidently the discomfiture of their leader had made them fear this strange new thing.

I turned back to the fire. I must get down the cliff path before their fears wore off. If there were any men within visible distance of the cliff, they would certainly be attracted by the fire. They might even now be coming up the cliff stairs to find the cause of the fire. The thought thrilled me. I had lit a beacon and was glad I had done so. Help might be already on the way. Danger might also be on the way from men, if they were hostile, but that thought did not trouble me. My action in lighting the fire had made certain that if there were men anywhere within range I should not miss them, whether they were hostile or friendly, and that was all that I cared for.

I looked round me. There were no lassoers in view. For the moment the country behind me seemed clear. I turned, and began to go down the cliff-steps.

Ever since my entrance into this new world I had been in a very excitable condition, but now, with this new hope of meeting men singing through my mind, I went down the cliff path in a mood of exultation that was heightened rather than diminished by the thought of the many possibilities of a violent death that lay in front of me before I reached my journey's end.

Whoever had hewn the path out of the cliff had done so by cutting a descent from the top on to a broad ledge, and widening this so that it was about four feet in breadth.

The light held good, and, as I went down, the landscape below got gradually clearer. I was descending into a great valley that lay between lofty mountain barriers. Where the river flowed to, or the valley ended, I could not see, but both obviously descended into lower lands, and I felt certain that it was in these I should be likely to find men, if there were men in this world. They certainly were not dwelling near me in the valley—or, if they were, they were invisible—for there was not the slightest sign of human life or human activity anywhere in view in the plain below me—nothing but the great river bordered by flat dim lands, and near me the other river that ran from the bottom of the waterfall to join the other.

At length I came out on a platform that overlooked the ground from a height of little over a hundred feet.

Below me, the boiling cauldron of water produced by the waterfall sent up clouds of spray. From the great pool into which it fell a long narrow lake ran along the foot of the cliff beneath me, and seemed to be full of floating trees that eddied back and forward and were now and again sucked back into the whirlpool. The banks of the lake were rocky and clear of animals, as far as I could see, but, lower down, the ground was a swamp, brilliant with phosphorescent gleamings in which I thought I could see large bodies moving, as if it were full of serpents or great lizards. There was no sign of man anywhere— no road or beaten path or track.

The river that ran from the waterfall had cut its way through the rocky ground, and seemed to rush at a great pace through the swampy lands, which I suppose it had produced by the overflow of its waters on each side.

I looked on all sides, but could see no path through the swamp, except the river waterway.

Near me, the water had eaten a curve into the ground, and made a sort of natural rectangular harbour in which all the flotsam that had escaped from the whirlpool and had not gone down the river was floating in a thick jam between the sides of my end of the rectangle. The stuff was chiefly trees, not all of the underworld type, for there was one, just under the bank on which I was standing, that looked like a sycamore.

I was particularly interested in the tops of mushroom trees that had been snapped off their trunks. There were four or five of these great mushroom cups mixed up with the wreckage, two floating on their mouths—the others riding on the water like boats. One of these latter attracted my attention particularly. It was on the outer edge of the pack, floating like a great bowl.

Its long, slender trunk had been snapped off about eight feet from the top, and appeared just over the rim of the floating bowl like a funnel. I decided to try to get to it across the jam of trees that floated between it and the bank.

I looked round me once again, then ran down the bank, sat on the brink of it, and tested the strength of the jam with my foot.

In a few minutes I reached the bowl. The rim of it was about three feet over the water, and I looked into it easily from a trunk that was lying alongside it.

I clambered up the side, which consisted of a tough rubbery stuff like cork, but not so dry and crisp. It rocked like a canoe, but the pack held it firm enough, and I managed to get over the side. This was nearly a foot thick. I made two deep notches in it, near each other, and hung my kit on the peg that I had left between the notches, then I slipped down into the bowl.

By dint of much bailing I managed to empty the great bowl completely. It was about six feet in diameter, and with a rubbery surface that was thick enough and tough enough to make it quite safe, unless I got rammed very badly by some tree. It was not a boat, for it could not be directed, but it was safer than a raft, and, if I could get it into the river, I was willing to accept whatever risk came my way, as being less than any I was likely to meet on land, and compensated for by the speed and ease of travelling.

The difficulty now was to get my scow into the river. I climbed out, selected suitable boughs, from among the wreckage, for poles, trimmed them, climbed back into the vessel, and put my kit into the bottom. I then got out again, and began to clear a passage.

After a long time and tremendous effort, I got my vessel at last to the outside of the jam.

I was afraid, once I got the vessel loose, to part from the bank, lest I should be sucked down into the whirlpool at the foot of the falls, so when I reached the bank I got out and began to tow the bowl towards the mouth of the river with some trailers made of long sea-weedy growths.

I was so engaged in this task that I forgot that there was any danger, until a slight rustle behind caused me to turn. A brute like a huge lizard was coming at me along the bank. I sprang into the vessel. The impetus of my spring sent the bowl spinning into the middle of the lake.

For a moment, in my pre-occupation with the reptile, I didn't realise the new danger. Then I saw to my horror that the spinning action of the vessel was bringing it towards the part of the water that was affected by the whirlpool.

The spinning was making my head reel. I caught the stump of the trunk, and tried to think. I was spinning nearer and nearer to the outer vortex, and it seemed only a matter of minutes until I should be sucked into it and drawn under the falls. Already I was drenched with their spray. If I jumped into the water, I might have some chance of escape by swimming strongly. In the bowl I should have none.

I climbed up the side of the bowl, and tried to balance myself on it, as it spun round and round, with the intention of springing into the water away from the falls before it was too late, when suddenly the dipping of the boat under my weight on one side swung her round in another direction. I thought she was going to heel over on top of me, and sprang back into her. The next moment she righted herself, caught the current of the river, and was dashing away from the falls towards the river mouth.

The landscape was whirling round me. I clung to the stump of the trunk, and tried to make out things. For a moment I could see nothing but a landscape that spun round and round with the whirling of the vessel, then I saw that I was through the outlet and rushing between the banks of the river at a great pace.

The bowl was spinning still, but more slowly. I looked over the side of the vessel, and saw marshes with serpents and big lizards; then I was past them, and running between wooded rocky banks.

On the left bank I saw two of the double-bodied animals staring, then, in front, the view cleared, and I saw the great river. At the same time I heard the noise of a waterfall. The big river was at a lower level, and the river I was on fell into it over a cataract! It would have been useless for me to try to swim for the bank, as the current was much too strong, and, even if I got to the bank, I should be completely stranded. I had little choice but to face the cataract.

I clasped my arms tightly round the "mast" and waited. My nerves had got to such a state of tension that I don't think I felt any fear. I merely waited.

The roar of the waterfall came up to me. I was rushing at it. Then, instead of falling, I was flying through the air. My light craft had been shot off the edge of the waterfall by its own speed. It fell on the water, bounced up again, fell again, and skidded along, shaking every bone in my body like a heap of dry bones in a sack. Then the rush of the greater river caught it and sent it spinning down mid-river.

My body had been rattled like a bag of dice and seemed to be falling asunder; my head was giddy with the spinning and bouncing of the boat, but I had managed to cling on to the "mast" through the whole of the skidding, though I had swung and bumped against it horribly. Then I slumped to the bottom of the boat and was violently sick.

Gradually the spinning of the bowl began to lessen, got slower and slower, and almost stopped. My giddiness was beginning to pass away. My body felt as if it had been brutally beaten. I felt bruised on the right shoulder and the left hip. There didn't seem to be any bones broken, however.

I stood up beside "the mast," and looked round me. I was in the middle of the great river about a mile from either bank. On each side the shores went past at such a pace that I judged that the river must be going at the rate of twelve or fifteen miles an hour. There was no sign of any human dwelling on the shores that I could see. On both sides they stretched away mile after mile towards the mountain barriers that I had seen from the cliff and the downward path. In front the river stretched into the dimness, and through the dimness I saw, a great distance away, a series of lofty mountains revealed under the gleams of the streamers of light.

The mountains in front ran away to right and left on both sides, to meet the great chains that ran parallel with the rushing river. Between them they seemed to form a complete barrier to the further passage of the river, unless it had carved an outlet somewhere between them. Probably it had made a way between the distant mountains that rose up in front. I stared at them, fascinated. I felt that beyond these mountains I should discover the world of men, if I could only get through or over them. Would the river bring me there? What should I find beyond? Men and towns, or a barren desert? Perhaps darkness.

Although I was becoming more and more drowsy, I wanted to see where the river led before I slept. Judging by the pace of the current, I calculated that another half-hour would bring me to the foot of the mountains. The river stretched almost straight in front of me for a long distance, and, unless there were very considerable windings farther on, it would soon be approaching the foot-hills.

I heard a noise and listened intently. It was certainly a cataract. Then I was round a bend of the river and rushing straight at the sound. Not two miles ahead the river met the mountain and disappeared with the noise of a cataclysm.

I stood staring ahead in dismay. What was in front? Perhaps a fall that plunged into some bottomless gulf! What was I to do? I thought of springing out and endeavouring to swim to the shore, but a moment's thought showed me that I shouldn't have the slightest chance of reaching it. Whatever hope of safety I had lay in sticking to my vessel. Then suddenly the bowl rounded a corner and dashed through a great arch under the mountain. As it spun round into the arch, I saw a waterfall that came down from the mountain on my left and that had been hidden from me by a mass of cliff—then I was in semi-darkness, rushing through a long cavern or tunnel lit into a dim confusion by phosphorescence from the sides and the roof. The latter was at least twenty feet over my head. The tunnel was not as wide as the river had been, but it was at least a hundred yards in width. I could see nothing living in it, and, when I listened, there was nothing to be heard but the soft swish of the rushing water. It came into my mind that the water might fall into so great an abyss that no sound could return—perhaps an abyss of fire—but I was at once too excited and too tired to be much troubled even by this thought. I had done all I could. If I were hurrying towards the mouth of a pit of fire or water, then I should soon be dead and at rest.

I think I must have fallen into a sort of doze, for I didn't see the exit from the tunnel. When I became conscious, the bowl was already rushing over a broad sheet of water. There was little light except the gleaming of the water, which seemed to be a mass of phosphorus. There was no sign of the streamer lights from above. But for the phosphorescence I should have been in complete darkness.

I looked round me. Everywhere was phosphorescent water. I looked behind me, but could see nothing, although I knew that the mountain that I had come through must be there. I turned again, and scanned the water for any trace of land. There was none that I could see. Nothing but a coruscating sea, under a dark canopy.

I was still rushing through the water at a great pace, carried along by the current of the river that had swept me into it, or by some powerful current that was in the sea itself. I was glad of this, for, if there were no current, I might remain floating on the dark water till I died of starvation. But although I searched the water on all sides for some glimpse of sails, there was none.

I could see a slight distance along the water, and I thought I saw, here and there, round bodies lifting themselves up from it, as if big water-beasts were swimming near the surface. I didn't want to attract their attention, as they might attack the boat. I had therefore to make my observation very carefully, without putting my head much over the rim of the boat.

After a while I sat down in the boat, leaning against the side. Thought was no use to me, only a trouble, since it suggested difficulties and disasters that it could not help to avoid.

I put my thoughts away, drew a piece of cooked meat out

of my bag, and began to eat. When I was cooking the flesh on the cliff, I had stowed away six grilled steaks in my wallet.

As I ate, the phosphorescence seemed to be fading, and by the time I had finished I had reached a region of almost complete darkness.

CHAPTER SIX

Men

I was in the worst plight in which I had found myself since my entrance into this world, rushing along blindly on a dim sea, of whose limits or bounds I could see nothing, under a lightless gloom, along a shore whose darkness might cover anything. I was rushing past a land that revealed nothing. From time to time, hoarse barkings and bellowings came to me from the shores flying past me on my left hand. Lights glimmered and flickered over them—spectral, blue lights. Now and again I imagined I could see tall moving figures.

My mind was so filled by fantastic things that I couldn't be sure that it hadn't deceived me—the shapes were probably only serpents coiling upwards.

I began to wonder what sort of creatures could inhabit such a place, and what other shores the sea might have. If I could only get back to the country of the streamer lights, I could start my search afresh. There, at least, there was some light and warmth, while here there was nothing but darkness and rotting phosphorescence. However, for the moment I could do nothing.

For a while I stood by the "mast," staring into the darkness. Feeling hungry, I took out a piece of my cooked meat and made a cheerless breakfast.

Then I sat down and waited.

Was it an illusion, or was it getting brighter? I stared upward. There were no gleams in the darkness above me. Yet, undoubtedly, it was getting brighter.

I peered cautiously over the side. In front there was a gleam of light, as if there were an opening of some sort through which moonlight was coming. To my joy the stream was sweeping me towards it. The light was growing larger. Already I could see the water dimly in front.

The river was getting more visible between shores of rock and slimy ground. Overhead a cavernous vault of rock was dimly visible, high up. In front it opened up into a wide gateway through which light was coming.

I stared at the opening with intense excitement. I was rushing at it—then through it, between rocky walls into the brightness.

I stared round me. I was on a great stretch of water, over which, high up, streaming Aurora lights were darting backward and forward. I could have shouted with joy. After the darkness of the great cavern or tunnel from which I had escaped, the sight of the Aurora was almost as great a joy as the sunlight would have been.

I looked round me with delight. In front, some distance away, I could see three islands. Beyond these, on all sides, the sea seemed to stretch to the horizon. I scanned it eagerly for the sight of a vessel.

There was nothing, neither ship nor mainland, only the islands and the expanse of empty water.

Behind me a vast cliff stretched from sea to sky on each side. I turned back and looked at the islands. Already they were much nearer. The current of the stream had been slowed down somewhat by its entrance into the sea, but it was still strong, and was flowing rapidly towards the islands. As they came nearer, I saw that they had tall growths, like trees, and that all three were larger than I had thought. The largest couldn't be less than three miles in length.

Now that I had seen no sign of a ship, I began to think that it might be wise to try to land on the islands. As we came near them, I examined the largest island as carefully as the light permitted. If it were merely a swamp of reptiles, I should be much safer floating on the great water. It seemed to be wooded and hilly, for there were dark, uneven masses like clumps of trees on uneven land.

The vessel was not moving directly towards it now, but towards a sea-channel, about a mile broad, that lay between one end of the island and the nearer of the other islands.

It looked as if I should be carried past into the sea beyond.

As the bowl rushed on, I was in exceeding perplexity. If I decided to land, I might have to jump out and swim before the current carried me past the western end, but that would mean abandoning the vessel.

I stared at the island, but, in the dim light, I could distinguish little.

Suddenly I grew rigid. A sound was coming from over the water—a sound like distant music!

I listened, tense.

There could hardly be any doubt that it was music—a soft strain of music, very low, through distance, but quite clear. And it was coming from behind the island!

I had been so often deceived, by my hopes, into believing that men were near, that now I could hardly trust my ears. The music ceased. I could hear nothing but the loud thumping of my own heart.

The music had come from behind the biggest of the three islands. I stared at it. Were there people living on it—houses, dwellings of men? Surely that music was made by man. There was no light visible—nothing, except the masses of wood that stood up dark under the streamers of light, but—that music! It could hardly be credible that I had reached men at last— but what else could have played that music?

All my doubts as to the wisdom of landing had ceased. I knew now that I must get to the island. I had fixed my kit firmly, and got ready to swim ashore when I noticed that I was moving towards the island, as if the current had deflected. It looked as if I might reach it without having to swim.

I was shaking with excitement. That had certainly been music. Even if I must swim, I would not abandon my vessel. I still had the stout trailers that I had tied round the "mast" when I was towing the boat out of the lake, and, if I had to swim to get to the island, I could hold one of these, so as to tow the vessel after me. If I failed to reach the shore, I should still be able to get back to the vessel with this rope.

All the time I was listening eagerly in the hope of hearing the music again. But there was no sound.

Ah! My vessel was turning away from the shore. The backward wash of the current had caught it, and it was beginning to drift out again.

I waited no longer, but seized the end of one of the trailers, sprang into the water, and began to swim strongly towards the island. At first I seemed to be making headway. Then the pull of the bowl began to drag me back.

After I had swum about thirty strokes, I saw that I should be swept past the island by the race of the water. I put out all my strength, and, for a few moments, seemed to make progress again. Then I saw that it was no use. Do what I would, I could not keep the bowl from being dragged away by the current. I was being swept past the island.

I began to get out of breath, and my strokes grew feebler. I had now to choose between abandoning the boat, or giving up all hope of reaching the island. The music might have been merely the fantasy of a weary mind. It seemed hardly credible that it could have been real.

I couldn't afford to abandon the bowl and leave myself stranded on an island that might be merely a festering swamp of reptiles. Now I was actually passing the point of the island. It was quite near. If I let go the trailer, I might reach it. On the other hand, I was tired, and might be swept away by the current and lose both vessel and land.

I was round the point. Then, suddenly, I found myself being carried towards the shore. My vessel passed me, stranded, and was just moving off again as my feet touched ground. It had not yet tautened the rope, however, and I held on to it. Then, for a moment, I thought that it would pull me out to sea. I tautened my body and jerked strongly backwards. The bowl resisted, then gave and came round with a spin. I pushed through the water without much difficulty. The ground under my feet was even, and not too sloping. I got to the shore, and hauled in the bowl.

I looked round. There was nothing in view but a steep shore that came down from a still steeper incline of land.

I began to work the bowl up the shore, pushing and hauling. It was heavy, but I managed to get it sufficiently high up to ensure its not being carried away by a rush of water.

All the time I kept watching and listening. No sound came to me, however, and I could see little except the shore and the water.

I began to climb up the bank. Near the top its slopes were covered with trailing growths.

At the top I looked round me. Then I stood staring, hardly believing my eyes.

Not more than a mile away, close into the shore, a ship was lying—an extraordinary looking vessel that seemed to be nearly a hundred feet long. It was no illusion. She was certainly there —standing high out of the water, and festooned with lights. I thought I could see figures moving on the decks, but she was too far away to make them out clearly.

For a few moments I stood staring, then I rushed towards her.

I ran across a sort of plateau, rushed down a slope that fell from it towards the shore, and found myself plunging through a swamp. I didn't wait to see whether it was passable or clear of snakes or other reptiles, but plunged right through it. Once I sank up to the knees, but I pulled myself out again and ran on.

I couldn't see the ship now, as some rising ground, on the other side of the swamp, hid her from my view.

As I ran, I hallooed, in the hope that, if the men had landed on the island, they might hear my shouts, but there was no answer. Then I was through the swamp and up the side of the slight incline beyond which I had seen her lying.

She was still there, standing out clearly under her lights and the lights from above—a long double-decked vessel, standing at least twelve or fourteen feet high out of the water, from her waterline to her top deck. I could see her decks clearly, and, on the upper one, a stern cabin. She had neither masts nor funnels, yet she was undoubtedly a ship made by civilised men, though not like our ships—more like the pictures I had seen of Roman galleys.

I stared at her, fascinated. I had only one idea now—to get to her! I had found the Romans, probably found my father!

I began to run again. The thought of danger never occurred to me. I was much too excited at the moment. My one thought, as I ran, was that I had at last found men; for there could be no doubt, at this distance, that the figures that I saw were really men.

What strange rational monsters I had unconsciously expected in this underworld, I cannot tell, but these were men. And not merely men, but civilised men, not savages.

I was so relieved at the sight of them that I began to shout for sheer joy. They were looking towards me, as if they were trying to locate the source of the shouting. I waved my arms to them. There was no answering signal. I shouted again. No answer came back. I was on the point of entering the water, to swim off to the vessel, when I saw a boat being lowered.

As the men swung over the side of the vessel I could see
their figures—small slim men, dressed in some sort of jackets
or tunics, under which their legs seemed to be bare. I could not
hear any voices, but the last man who got in was evidently in
command, for, when he sat in the stern of the boat, the others
began to row.

As the boat came near, I thought that its occupants must
be boys. They were certainly not full man's size. Indeed they
looked more like slim girls than big boys, their shoulders and
waists were so small. They were rowing with a perfect co-
ordination. Evidently they were excellently trained. Very dis-
ciplined also, for no man was speaking.

I listened and watched with intense excitement. In the
silence I could hear the sound of the oars in the rowlocks. The
men were moving with the regularity of machines.

I took in every little detail. The boat was clinker built, and
the oars were attached by some sort of straps to the rowlocks.
The men were rowing as we row—by pulling the oars towards
them.

The boat was now running in to the shore beside me, and
the face of the man in the stern was becoming clear.

I stared at him with intense eagerness. I saw a small face,
so impassive that it might have belonged to a lay figure, but
it was the face of a European—unquestionably it was the face
of a European—with very regular features, extremely delicately
cut—a feminine face.

His was the only one I could see, as the men who were rowing had their backs to me, and, as the boat ran in to the shore,
I kept staring intently at him, smiling and waving my arms.
He took no notice of me, but stared in front of him, as impassive as a mummy.

As the boat touched ground, I caught hold of the bow in
my eagerness. At the same moment the two men who were
nearest to me, at the bow, jumped out, and took me by an

arm each, without any salutation. I stared at them, surprised
by their sudden movement. They weren't looking at me. They
were staring in front of them, as they laid hold of me—not at
me, but through me!

Their eyes were so large that the light seemed to run through
them from side to side, but they were fixed and staring, absolutely devoid of expression, even of the expression of an imbecile; for an imbecile looks at you, but these men looked
straight in front of them as if they were unaware.

If they hadn't caught hold of me, I couldn't have known
whether they had seen me at all or not. If this were discipline,
I had never seen such automatic discipline.

I felt suddenly chilled. A touch of apprehension caught my
mind.

They were urging me into the boat, but they were doing it
gently, although firmly. I didn't resist, but stepped in. The men
followed, and directed me in silence to the seat nearest the
stern-seat. The man sitting in the stern-seat was facing me, his
knees touching mine. I bowed to him, and smiled. He seemed
not to see me. His eyes were looking through me, as if I were
invisible!

I stared at him, considerably taken aback by his extraordinary attitude to me. His delicately cut face was of an earthy
fawn colour under that light, but it was entirely devoid of expression—as blank as if it were carved in wood. His eyes, which
were large and slightly protruding, with very dilated pupils,
had the same absolutely empty stare as the eyes of the men
who had seized me. As I looked at him, the thought occurred
to me that these men behaved like some primitive peoples, who
pretend at first not to be conscious of strangers. If this were
so, then presently he would speak to me, ask some questions,
come to sufficient consciousness at least to look curiously
at me.

I settled myself in my seat, and waited patiently. The men

pushed off the boat, and began to row to the ship. The man
still made no sign that he was conscious of my existence. I
began to get a feeling of foreboding. As I watched him, I knew
that my first surmise was wrong. This was no primitive man
who looked through me as if I weren't there. There was something fundamentally wrong in the whole situation.

I wanted to speak, but couldn't. I was being frozen into
immobility by the look on the man's face, by the look that I
knew was on the faces of the men who were rowing behind my
back.

For a moment I got a wild idea that these men were not
living men at all, that I had come to a world of ghosts; "living
dead" was the thought that came into my mind as I stared at
the empty eyes that looked straight through me as if they
didn't see me, but were caught in some pre-occupation or life
that shut out from their vision the world of men. Yet these
men could not be mere ghosts. I had felt their hands on my
arms.

I turned and looked at them. Their faces were flesh and
blood. In spite of that inhuman stare, they were men. In front
of us the ship was there clear to see. The boat was firm under
me.

They were men—human beings like myself. I would not
allow them to paralyse me by their immobility. I would submit
to the silence no longer. Whatever was to happen, I must break
the spell.

I looked back at the man in the stern. Once again I felt the
compulsion of his silence. I wrenched myself out of it, and
threw my head back. My voice burst forth:

"I come in peace," I said loudly, in Latin.

The moment I spoke, I felt as if I had committed an in-
decency! I stared shamefacedly but expectantly at the man.
What was going to happen?

Nothing happened. He didn't make the slightest sign of

having heard me, not even by the flicker of an eyelid or the faintest movement of the head!

I turned round to the others. The man nearest me was looking straight in my direction, but he, too, was looking through me. There was no sign in his eyes that he had heard me either!

I turned back, and stared at the man in the stern in consternation.

My mind shrank back from the fear that was invading it, and began to try to fashion human explanations of the inhuman situation that confronted it.

Perhaps this world was one in which the human beings lacked some of the senses of men on the upper earth. Perhaps these men were completely deaf and blind, but had some other sense that enabled them to find exact direction.

Then I thought that that could not be the explanation. The man sitting opposite me was like a delicate statue moulded by a Greek, and with all the natural restraint of a Greek. He could not be a human monstrosity that had neither sight nor hearing. That colourless monochrome face was yet the face of a man. Even those eyes—— No! No! It must be some extreme discipline that had imposed on these men the logical conclusion of the discipline which soldiers have to bear, even on the upper earth. Probably they were soldiers or marines—subjected to a discipline that had gone to insane extremes. On the vessel there would be higher-grade men—officers, the commander, the captain—these would surely be different.

I looked round. The vessel was looming up over me. The next moment we were alongside. She was even larger than I had thought, and I could see, along her sides, banks for oars—one above the other in rows. To that extent she was like the Roman trireme, as I had seen it in illustrations. These men must be the descendants of the Romans who had escaped to the underworld from the Wall—the descendants of the Conquerors of the World, these shells of men! That might explain it. The discipline of old Rome had become a madness here below—a strait jacket that had killed all individuality. What was going to happen to me in so strange a world?

One of the men went up to the side. Another put his hand on my shoulder, as a sign to me that I was to follow him. Even that recognition of my existence comforted me.

There was a sort of rope-ladder hanging down. It led, not to the top deck, but to the first deck, about half-way up. The man passed through this and I followed, and found myself in a sort of corridor at the end of which there were two men standing.

My guide went down the corridor, past the men, who stood staring into vacancy as if they hadn't seen us. Beyond the corridor was a wide space, but I had no time to look about me, for my guide went down a hatchway.

As I descended, I got a glimpse of places for oarsmen— benches placed behind one another in oblique tiers. Then I was in a long, low-roofed cabin, lit by rows of globes that hung down from the roof.

The cabin was full of men. Some sat at a long table, eating; others sat or lay on bunks round the walls, but there was no murmur of talk, no sound but the slight movements of the eating men. None of them paid the slightest attention to our entrance, or to one another. Each was acting as if he were alone! Each seemed to be unaware of the others, or of anything outside himself—unaware even of the food that he was eating!

Had the strain of the journey turned my brain? Could this world, that I thought I saw, be real, or was I the victim of some extraordinary dream? Had I eaten or drunk some strange drug?

My guide brought me over to one of the bunks and left me. I sat down and looked round the cabin. It was no dream. It was as clear and real as any room I had ever been in; hard and real—quite bare, except for the tables and benches or couches, and clean, very clean. It was the product of a very definite standard of civilisation. But for the demeanour of its occupants, I would have thought myself in the cabin of a European ship; I would have been feeling full of joy at finding myself in the presense of so highly organised a civilisation. But this thing that I had come to was more hideous than the lowest form of savagery!

I stared round at the men. Could the minds behind these masks be the minds of men—the minds of sane men? If not, into what inferno had I fallen?

Yet they were eating daintily. Their movements, though queerly automatic, were not ungraceful. It could not be possible that insane men could have produced this highly organised life.

I looked at the food. There were large dishes along the middle of the table, containing assortments of foods like *hors d'oeuvre*. The men took morsels out of the dishes with their fingers and ate them quite daintily.

I looked at the food. Most of it was pale stuff that looked like preparations of fungoid plants or the sea-weedy growths that I had met already, but there was meat, too—pale meat like serpent flesh or the flesh of slugs or lizards. Strange though it was, the sight of it was comforting. Men who cooked their food and served it as these men did could not be altogether inhuman. Somewhere there must be a connection between them and ordinary humanity.

Two men came into the cabin, came straight up to me, and took me by the arms. I got up. They were leading me out of the cabin. I should soon know my fate.

I was brought along a corridor, up two short flights of stairs, and out on a deck. I looked round. We were on the top deck near the stern of the vessel. There was a structure at the stern with a curtain drawn across it. We had come up

beside it, and, as we stood in front of it, the curtains parted
in the middle and revealed a man sitting at a little table. He
was sitting with his back to a lamp that flung its light full in
my face. I looked at him, then straightened up, astonished.
What I had expected I don't know—another of the "living
dead," I suppose. What I got was very different—an eagle-like
face with an intensity of life so concentrated that I felt almost
as if I had received the impact of physical force. I stared at
the man. The eyes were vacuous—extraordinarily vacuous—
yet penetrative like searchlights, and they were turned on me
in a fixed, paralysing stare.

For the moment I was completely dumbfounded. The eyes
were not hostile or angry, but their effect was more frightening
than that of the eyes of a tiger about to spring. They seemed
to hold and dominate me with an almost sickening effect. I was
being overpowered! Stunned! Then I realised that I was also
being invaded. The man's eyes had entered my mind. His mind
had entered mine, and was searching it.

It would be impossible for anyone who has not experienced
it to understand the sense of violation that I felt when I found
another mind in possession of mine, overpowering it, seizing
my will, laying hands on my personality. The recoil was so
great that for a moment my mind shook itself free of him.

Looking back now at that moment, I believe that in it my
fate was decided. If the outrage had been less, the recoil not
sufficiently strong, I should have foundered, as a person, there
and then. If my first reaction had even been fear instead of
anger, I should have probably been overpowered. But my only
feeling was anger. There was in my mind something akin to
nausea, but it was not the nausea of fright but of disgust and
rage.

So great was the recoil, that the man drew back as if I had
been on the point of hitting him. I had an insane desire to
spring on him. I moved forward, met suddenly with some

strange force, and stopped. The man's power had reasserted itself and checked me.

The next moment it had hurled itself against my personality. This time, however, I was ready for it. Every force of my mind and every nerve of my body were strung up to meet it, and I took its spring with the full weight of my powers. I felt my eyes glaring into the eyes that gripped mine. I don't know how long our eyes were locked in that struggle, but to me then it seemed an eternity. Time had ceased. Everything had ceased, except those eyes that tore at me. I could feel waves of some strange power pouring over me. I was giving way. The thing was again entering my mind. The outrage was about to happen again. I shook with hatred and disgust. All fear left me. I would die rather than give way. Straightway my mind sprang upward. Some force seemed to rush to its aid from the depths of my personality. It was as if my soul had come into action and flung into the contest powers greater than my own.

Suddenly my mind was free of the grip that had been strangling it. I flung back my head and laughed—a peal of triumphant laughter that rang through the silence like a trumpet. The man stared at me now quietly, with the same concentration, but without attempting to interfere with my mind. He seemed to be trying to understand the situation, but there was no expression of anger or fear or any emotion in his eyes. Except for the fact that they were full of concentration, they were empty of all expression.

"Why did you do this thing to me?" I cried out to him, in Latin.

He made no answer, merely staring fixedly at me. I turned to the men. They were staring through me, seemingly indifferent to the struggle that had taken place. I now understood what had happened to them. They were slaves in mind as well as in body.

I felt inclined to cry out to them to save themselves, but the sight of those empty eyes, mere pits of nothingness, brought me to my senses. I looked back at the man. He was no longer there. The space in the cabin was empty. Where he had stood, there was now nothing but a wall covered with some sort of soft tapestry.

I turned. The men were advancing towards me. Suddenly I felt exhausted. I began to tremble, and a cold sweat poured over me. The reaction had come. I don't think that, even now, if the man had come back to attack, he would have won, for I was too full of loathing of what he had tried to do, but I felt no power to resist the mere physical force of the men. I dropped my hands to my sides, and stood quietly. Two of them took me by the arms and gently led me away.

CHAPTER SEVEN

"Absorbed"

WE WERE on the deck of the ship—a long floor-like space that glittered with a phosphorescent polish. In the middle of it, half-way to the bow, a number of men were standing like statues. Otherwise the deck seemed empty, but I could not see clearly beyond the group of men.

A short distance away, the island lay glimmering under the upper lights. As I looked at it, it seemed to me incredible that it was not even an hour since I had come running down to its shores calling eagerly on the ship. The man who had done that seemed to me now to have been a man in some former life, far away, so remote did his hopes and fears now appear.

I felt a gentle pressure on my arms. I had stopped involuntarily, and they were moving me forward. I went with them, because there was nothing else that I could do, and I felt exhausted. The situation was so incomprehensible that there was nothing I could plan except to steel my will to face whatever further horror tried to seize it. The struggle was not to be won on the physical plane—that was clear; but beyond that I could make no guess. Perhaps they would now beat me down by physical attack and seize my mind while I was stunned, or they might try to drug me or deprive me of my senses in some other way.

They led me through an opening in the deck, down two flights of stairs, and back into the large cabin, where the men had been eating. Here they placed me again, sitting on a bunk against the wall.

I looked round at the men who were in the cabin. I was seeing them differently now, in the light of my own experience. I was beginning to grasp what had happened to them. The man that I had encountered, and others of his kind, had done to them what he had tried to do to me. They had entered into these men's minds, substituted their own will for the life force of their victims, and made them what they were. The men had been murdered mentally while kept physically alive—not merely dominated completely in their minds, but deprived of them!

The realisation of this came on me with a sudden shock. None of these men had any individual life. None of them existed except in and through the will of the commander. None of them existed as a person for himself or for the others. In the guardroom, perhaps in the whole ship, I alone existed personally, besides the master who owned their souls.

At this moment a man came into the cabin and came over to me. He made a sign to follow him, and I did so. I thought that I was being brought back to face the commander, and I steeled my mind for the ordeal, but, instead of going up the stairs that led to the deck, my guide turned down a corridor at the side of the vessel and stepped aside before a cabin to let me enter it. I did so. It was a bathroom, with a long trough, full of water, in the middle of the floor, and strange-looking toilet utensils. I put my hand into the water. It was hot. They evidently wanted me to take a bath.

For a moment I paused. Possibly this was some way of drugging me. Then I thought that, even if it were, I could not avoid it. If they wished to drug me, they could do it, no matter what I did. A bath was a very unlikely method, in any case. I began to take off my clothes. My guide left me and shut the door.

That first bath of mine, in that extraordinary world, was a strange experience. I lay in the hot water as if I were at home —so stunned by the incredible turn of fate's wheel that I was in some way suddenly at rest. I looked round at the strange utensils—the metal mirror, the soap that looked as if it was made of some sort of yellow earth, the curious brushes and scrapers, the soft phosphorescent light that glowed from the ceiling and the walls—and I found it hard to believe that the whole thing was not a dream. It seemed incredible that in a day, or a few days, I might be dead or mad. Incredible: yet I knew that it was not only possible but probable.

Suddenly I sprang up out of the bath. My father—during the last hour I had forgotten him. Where was he? What was he, in this terrible world? Was he dead, or mad, or a prisoner? I could not believe that he had become an automaton. My mind shrank away from the possibility of such an end for him. No; he, of all men, could not have fallen to be one of the living dead—it was not thinkable. But, if he hadn't fallen into that grave, where was he? What was he?

The door opened, and a man walked in with a bundle of clothes, which he put on a low table, and then went out again, taking my clothes with him. I called to him to leave them, but he was gone and the door shut.

I dried myself and took up the clothes. They were of a soft delicate material. When I shook them out, I found that they consisted of a shirt or tunic, and a pair of short trews. I put them on. They were as delicate to feel as the finest silk.

My mind kept running on my father. Where could he be in this world? If he was not dead, where could he be? If he had resisted, as he surely would have done, they might merely have made him a prisoner. But that was several years ago. My mind was in a whirl of anxiety and questioning.

The door opened, and a man came in and put his hand on my arm. I went with him, back to the guardroom, and to a vacant place at the table. In front of me there was a large dish of assorted foods, like those I had seen before. One piece of meat on the dish looked exactly like a stewed beefsteak.

There was a knife and a wooden platter beside me. I cut off half the beefsteak, put it on my platter, and put a piece in my mouth. It was not meat, but a rich sort of fungus, and tasted quite good. It made me feel hungry and I began to eat heartily. A man came up behind me and put a jar beside my platter, and a tall narrow mug. I looked into the jar. It was full of liquid, which I was evidently intended to drink. Each of the other men at the table had a similar jar beside him. Possibly mine was drugged.

I felt that the struggle with the commander of the ship had only begun, and that, having felt my power when awake, he would probably try to put me into a drugged sleep and so deal with my mind while I slept. Then I thought that, even if this were so, I should have to face it some time or other. As well now as later. If I could only screw up my will to resistance before I slept, I should still baffle him, for my mind, when asleep, had its own power, if only it were moved beforehand to resistance.

I took the jar, poured some of its contents into the mug, and tasted it. It was insipid but not unpleasant. I drank a mouthful and watched its effects. It warmed the back of my throat rather pleasantly, but otherwise I could feel nothing, nor was there any sudden stupor or exhilaration.

I went on with my meal. As I did so, a deep sound vibrated through the vessel like the booming of a heavy gong. It rose, fell, died away. Then it boomed again, and once again. At the third stroke the ship rushed forward, trembling under the sweep of its banks of oars. At the same time a soft music began, with a rowing rhythm in it. We had started for our unknown destination.

My mind began to see things with lucidity. This people had taken an entirely different road from our people on earth. Whatever the powers of the rulers, they evidently did not include any scientific knowledge of methods of propulsion such as ours, for the ship, as far as I could see, was merely a repetition of those used by their ancestors two thousand years before. Since they had not made any discovery in method of transport, it seemed unlikely that they had made any other discovery in the regions of material science—at least, any discovery that mattered.

They had acquired some great powers which I didn't understand, but these new powers were over mind, not matter, and, judging by their methods of driving the ship, they were probably in the physical world feeble and imitative compared to the white races on earth.

As these thoughts poured through my mind I felt more confident. I had powers and knowledge that they did not possess.

Then I sat up. If they could lay hands on my mind they would seize that knowledge, those powers, or, if they could not do that, they could force me to use my powers for them. Perhaps that was what the commander of the vessel had already been trying to do when he had sought to invade my mind.

My father, if he had fallen into their hands, could have given them little, for he had an entirely unscientific mind, and no interest in science, either applied or theoretical. He knew, in fact, no more than they did; but I was different. In plundering my mind they would gain rich loot of knowledge, if they could apply it. Even if they could not, they might be able to force me to use my knowledge for their benefit—by consent if I would agree; if not, by reducing me to the condition of a scientific robot.

After the first shock of the thought, my mind began to contemplate the position with calm. Now that it was beginning to grasp things and arrange the facts, it did not shrink from this strange world that was emerging to its view. Indeed, I felt restful, almost sleepy. A drowsy ease was beginning to come over me.

I realised that I had been drugged after all. I tried to rouse myself, but struggled in vain. A sea of sleep was pouring over me. With one last effort I fixed my mind on the idea of resistance—resistance—resistance to invasion of my personality, and so sank into a gulf.

I woke with a feeling of restfulness and well-being. A long rhythmical movement was rocking me pleasantly. I lay on my back looking at the roof of the cabin. The rhythmical movement was the sweep of the oars of the Roman galley. I looked round me. I was on a low couch in a narrow cabin dimly lit with phosphorus. I stood up. What had happened to me?

I stood listening, collecting my mind. A soft music was keeping time to the rhythmical hum of the vessel as she rushed forward under the sweep of the oars.

I sat down again and tried to think out the position. What had happened during my sleep? Had my mind been explored by the searchlight mind of the commander?

I could not remember my dreams, nor did I feel like a man who had been through a struggle, yet I had a strong conviction that an attempt had been made to get into my mind and find out my purpose, my thoughts, and my powers.

But why, if they wanted to discover my intentions, had the commander not questioned me? These men were Romans. No matter how changed they were, they were Romans. They had kept the Roman ship, the Roman dress. It was unlikely that they had not, in some way, kept the knowledge of the Latin speech. The natives of European countries on earth, even those who were not descended from Rome, had kept Latin as a language to be learned by their educated people. It was hardly credible that a mind as powerful as that of the commander could not know something about Latin. Yet, if he had known, he had made no sign when I spoke to him.

I looked round the cabin. It was a strange place, with its green phosphorescence that came from roof and walls with a hypnotic effect of repose and confused edges. Everything was soft and slightly blurred when seen through this dim radiance.

My mind swung back to my father. Where was he? Where

was I being brought? This ship's commander could only be a comparatively minor man in their State, yet he had shown a power of attack on my mind such as I had never conceived possible. Were the powers behind him so much greater that I should have no chance before their attack? Had my father gone down before them? Had they reduced him to a pitiful automaton like those men on the ship? Was that to be my fate also? If I was perfectly honest with them, and told them everything, could I avoid the worst, or would I merely put them on their guard and so lose all chance of saving my father?

These questions went round and round in my mind, but I could see no answer to them, in my lack of all knowledge of the nature and extent of the powers and purposes of the beings into whose hands I had fallen.

I wondered if I could in any way get more information. It was fairly certain that I could not get it by remaining in the cabin, but I could see no door. The walls were perfectly smooth and undivided, except at the corners. I got up and began to feel them. They felt like satin, soft and yielding, yet they were as firm as hard wood.

I went over the surface of the wall opposite the couch. There was no slit or line of division that I could find as far as the right-hand corner. I tried the corner. It was not a curving corner, but an angle. It felt as if there was a division there between the two walls. If so, it was too narrow for my fingers to find it. I made an instinctive movement for my knife. Then I realised that I had no pockets; I was dressed in the tunic. All my belongings had been taken from me. I tried to move the wall at the corner with the flat of my hands, in the hope that it was a sliding panel, such as I had heard of in Japanese houses. I could not move it. I began to work backward along it. Nothing happened until I had got to the middle of the wall, when suddenly it slid back, leaving a wide space opening on a big cabin.

I stepped into the guardroom. Men were lying and sitting on bunks and benches round the room, but no one took any notice of me. It was as if I had stepped into one of the dens of opium-eaters that I had read of.

Across the room there was an opening. I began to move towards it. Still nobody moved. It was impossible to know whether those automatons were aware of me. Then I saw that two of them had arisen and were coming towards me. I waited. They put their hands on my arms and led me out of the room.

We went along the same corridor, up the same flights of stairs, and emerged at the cabin where I had met the commander. The curtains parted. He was sitting there again, staring at me with his concentrated glance. At once I was on the defensive, but this look had none of the domination that had outraged me before. Instead of searching my mind, it seemed to be trying to tell me something. I got a feeling that there was something he could not understand, and that he was trying to express this to me. I dropped my attitude of hostile defence. Yes, he was trying to convey to me that he did not understand what I had done to him. The message came to my mind through his eyes, as if he had allowed me to read his thoughts. He wanted to know why I had acted to him as I had. The question surprised me. I thought that it must be as clear as light to anyone that I had to resist the violation of my mind. Yet the man in front of me did not understand it. Again he was asking me insistently why I had done it. I couldn't let him into my mind again to read the answer. I could allow no being to enter there. But how was I to establish contact with him?

Instinctively I began to speak in Latin, since my mind associated him and his surroundings with the Latin speech. He stared steadily at me. His questioning of my mind stopped. His eyes were now full of a different sort of concentration. He was sending me some message again: "Slowly, slowly," it said. "More slowly. Your speech is difficult to understand."

My heart leaped up. He found me difficult to follow, but he was following me; he was trying to understand. I began to speak word by word, as if to a foreigner who knew little of the language. I tried to explain to him that, if he wanted information from me, the only way to get it was by asking me, in which case I would tell him everything.

He showed no sign that he understood my answer. At first I thought he was unable to understand my words, then I knew that this was not so—that he had grasped my meaning, but that he could not understand my point of view. His mind was sending a message back to me—a question:

"Why, if you are willing to tell me everything, did you strike at me when I tried to see everything in your mind?"

I began to explain slowly, word by word, that no man had a right to enter into my mind or to try to take hold of my powers of will and thought. I must be free to give these or withhold them as I thought right.

"Free?" came back his query. "Free?"

The word and the thought were equally unintelligible to him. I saw that he could get no further in that way, and I began to speak again.

"Perhaps you would tell me what you want to know?" I said. "Then I shall tell you everything I can."

There was a pause. Then my mind received the question:

"Why did you come?"

"My father had come here before me," I answered. "I came to look for him."

"Your father?" his mind said. "Your father?" Then he went on: "Why should you look for your father?"

This question amazed me, and for the first time, I think, I began to get some inkling of the impassable gulf that separated my mind from that of the man in front of me.

"I love my father," I answered. "He has been lost to us. It was natural that I should come to look for him."

There was a long pause. It was clear that my explanation meant nothing to him, and that he was trying to fit it into some conception of his own and so get some meaning from it. His next question showed me this clearly.

"Is your father a Master of Knowledge?"

"For me, yes," I answered.

He paused again, pondering.

"If for you, then for all. Otherwise your words have no meaning," he answered.

I remained silent. How could I explain anything to such a mind? He felt my doubt, for he went on:

"You do not know. You cannot answer. If you are a High One, there is something wrong with your mind."

"No," I answered, "I am not a High One."

"Yet," he said, "you are not a Submissive One. You are willing, not obeying. What do you mean——?"

"I cannot explain to you," I said hopelessly. "Can you tell me if my father is in this country, and, if he is, where I can find him?"

He paused a long time, then his answer came:

"How could I answer such a question? How could any man know him?"

"But he would be different from all other men," I said.

"He could not remain so," he answered. "You, too," he added, "now you are beyond understanding, but you cannot remain like that. You will be absorbed."

"Absorbed!" I cried.

"Yes. The High Ones will do it. You will not remain ill, as you are, and wrong in your mind. You will be cured and absorbed."

"Absorbed!" I repeated. "Absorbed! Do you mean that my father has been made an imbecile like these poor creatures?"

"It is you who are an imbecile," came the answer. "Strong in the will but feeble in the mind, like a very little child—yet violent also like a madman at times. It cannot be that you have not once been a High One, for you have the power, but you have no longer wisdom or knowledge such as the High Ones have, nor love such as the workers live by. Where did you come from?"

I pointed upwards.

"From the surface of the earth," I answered, "where the sun shines, and there are bright days and green grass and all beautiful things."

He stared at me in silence. Then the message came again:

"The disorder of your mind is deep, but there is no ill that the High Ones cannot cure or ease. You may go."

I turned and went out of the cabin. If my father had arrived at this land, I knew now that he was either dead or in a worse condition. Soon I, too, would share the same fate, if I could not escape. But where could I escape?

I stood on the deck, looking over the rail at the phosphorescent darkness. The water fled from the ship's prows in lines of green light, but, beyond the shimmer in the near waters, I could see nothing. Then I saw a form, a heavy brown back that heaved up in the green light, wheeled round and round, and then sank slowly. No, I could not attempt to escape by swimming. Even if there were shores near, I should probably not reach them, and, if I did reach them, I should be no better off, since they would be either in the possession of this people or of dangerous brutes or reptiles. I was tied to the stake, and must stay.

What troubled me most were the words about my being absorbed. Had my father been absorbed, made imbecile? Was I to have the same fate? I could have faced physical danger with a sense of adventure at the thrill it brings, but the thought of the violation of my mind and soul nauseated me.

CHAPTER EIGHT

The Silent City

DURING THE WHOLE of the rest of the voyage the ship ploughed her way through an almost complete darkness.

I had no opportunity of observing the stretch of water that we were traversing, or the nature of its shores or its islands, if there were any.

The ship herself was a circle of light, owing to the fact that she was festooned with a network of large, brilliant globes. These threw a light on the waters within a short radius, but beyond that there was a circle of total darkness.

Twice, in this darkness, lights loomed up near us. Once, about two furlongs away on the starboard side, a broad, low vessel was revealed, like a canal barge, piled up with some sort of cargo. I could make out the forms of men rowing, but we were not near enough to get any clear view. I stared at her eagerly, but, though she was going in the same direction as our vessel, we were making a much greater pace, and we passed her in a few minutes.

The second lights emerged from the darkness a short time after the first, and revealed a much larger vessel, with a double deck and two banks of oars. She was going in the opposite direction, and was out of sight in a couple of minutes.

The men on our vessel took not the slightest notice of either boat, nor was there any recognition of us from the others, as far as I could see—no waving of flags or dipping of lights, or any sign that they had seen us.

When the second boat was passing, I was watching her from the bow. Near me a look-out man was posted, with an enormous metal disc beside him, like a huge gong, and a heavy metal clapper in his hand, obviously to give warning if there were any danger of collision. When the vessel had passed, I went over to him and asked him, in very slow, clear Latin, what sort of vessel it was. He did not seem to have heard me. I put my hand on his arm. He brushed it away like a man in a dream. I caught him more firmly by the arm. He unloosed my hand with a flexible movement of powerful, sinuous fingers. I gave up the attempt to get his attention, and moved away. This incident was typical of what was happening to me on that voyage. No matter what I did, I could not get any of the crew to take the slightest notice of my words or my presence.

At first I could hardly believe it. My mind grasped it in a superficial way, as intelligence grasps things before they are felt as well as perceived, but I had not assimilated the knowledge. I could not believe that they were completely unaware of me. It was too incredible, too alien to everything that had ever been known. I could not keep from trying to make contact, to produce some little connection with them, some incident that would give even a semblance of recognition of our common humanity. I kept on trying to speak to them. I asked them questions; made comments on the food, on their appearance, the darkness, my own adventures. There was no answer, no sign from a single person that he had heard me, or even dimly realised my existence. I might as well have been trying to get into touch with a gramophone or a motor-car. That they were conscious at times of my existence was obvious from the fact that they had brought me to various parts of the ship when I first arrived on her, but, apart from this, there was no evidence that they ever perceived me. With the exception of the commander, who did not appear during the rest of the voyage, there was not, as far as I could see, a single person on the ship who had in his mind any solid picture of my personality, or who was aware of me as men on earth are aware of one another.

As I walked amongst them, and watched them pass me and each other as if they and I were non-existent, there came to my mind a story I had heard at a scientific lecture in York— of how pike could be made permanently indifferent to trout in the same tank if they were separated from them for a sufficient length of time by glass partitions. After a while the trout, the lecturer said, became non-existent for the pike. The barrier produced by the glass had remained, as an insuperable psychological fact, at the back of the mind of the pike, even after it had been removed. In the same way some insuperable, psychological barrier seemed to me to have been erected in the mind of each of these men that made them non-existent for each other.

It was not, however, their lack of awareness that weighed most on me. Even if they had been totally unaware of me, but showed any of the normal reactions of humanity to external things or events, they would have been company of a sort; but, no matter how closely I watched, I could not detect a single one of the reactions that life calls up, not merely in men, but in animals, and that make a prison rat, or even a tortoise, a comfort and a healing influence for an isolated man.

It would be difficult for anyone on the upper earth to realise the feeling of desolation and hopelessness that the absence of this, in these men, began to produce in my mind as I walked amongst them; and with this feeling there was mixed a growing apprehension of something else that emanated from them— some strange influence—as if, in spite of their isolation and their lack of awareness of me, they had been combined against me, and had all their thoughts and emotions pooled into a single compelling force that was dragging me into its orbit.

Looking round at their sightless, indifferent faces, I told myself that the thought was a ridiculous one; that in my excited
condition I was the prey of absurd imaginings; but, as I
watched them, I knew that this was not so—that I was, in
fact, in the presence of some force that I could not understand,
a force that was invading me and compelling me to conform
to its rhythm. The mysterious force generated by an angry
mob on earth, when it has become fused by some flame of
passion, is the only force that I could compare to this influence that was constricting and dominating me; although nothing could be farther apart than the pushing, noisy, excited
collections of human beings that we call "crowds" on earth,
and the crew of that extraordinary vessel.

As I watched them, I realised that a cat or dog might as
well try to understand the feelings and thoughts of a fish as I
to fathom the life of that band of silent ghosts that was bringing me, on that antique vessel, to a destination of which I
could not even guess the nature.

What should I find when I got there? Were there towns
and cities with civilian populations that had not been subjected
to the surgical discipline that had emptied the minds of these
men? It was hardly credible that a whole population could
have been subjected to such complete slavery. There was
nothing on which to base any judgment, or even any conjecture
as to the characteristics of the civilisation towards which I was
being carried, and at length I gave up the futile task of trying
to unravel the problem, and waited with as much patience as
I could muster.

As they had taken my watch from me, I don't know how
long the voyage lasted, but it could not have been more than
about fifty hours, according to my reckoning, based on my
sleeping times and the number of meals I took. During almost
the whole of that period we travelled, as I have said, in complete darkness, and, apart from the two vessels that had

emerged near us from the gloom, I saw nothing beyond the circle of the ship's lights, except occasional dim flickers that appeared in the distance and might have been the lights of distant vessels. After we had been about forty-five or fifty hours travelling, however, the Aurora began to show itself again in long streamers that darted over our heads.

I was on the upper deck when it began, and looked around me eagerly. At first I could see nothing but the water. Then, as the lights grew brighter, I saw that we were running towards land. The lake was narrowing, so that its banks were visible on both sides—very close on the right hand—a flat dark shore. In front, more land seemed to bar our way, and I could see lights.

The land closed in still more on us, and presently I saw that we were running into a harbour of some sort, for I could see a circle of lights, and, beneath them, shapes that looked like canal barges moored to the sides of a big horseshoe curve of land that was opening up in front of us.

The Aurora had now come together in a glowing centre that poured out a brilliant and beautiful moon-like light.

I started forward, trying to find out what sort of city I was coming to. My eyes searched the darkness for the buildings; my ears listened eagerly for the noise of traffic, for any sound that would indicate the activities of men. There was none—no hum of humanity, no lights beyond those of the harbour, no buildings of any sort. No matter how I strained my eyes, I could see no sign of houses—nothing, indeed, but a collection of hedges, as if the land near the harbour had been divided up into a great number of individual fields.

I began to think that the town to which the harbour belonged must be some distance inland, behind the enclosed fields, but the country was becoming clear—a sort of flat plateau standing over the harbour—and I could see no sign of houses anywhere in the distance.

As we came nearer, I saw groups of men on the banks of the harbour around the boats, as if they were loading and unloading cargoes or going or coming by water. Also there seemed to be lights behind the hedges that lay at the back of the harbour, but, beyond that, there was no sign of a city or town or group of human dwellings. If there was a city anywhere near, it was difficult to see where it could be hidden.

Could it be, I found myself wondering in amazement, that the people lived like beasts, without any houses or streets or any of the other things that one associated with human life?

Even though I knew that in that land there was no need of houses such as we have, the total absence of them began to fill me with dismay. Perhaps it was the shape of the ship that led me to expect the other outward manifestations of the civilisation of Ancient Rome. Perhaps also the powers shown by the commander had led me to expect civilised dwellings, streets, and other things associated by us with power on the upper earth. Whatever the reason was, I had, in the foolish way in which one imagines unknown things on the pattern of known ones, been letting my mind dwell on visions of urban civilisation, and the sight of this settlement, compared to which the lowest form of kraal would have been human, deepened my foreboding. It was not merely that it made me feel that my hopes of the civilian population being different from the others were illusory, but that it destroyed those other foolish dreams of roofs and windows and the external things that humanity has created round itself. I had thought that the sight of these familiar things would, in some way, make up for the inhuman aspect of the people. I had been hungering for at least that crumb of consolation. Now I knew that that hunger would not be satisfied.

I switched my mind violently away from its fears.

After all, there was nothing in them. It was my own folly that had produced the imaginings of streets and houses. There was obviously a very highly organised civilisation in this land, and I was coming to one centre of it. The fact that it was constructed on entirely different lines from ours did not necessarily mean that it was not equally complicated. At any moment I might meet my father.

At this last thought my excitement grew intense. My mind had, in fact, substituted a new imagining for those of which it had been deprived.

As we ran into the harbour, I stared eagerly at the quays.

Extraordinary as it may seem, I know now, on looking back, that I half expected my father to be waiting for me on the quay; for I kept scanning the groups of men for one much taller than the others.

The quays were well lighted, and, if there had been any such figure there, I should by now have been able to distinguish it from the others. There was, however, no such figure to be seen. At the back of the quays there was a wall with heaps of stuff piled against it, and the men that I had seen were engaged in shifting this to and from the ships, on their backs or on long low carts with wheels. Apart from them there were no people on the quays, no crowd waiting for the ship—and, needless to say, no sign of my father.

The hope of seeing him having departed from me, my mind went back to its other trouble about the unnatural appearance of the settlement. The quays were well built stone quays, with pillars and rings for mooring the ships. The men were engaged in dealing with cargo. In spite of their inhuman aspect, their occupation at least was indicative of some form of trade and commerce. Why then was there no town? Could it be that the people lived underground? If so, what reason could they have for so strange a way of life? My mind kept revolving the question in a futile, troubled way. It was useless to ask the automatons who surrounded me, and who were now bringing the ship carefully to the quay-side, while a few similar robots on the quays waited to catch the mooring-ropes. I was at my destination, and would soon know the secret of this enigma, and with it, probably, my own fate.

All the time I kept looking up and down the quays for a sign of any tall man. There was none. They were all the same undersized, boyish figures—all men, too, as far as I could see; no women amongst them, and certainly no children nor animals.

As I waited at the side of the ship, a man touched me on the shoulder. I turned. One of the men was waiting to conduct me somewhere. I followed him, in the direction of the commander's cabin. As we came to it, the curtains swung back and the commander came out. I stood in front of him and bowed slightly. He watched me with his steady, unwinking stare, yet I drew comfort, after the days spent with the solitary robots, from the contact with his eyes. The message was coming to me.

"I am sending you over to the Masters of Will and of Knowledge. They will understand you and cure you."

"I hope they will understand me," I answered slowly. "If they do, they can help in the only way I ask to be helped—by bringing me to my father."

"They cannot do that," came the answer. "Even those who combine will and knowledge cannot do that, since there is no such person as your father."

"But there *is* such a person," I said. "He came down here, and he is either here or he is dead."

"He cannot be here now—not such as you think him to be —as you yourself will not be after a little while. However, I do not understand you nor you me. The Masters will understand, the Masters of Knowledge, and, when they have understood, they will cure you."

He began to walk past me. When I asked, "Where is the city?" he stopped.

"The city?" came his question.

"Yes, yes, the city, the settlement, the collection of dwellings of men who live here together? Where is it? I see nothing."

"That is it," he answered, turning his head slightly in the direction of the hedges.

"But there are no houses. I can see no dwellings of men, no streets."

"There are dwellings and paths between them," came the answer. "You will see. They await you now to bring you to the Masters of Knowledge."

He passed on. Two men came and stood beside me, took me each by an arm, and led me after him. He passed down the deck, and went off the ship to the quay by a gangway. Then he turned along the quay to the right.

As we followed him, I kept looking round eagerly, expectantly. Soon perhaps I should see real people. We passed several men, but they were the same type of automaton as those on the ship, and seemed unaware of our presence. They were dressed merely in short kilts that fell from the waist to the knees, and were obviously working men. There were no others.

The place was lit with some phosphorescent stuff, that was smeared on the ground and on the walls, and by globes of phosphorescent light that stood at intervals on the tops of round pillars. If there was anything to see, I should have seen it, but there was nothing but the automaton men and the piles of stuff on the quays and the boats.

Some of the cargo in the boats seemed to be bales of cloth, but mostly it consisted of foodstuff—fish, clumsy-looking beasts like seals, serpents piled on one another, and heaps of different sorts of vegetable growths. Of machinery I could see no sign.

After a few minutes' walk along the quay to the right, the commander turned from the waterside. There was an opening in the quay wall to the left, and we went through it. I stared around. We were on a path of hard-beaten earth, as broad as one of our big public roads. In front of us, a series of hedges formed enclosures, and the road led to the middle of this, but the place was empty except for three men who were coming along the road, and who, when they came near, I saw were automatons.

By now I had become adapted to my surroundings. The glimmer of phosphorus that gave light would have been confusing to eyes accustomed to the clear, hard light of the sun, but my eyes had grown used to the general dimness, and, indeed, found the roadway well lit after the comparative darkness of the waters.

The hedges were of some sea-weedy tree, and were fairly thick and about six feet high, and I could see that there were lights behind them, as if people lived there, though there was no sound except the padding of feet on the roadway.

As I walked along I tried to keep up my courage, but the silence of this abode of men, the lack of all the ordinary noises of streets and horses and traffic, was depressing me. In spite of all the warnings of my reason, I had been expecting something human, and the lack of it was weighing on me, invading me, with its suggestion of unknown sinister powers. I felt influences pressing in on me, and could not know whether those were coming from the darkness that had subdued this branch of the human breed to such inhuman silence, or from the powers which the darkness had called forth in that race in their efforts to combat it. Whatever cause had stilled all the noisiness and tumult of life that one associates with the groupings of men, it made me afraid.

Although we met several people, they were all men and all automatons.

Apart from them, there was nothing to see but the hedges grouped round big squares or circular spaces of considerable size. We moved in a complete silence. Since there were lights inside the enclosures, it was clear that there must have been something going on inside, but I could not tell what it might be, since there was no sound. I was encompassed by a brooding menace.

CHAPTER NINE

The Sentence

AT THE CORNER of one of the hedges we swung round to the left and then again to the left, through a passage in a side-hedge. We were inside one of the enclosures. The commander had disappeared.

I felt my heart beating against my ribs, like the thumping of an engine. I looked round me. In the middle of the enclosures men were standing in a row, like statues, under globes of phosphorescence. They were dressed in some soft stuff that shimmered in the light. My guides stood at the door of the enclosure and let go my arms. Two of the men came forward. I stared intently at them, then relaxed. Whatever was coming had not come yet—the men who were coming towards me were mere automatons. They stood beside me, but did not move. I stood staring at an opening in front of me that seemed to lead to an inner enclosure. I felt that in that inner space my fate would be decided, my life perhaps ended.

I closed my eyes and tried to pull my forces together. I hadn't thought that I should meet my fate trembling in this way. I tried to hold my knees firm. The men were now bringing me forward, past the row of men who stood under the globes of light, to the opening into the inner enclosure. We went through.

Inside, there was an empty space with two men standing in the middle—not automatons. I thought that one of them was the commander of the ship, but I could not tell. Both men

112

were very like him, but both ignored me—stared through and past me. It was not to these either that I was being conducted.

We passed them. There was an opening in the farther side of the square, and my guards were leading me to this. At the entrance they halted.

I was on the point of going through, but they held me back.

I stood staring at the opening. At last I was coming to the place. My body was firmer, though my heart was still pounding hard.

I looked around, trying to fix my attention on external things. The place was a sort of yard, with benches and presses round the sides and nothing more in the way of furniture. There was nothing to hold the attention.

A man came out of the enclosure, a man with a face like the commander, and motioned me to pass through the opening. I went forward alone.

My body was rigid, but my mind was clear and ready. Then I relaxed deeply. I was in the presence of a man—not a monstrous being such as I had expected, but a man comparatively young, a man with a face far more human than any I had yet seen.

I almost smiled with relief. The easing of tension was profound; I drew deep breaths. It was not a human face—not really human; it was the face of an eagle—vacuous, all-seeing, hypnotising in its fixity—but there was something else in the face, something beyond mere brute will and driving-power. There was knowledge—whatever sort the knowledge would prove to be—there was knowledge and understanding looking at me—searching, almost sickening knowledge—pitiless, passionless—no sympathy, no more contact in those eyes than in those of the others. But I had expected none, and my heart sprang up at the mere sight of deep knowledge, however inhuman, in the strange eyes that were regarding me so steadfastly.

He was watching me, reading all I thought. Now he was ordering me silently to come nearer.

I went over near him and stood, at some direction of his, in such a place that the light from the globes over his head fell full on my face.

For a long time—or what seemed a long time—he gazed at me. I was not afraid, but paralysed, fascinated, motionless under that fixed stare. Then suddenly I realised that he was not merely reading my thoughts. He was entering my mind. I felt him almost physically entering my mind.

Immediately I took fright and resisted.

When I say that I took fright, I do not mean fear. I know now that, if I had felt fear, he would have got me. My fear was gone. He was entering my mind, but he had not seized my will. It was standing upright, not cowering. My fear was the horror of violation again, and the instinct to resist with all my forces. I flung the whole of my will into it. At once he accepted my resistance and withdrew.

"Be quiet," his mind said to me. "Be quiet! If you do not wish me to understand you fully, you are unwise, and I cannot understand you fully if I cannot enter into your mind and see for myself what is there. Questions and answers will not be enough, since they are knowledge at second hand. The mind itself must see directly."

Again my body relaxed, became calm, soft. He was helping me, not attacking. I heard my own voice saying aloud in Latin, but quietly, as if he were directing me:

"I have been trained in such a way, or born in such a way, or both, that I cannot let any man enter my mind. It is not possible for me while I live and am conscious, and, if you try to do it, I must resist. I cannot help it. Even while I am asleep or unconscious, I will resist. I must resist to the last of my strength."

"Why then did you come to us?" came the question.

"I came to look for my father, who came down here from

the surface of the earth some time ago—years as we count time."

I stopped. I was panting. I must wait, though words came pouring into my mouth.

He stared at me without reply, then his mind sent me the first mention I had had of my father:

"There was such a man. He is no more. You cannot find him."

"He is dead?" I cried.

"The man you knew is no more. He came here to us to be reintegrated. His mind was remade. He is absorbed. There is no such man now as the man you call your father."

"But," I cried, "he is still here. If you haven't killed him, he is still here!"

"No," came the message, "he is not here; there is another here, created from the being that you knew, with all the warring elements left out."

I stared at him in silence. Then I found my voice.

"Where is he?" I cried. "No matter how mutilated he is, I want to find him."

"The man who is here now has not the memories of the man you knew. He could not remember you."

"Even so," I cried, "I want to see him."

"You cannot," came the answer. "No one can see another in this land for any purpose except one arising from his work for the State. You have no work and no purpose that we can understand. If you wish to have purpose or meaning, we shall give it to you, when we know what purpose your powers can best serve."

"I have purpose and meaning," I said, "even though you cannot understand them. I have come to find my father. A man could have no greater purpose."

"That purpose can exist no longer," came the answer. "There is no such man, no such purpose, now.

"A man came here to give himself to the Roman State. He

has given himself. The State has absorbed him. He is happy at last. The People are the better for his coming. You want to find him and take him from the State and from his happiness. It could not be done.

"Even if we were to try to help you, it could not be done. You are lawless, and want to do what you will, not what the State needs nor what the man you speak of wishes."

"But," I said, "if I find that he does not wish it, I shall trouble him no more."

"You are weak of mind," came the answer. "Therefore you cannot understand that he is all one—a single mind."

"Then," I said, "you will not tell me where he is?"

"There would be no purpose served by telling you. There can be no waste, no distraction——"

"Even you," I cried, "even *you* do not know where my father is!"

His mind stopped me.

"He is not here. The man who has taken his place is here, and I know where he is, since it is my duty to know all things here below. Such knowledge is necessary for my task. If it were not, I should not know."

I stared at him in dismay. I felt as if I were being strangled in the meshes of a net. I heard my voice saying:

"I want to know where the man who has taken my father's place can be found—only that.

"I don't ask for knowledge that isn't necessary to me. What I ask for is necessary—essential; it is what I have come for."

"Your mind is full of confusion," came his answer. "You do not know the meaning of the words you use or the thoughts you think. The knowledge you seek is not necessary to you. Therefore you will not get it.

"Knowledge that is not necessary is as poisonous as super-fluous food. Knowledge cannot be necessary, except when it is needed for work. No other knowledge *is* knowledge."

"There is other knowledge," I cried. "Knowledge that is necessary because one loves—all knowledge that touches life—all knowledge is necessary in the end—all knowledge. There is no knowledge that does not touch life—no knowledge. You have no knowledge if you think otherwise, no joy or knowledge, no meaning——!"

I was trembling with excitement. It seemed to me that I was fighting the battle of the whole human race. His mind stopped me:

"There can be no true meaning attained from knowledge. Only from feeling can man draw meaning and joy. We have joy from feeling; every man has constant joy, here in our State, from feeling——"

I stared at him in amazement:

"From feeling!" I cried. "Joy from feeling! You and your poor automatons have joy from feeling!"

I felt equal to him—not afraid—not trembling now—standing up straight before him.

His mind stopped me, this time with a question:

"How else than from feeling? Our lives have meaning through our emotions for the common good, for which all work, some with Knowledge, others with Will, others with their hands, each according to his capacity——"

"And these automatons," I interrupted in amazement, "these poor creatures whom you have robbed of their minds—they are happy?"

"They do not need their minds for their work," came the answer. "Little minds such as theirs could be of no use to them, any more than their little emotions. These could only do them harm. We have taken all the little minds and little emotions and we have pooled these into one deep emotion—a love for the common good of all—so that they have more joy even than I have, who have had to keep my mind."

I stared at him, unable to answer. His version of life here

below was so strange and incredible. My mind was not triumphant now in its defence, as it had been a few moments ago. It felt weak—ignorant. There was a strange power numbing it. I shook off the confusion that was coming over me.

His message was coming again:

"Yes. It is true. This State is built on a great emotion, such as the men of old, from whom we have sprung, did not know.

"Their books tell us that they loved little things and various things, with little loves—little things that died and left them desolate. They let their minds war with their wills, their feelings war with both. They had lives that were torn apart by meaningless struggles, and they lived and died without faith or hope.

"Before they came here they had lived above. They thought that they could go on living here as they had lived above. They died or went mad—scattered and died.

"Then a Master of Knowledge was born with deep knowledge—the knowledge that, if lives have no meaning, they will perish. Our people accepted that. After a struggle, they accepted his message.

"Otherwise they would have all died here below, where life must have a meaning in itself. If we had remained as you are, we should have died, but wisdom was given to us equal to our need, and, when we accepted it, we discovered powers in man that were great enough to save us from meaninglessness and despair and death."

His message stopped, but I made no answer. I was too overwhelmed by his statement of the solution those men had found to their dreadful problem.

I looked at the dark, beaten earth, on which no grass had ever grown. I looked round at the darkness that encompassed us on all sides, feebly tempered, in our little bit of space, by the glimmer of a green phosphorescence.

I thought of how these men had never heard a bird sing,

nor seen the sun shining on fields of corn, nor the soft green of grass just coming up from the earth, they whose fathers were children of the sun and the wind and brothers of the joyous birds and happy creatures of our upper earth.

How could I talk to men who had suffered such deprivations and yet endured—I who had had to meet only the common lot of humanity?

His mind read mine, for it came to me again.

"You are growing wise—you are beginning to understand. When it has sunk into your mind, you will know that from the greatest misfortune that has befallen men we have reached the greatest happiness to which man has attained."

"I cannot accept your happiness," I answered, "if you are happy. I cannot tell whether you are happy or not, or anything about you.

"I have grown wise enough not to give you advice or counsel, or even to deny that you may have reached happiness of a sort. But I am not as you are. Your happiness, if it exists, would be death to me.

"If you will not tell me where my father is, let me at least go out to look for him. You have no right to keep me, who have not come to seek you and cannot accept your happiness. My happiness can come to me henceforward only if I can find my father and have his word that he is happy and will not come back with me——"

His mind stopped me:

"You have already been told that you cannot find the man you seek, since there is no longer such a man; but you cannot grasp it. The sight of our people may perhaps enable you to do so. It may bring you wisdom, if your mind is capable of wisdom, since you may learn by vision what you are not capable of grasping by thought."

"No matter what I see," I said, "I shall never accept your system."

"You think so now," came his answer, "because your thought is feeble, but wisdom lies deeper than the regions where thought is made. Your deeper regions of mind are overlaid with little thoughts.

"If you would let me into your mind, I could cleanse you of these, but, since you will not do that, we will let you learn by studying our people. When you see the truth, it may dispel your fever of thought and your own wisdom may heal you."

"And if I keep my thoughts," I said, "even when I have seen the life of your people, what is to happen to me?"

"We shall decide that when the time comes," came the answer. "There is no need to decide things that may not arise for decision. It is probable that your wisdom will heal you when it is allowed to work."

"And if I have no wisdom but the wisdom of my own thoughts?" I asked.

"All human beings have wisdom," came the answer. "In our children it is also overlaid with thoughts inherited from our ancestors. We clear their minds of these thoughts and their wisdom is free. Then we rearrange their powers. We develop that in which each is best, and suppress the other powers that might conflict with it. Thus each is a unity, with one aim and one desire. There is no more pain in conflict and uncertainty.

"You will see the happiness of our people, and, having seen it, you will also wish to be as happy as they are."

"And if I do not wish for that happiness?" I asked.

"Then we may have to rearrange your mind, take away from it those parts that cloud it and make you unwise. You will then desire real happiness."

"Even if I refuse to submit to your will?"

"You cannot refuse, if we will it. No single will can resist the power of the combined will of the people. The cure is more perfect when it is made with the acquiescence of the subject, but, if the subject is so ill as to desire to remain ill, we cure him by depriving him of the diseased will that is killing him."

It had come at last! My sentence had been passed! If my mind would not commit suicide, they would murder it, efface my personality, and take over such of my powers as suited them, using my body as a tool for their purposes.

I made no answer. I couldn't speak. I could only stare at the being in front of me.

He watched me with fixed, expressionless eyes. If he could not read my thoughts or my feelings from my expression, he must have been a thing of stone, but I knew that he could see them as clearly as the eyes of men see objects under a bright light. Yet he made no sign. No slightest flicker of feeling of any sort came into his eyes—neither anger, nor pity, nor surprise.

As I looked at him, I got an overwhelming desire to hurl myself on the inhuman mask, to smash it, trample on it, tear the heart and brains of the creature that had dared to pronounce such a doom on me.

He must have read my thoughts at the moment they came to me, for instantly I felt my will gripped and held.

There was no struggle. Something powerful had been launched at me from those eyes—not merely a power that searched my thoughts, but a force that struck my will down, held it there, and made it impossible for me to move.

My passion was gone, my impulse to act violently, paralysed.

Then the grip on me was released. I was free to will again, but my feeling of rage was gone. I did not desire to act any longer against the being in front of me. My mind was calm.

I looked at the position clearly. He had no choice but to do what he was doing. He could have paralysed my will from the beginning, but he had not tried to do so. He had tried to appeal to my wisdom. I also had no choice. He had offered to allow me a respite, to go and study the lives of the people. I had no other choice but to take his offer. I did not know what I might find. Perhaps I should discover my father. I should at least get some knowledge of the circumstances of this world and the conditions that I should have to face. My only hope of safety lay in getting such knowledge.

His mind was speaking to me again. "You are free to go; you have learned that physical violence, such as men used of old, is not possible here. We are not the slaves of our passions. We are no longer like animals. Love of the common good directs our minds, controls our wills, and rules our bodies. You will learn by watching our world how that is so."

I bowed, turned, and went out.

CHAPTER TEN

The School

I CANNOT REMEMBER passing through the outer enclosure or seeing the men who stood there. Something had happened to me that had made the outer world invisible to me. A darkness more profound than the darkness that enveloped the world around me had fallen on my mind. My dreams of a human city, of all the outer external things that I had been hungering for, were gone, swept away as something childish and irrelevant. All the knowledge that I had got on earth, all the associations of my life there, seemed to me now remote and absurd —as meaningless as the collection of rubbish in a small boy's pocket.

I pulled myself together and tried to think out the situation. They had seized my father, and they intended to seize me in the same way, mind as well as body. If they had been able to seize my father, who was so strong in his will, how could I succeed in resisting them? Then I remembered suddenly the words of a doctor who had come to see us after the war, an old comrade of my father's. This doctor had served in the East, and was talking of the psychic powers of some Orientals. I remember his saying that my father would be a good subject for hypnotists and I myself a bad one.

"If they got you on your emotional nerve," he said to my father, "they could do what they liked to you."

At once the matter became clearer to me. They had got my father on his one deep emotional ground—the Roman State.

They were the Roman State that he had dreamed of and lived for. He had willingly given himself up to it and them. The last words of the doctor that evening came back to my mind:

"Yes, yes, Mrs. Julian," he said, "a man of most unusual powers, your husband, but a neuropath. Subject him to great emotion or profound fatigue and you may get a dissociation of his personality. I would try to keep him engaged with ordinary things, if I were you. Get him away to some city and the common life of man." He turned to me:

"You too will gain by leaving here, young man, though I will not pretend that it would be easy to knock you off your perch, wherever you settle."

I tried to think back on earlier parts of his talk.

"Not more than a quarter of our Western people can be completely subdued by those hypnotic dominators," he had said; "that is, deeply invaded and subdued. The rest are safe if they don't get afraid. Once you get panicky and afraid in face of the master, you are in his hands. Have confidence in yourself and you can defend your personality—at least seventy-five per cent of white men can do it, for the stuff of the race is tough and strong."

If these words of his were well founded, there was still hope for me, even if my father had failed to save himself. But how to save him if he had been absorbed? I hadn't come down to save myself. I had come for him. He didn't want to be saved, they had said; he was happy; he belonged to the Roman State; I couldn't find him, since he wasn't there, and, even if he had been, I couldn't have found him.

My thoughts kept going round in a circle—"absorbed"; "happy"; "belonging to the State." The words had no meaning for me. I knew that they had a meaning but I couldn't feel it. It wasn't that I was excited now—I had never felt less excited—but I was so full that I could feel nothing—I couldn't even feel the meaning of the words, "there is no such man."

My father was somewhere near me—paralysed in his mind perhaps; silent and staring and empty like one of the automatons; but perhaps not—perhaps empty and staring like a hawk.

Even before he had come down his eyes had got empty, vacuous, powerful, inhuman almost.

How long I stood outside that enclosure I cannot tell. Again and again in that land, in periods of waking, I seemed to lose outer consciousness, so that time and space ceased for me, as if I were in a deep sleep. This occurred usually if I got a heavy defeat in my hopes, or was faced by so fundamental a difference of belief that I could not even begin to grasp it. It also occurred when I was profoundly fatigued, and in a sort of physical as well as mental despair. This was one of these moments. I had gone back to the depths of my own life in my effort to grapple with this monstrous life that was encircling me like a great silent bird of prey. In the search in the depths of my own soul for what was real in me, I had lost consciousness of outer things.

I was called back to consciousness by a message from another mind that was trying to communicate with me. I woke up and looked round me. There was a man at my right-hand side with eyes that called to me to follow him. He went forward. I walked in the rear. I noticed the poise of his body, the little head; the softness of the movements, supple as those of a cat; the silence. My mind was circling round, still circling round and round. Was my father beyond saving? Could it be true?

The man's mind was speaking to me: "We are going to the schools for the young."

My feeling sprang from the depths into which it had been plunged. "Schools for the young." The thought brought back the familiar things in a flood—the faces of children, the joyous cries of them as they poured out of the schools above and filled buses and trams with their chatter. Then, as suddenly, it stopped. It could not be possible that the children here below could be such as these. There would be the same silent emptiness, the same shock, if I let myself hope for anything; the same despair. I closed my mind and moved forward beside him.

There were no people on our path—nothing but the enclosures on each side, these and an automaton or two on the roads. No women. A strange "city."

The enclosure on the left ended abruptly, and I stopped short, staring at a sight I had not expected. In a broad open space, lit by a multitude of phosphorus globes, a number of children were coming out of an enclosure on the far side from us. As I looked, a very soft music came to me. The children began to move to it, to sway, to form lines and curves and melt in and out in circles that came together and dissolved like smoke-rings. Their movements were like the movements of shadows—or water under shadows. The music was so low that I could scarcely hear it, and their movements seemed to be part of it—unreal, shadows in a dream. They were weaving rings in a dance that made me think of the dancing of snakes under the spell of Indian snake-charmers. Now they were whirling round like autumn leaves. I could see their faces—not very clearly, but clearly enough to note that they were not the faces of European children. Even from where I stood I could see that they were impassive, yet it seemed to me that they were live faces, quite different from the faces of the automatons or of their masters.

As I stood watching them, a murmuring voice came to me. I started in surprise. A woman was coming towards the centre of the space, saying something on a low piping note, like the first call of a bird at dawn, or its last sleepy twitter—the first human voice I had heard here below! I listened, entranced. A human voice at last! Strangely thin and quite unintelligible to me, but a human voice! I stared at the woman with extraordinary joy. She was, except for the rounded breasts and softer cheeks, little different from the men that I had already seen. She had the same earthy colouring, the same large, prominent eyes with the light gleaming through them, the same little head and slender body. But she was speaking, and it seemed to me that her face was not as empty—not altogether as empty.

I came nearer, staring at her and listening. No; she was not different from the others after all. The eyes were not our eyes. They were vacuous—empty except for their gentleness, and as alien, in their remoteness, as the eyes of a tortoise or a serpent —incredibly remote. But she was a woman in charge of children, and she was actually speaking.

I moved forward, very quietly, and strained my ears to listen.

The class was speaking now, answering her. I couldn't catch their speech, it was so thin and strangely pitched and so low in tone, but it was certainly human speech. It seemed, indeed, to be a training in the practice of speech, for now three children were acting some sort of scene, and as they did this, the other children seemed to be describing it.

I kept on moving nearer to them, ever so gently, with my ears strained to catch the sounds. Not a syllable of what they said could I understand. Then the sounds stopped. I stopped also. The children were going through a sort of dumb show in which each came out in front of the teacher and stared at her. Possibly this was some sort of training in the sending and receiving of thought without the medium of words, but I was hardly taking it in. I was strangely confused. The sight of a woman, the sound of human speech in this dreadful place, had stirred up depths of memory and of association that were shaking me with emotion.

How long ago was it since I had been on the earth? Less than a week ago! It was incredible that only a week ago I had been coming up to the Pond to spend the week-end with my mother and explore the Wall again, and see the May flowers blowing on it—away from the smoke of the towns. That all this could have happened in a week—happened in England! When I had arrived I had gone out with my mother to the garden. The pear-trees were in blossom there—and a cherry-tree; she had wanted me to come to see them before the blossoms fell. She had stood with her head thrown back, beside the cherry-tree, looking up at the ash, where a thrush was singing as if his speckled throat would burst.

I sighed heavily, expelling the weight that had been lying on my heart. At the sound the children stopped and looked at me. The teacher paid no attention but they had reacted.

I pulled myself together. It was the first human reaction that I had seen here. These children were still human beings; they were like myself—victims waiting to be slaughtered—but still alive, like lambs at play before they are ready for the butcher. I felt an intense pity for them. How could I have patience, hold myself in, wait and watch and learn, when this thing was rushing at me, rushing at them? I wanted to run over to them, to put my arms round them, to hug them, to take them away from this horror that was advancing on them and on me.

I began to move towards them again, gently, like a man who is afraid to break a dream. As I came near, the illusion began to vanish; they were so alien, so vacant and aloof—they were part of their people.

I stopped. The teacher was looking at me, and, when I looked at her, I knew that she had willed me to stop. Her message came to me:

"What do you want to know?"

I looked at her in despair. What was the good of telling her that what I wanted was to feel the touch of children and hear their voices, to see the expression in a woman's eyes? Her eyes were not a woman's eyes—they were gentle, full of a calm, deep gentleness, but it was not the gentleness of a woman's eyes, it was a gentleness that was desolating because of its emptiness.

Again my confusion was settling down on me like heavy fog. I pulled myself together. She was right. It was knowledge I needed—I must get knowledge to escape from those eyes—and I should begin now, not waste any more time in brooding. But where was I to begin?

There was no use asking her about my father. What else did I want to know—where could I begin? Yet I must begin somewhere. I must ask her questions—about anything; it didn't matter what—so as to make some beginning. I heard my own voice—a loud voice—asking, in slow, distinct Latin, what language it was that she and the children had been speaking. There was a pause, as if she were trying to get clearly the meaning of my words. Then her answer came—not in speech, as I had hoped, but in silence:

"We were speaking Latin. There is no other human speech."

"Will you not speak it to me, then?" I cried. "I am lonely for the sound of a human voice. Will you not speak to me with your voice?"

Again there was a pause. I waited eagerly. Would she speak to me?

If she did, could I follow her Latin speech? I was full of expectancy. Perhaps, if she would deal with me through human speech, I might make real contact at last.

In a moment my new hopes were dashed. Her answer was coming to me, not through speech, but through thought transmission, recording itself on my mind as if it were tapped out on a machine. She was telling me why she would not speak to me. She was communicating with me, but handing me the answer as if it had been made up in a packet for her and she was merely the machine that ran it off.

"There is no need for oral speech between adult people,"

came her message, "unless they are so feeble in their mind that they cannot transmit their thoughts without it. Oral speech is merely a gesture to help the sending of thought in the case of those who cannot send it without such help."

"But," I cried, "you spoke aloud to the children just now. Why will you not speak aloud to me?"

"I have used speech with the children," came her answer, "because human thought has been so accustomed to shape itself through the gestures which are words that children still have to learn to think first through words. But, when we have taught them how to think by the use of word-gestures, we make them put aside such clumsy methods of communication. They can do without them if they become Masters of Will or Knowledge, but not always if they remain in the lower grades of mind."

It was a good answer—clear and strong—and it came to me as it might have come from a penny-in-the-slot machine. For all the human contact I received through it, I might as well have been listening to a speaking robot.

If the woman were capable of astonishment, she must have been astounded by the strangeness of my voice, so loud and strident compared with theirs. She must have been surprised at my question and my request, since both showed that I was completely strange to their system, and she could not have met many such strangers. She must have been surprised by my appearance, by my curious Latin, by my movements and gestures and expression. But she showed no sign of noticing any of these things, as if her brain were boxed up in some compartment in which it could busy itself only with one thing.

I felt baffled, beaten down, once again encompassed by the thing from which there seemed to be no escape. I had failed in my most hopeful effort to make contact. I must give up that hope. But, if I could not get contact, I could at least get knowledge, and I must get it. I must learn what these people were doing, and I must begin with the knowledge of how they were shaping the human material before it had become absorbed. This was the road that I, too, would go, if they could get me.

I heard myself questioning her about the nature of her work, the purpose that she was to attain through her teaching. I was forcing myself to talk about these things, not because I wanted to know about them, but because I felt impelled to ask her questions such as she could answer. But, although I was asking her these questions, my mind was not in a condition to receive her answers. I was in too emotional a mood to be interested in them at the moment. What I wanted was not information, but some touch with a human being, and, instead of leaving my mind open to her answers, I was watching her face, her eyes, every movement of her, with a craving for some little gesture, attitude, expression, that would link us through our common humanity.

As I watched and listened, my hopes died. There was not the slightest response on her part, not the slightest awakening of any human expression, or of any awareness of me as anything but material on which a message was to be recorded. As a human being I had for her as little personal existence as I had for the other automatons.

Then, as I stood there, passive in my disillusionment, her message was able to come through to me, and, with a shock, I began to realise the purport of it. I was getting contact now of a very different sort from that which I was seeking. I was getting contact with the system, an impact from it that was arousing me into a state of full awareness.

The woman who was standing in front of me was explaining that the purpose of her work was the destruction, in the children placed under her care, of all the essential life of childhood—its joyous curiosity, its wakening intelligence, all that upward surge of life that gives childhood the glory and the beauty of the awakening spring. It was her task, and the task of her fellow-teachers, to root up and destroy the deepest sources of those torrents of vitality.

I stared at her in amazement. Such a message from so gentle a person was almost incredible.

She realised nothing of my thoughts, or, if she did, she gave no sign.

Her message went on, explaining that the music and the dancing were part of the machinery by which the children were drugged into hypnotic suggestion—that the amount of knowledge that was taught was the minimum necessary for the work the pupil would have to do in life. But my mind was becoming too disturbed to record the message clearly. She had ceased to exist for me as any kind of human being, but she had come to life as the priestess of another Moloch.

I can remember no more of her explanation. Up to this point my memory of everything is quite clear, but from this stage I find it difficult to recall the detailed happenings. I cannot remember, for instance, leaving that enclosure, nor can I remember distinctly my experiences in the other school enclosures that I visited after the first. The reason for this lack of clear memory of events is that something peculiar had begun to happen to myself. It was not merely that my mind was getting clouded with feeling. It was also being confused by fear—not a fear of the system that I was seeing in its workings, but of something deeper.

My first feeling was, as I have said, a natural revulsion produced by the explanation of the system. But, almost immediately, this feeling of revulsion began to give place to a quite different feeling—a vague but very deep fear of something else that I could not define. It was as if some inherited dread, of which I had never before been aware, was coming up from the depths of my subconsciousness, so that my mind saw everything through a cloud.

Looking back now, I feel as if an exhalation from some abysmal swamp of the subconscious had taken the place of the ordinary clear atmosphere in which the mind does its work. Whatever it was that caused it, my mind was being seized by panic.

I found myself moving from school to school like a man who is conscious of some dreadful thing that encompasses him, and is looking on all sides for a road of escape.

Through the miasma in which I moved I saw the faces of the teachers appearing and disappearing like faces in a dream. They may have been sending messages to me, trying to communicate the explanations of their system, as the first teacher had done. If they did so, I cannot recall any individual message; but, while I can remember no contact with the mind of any one of them, I began to feel a profound conviction that they alone, and the system they stood for, could save me from the thing that threatened me.

Now at last I understood this and the great thing that they had accomplished.

Even though I was not getting their explanations, because of the trouble in my mind, the full meaning of their system and of their work was coming to me from them, as if I had entered into their minds. But I was receiving something else from them also—something deeper than knowledge—some emanation of encouragement and protection as if they were impregnating me with their belief, their intense belief, that in their system and in it alone could I find safety.

When I try to analyse it now, I cannot tell how I was being possessed by this body of conviction, except that I seemed to be receiving it, not through the mind, but through the influence of some pulsation of deep emotion that was welling up from them.

I know, however, that at every new enclosure to which I was brought I felt the need of them more strongly.

I felt myself longing to be one with them, to find myself in the shelter that they had provided for me, to be absorbed.

"Absorbed!" My mind suddenly recoiled from the thought. What was happening to me?

This urge to run to earth, to give myself up to them—they were hypnotising me!

The shock of the thought brought me to myself.

What was happening to me? This dread that was coming up in my mind—what was it that I was afraid of? Nothing. A mere phantom.

They were causing it in some way, drugging me, frightening me into being one with them. It was they who were the danger —their system that was seeking to seize me, enslave me, possess me.

They were creating phantoms of fear, mere phantoms.

Already, now that I was becoming conscious of their unreality, the fears had begun to shrink. They were not gone, but they were not so overpowering.

There was nothing to be afraid of but these people themselves. I must fight them with all my strength, hold on to the truth against them. Vehemently I told myself again that my doubts were nothing, mere shadows; that it was the people round me that were producing them, in order to frighten me into being one of them; that, if I yielded, I should soon be travelling the most ghastly road ever trodden by a man—the slave of creatures who were mere monsters of concentration, without pity or love or the knowledge that can come only from these things.

I kept repeating to myself that there was but one thing left for me to do if I were to escape madness—to find my father as soon as possible and rescue him and myself.

Gradually the alarm died away. My mind cleared. I felt physically free.

I turned and walked out of the enclosure.

The drag on my mind ceased. I felt myself panting like a man who has been running away from some danger.

I was brought to myself by a touch on my arm. The guide

who had led me to the schools, or some similar person, was standing beside me.

At first I thought that he wanted to bring me back. I resolved not to go, but he turned in the opposite direction, and I followed him. I was breathing more freely. The jaws of the trap had almost closed on me, but I had escaped. The trouble that had lain like a heavy weight on my mind was gone.

I raised my head and looked round me. We were coming to a very large enclosure, brightly lit. In front of us a gateway opened into it. We crossed the path. I thought that it might be another of the schools, and I stopped at the entrance.

It was not a school but an enormous square in which a great number of men were sitting at tables, eating.

I went in. The tables were in long parallel rows, and my guide brought me to a vacant space in the row nearest to us and sat down, motioning me to sit beside him.

I felt a sense of liberation, of great relief.

I hadn't expected that danger, and so I had almost been trapped. It would not be so easy for them to get me, now that I was forewarned, but, even here, I must watch.

I looked closely at the faces of those nearest to me. They were automatons. There was not a single concentrated face to be seen, nor even the semblance of power in one of them. There could be no serious danger here.

I breathed more freely.

After the schools the place looked human and almost familiar. There were no cloths on the tables, which were of some sort of soft-looking wood, but they were very clean, and the whole scene would have looked comforting and familiar were it not for the row of blank, silent faces, like faces from which the eyes had been plucked, and the awareness of those lives from which the minds had been torn with the eyes.

I dragged my mind away from its thoughts and tried to concentrate it on outer things.

A man brought us basins to wash our hands, and towels to

dry them. After that, servers brought round wooden plates
with the same sort of pale meat on them and a collection of
vegetable stuffs. There was a knife beside my plate, and with
the help of the knife I began to eat.

The food was hot and satisfying, and though here, as on
the ship, I found it tasteless compared with our food on earth,
the eating of it helped me in my effort to return to a normal
condition.

The memory of that strange fear which I had felt in the
schools was still in my mind. I tried to shake it off. I spoke to
my guide, who was eating beside me. I have no memory of
what I said, but I know that it was a question about something.
He merely stared at me when I asked the question, as if the
noise of my voice mildly surprised him, and made no answer.

Even to myself my voice sounded loud and absurd in that
silence, as when one talks aloud deliberately when alone. But,
though the people at the table actually looked towards me
when I spoke, they showed no real sign of surprise or of any
human feeling in their eyes. Indeed, though they looked
towards me as the source of the sound, they gave the impression of looking through me, as if I were invisible.

I felt inclined to cry out, to laugh, to produce any sort of
noise that would fill the emptiness and drive away that fear
that seemed to be hovering in it.

There was nothing visible to prevent me, no person of Will
or Knowledge to constrain me, yet I felt constrained to silence,
as if the communal atmosphere of the place had as compelling
an effect on me as the hypnotising will of a single powerful
personality.

This was no collection of powerful single forces like the collection of teachers in the schools. It was evident from the faces
near me that I was in the presence of a crowd of the lower
type of automatons. The feeling of undefined dread was gone.
Yet, though the atmosphere these people were creating was

not as powerful and sinister as that of the schools, some influence that emanated from them as a body was fettering me, as if a force had fused them into a single organic unit and was now working upon me, from them, to draw me into its orbit.

After the powerful pull that had been exerted on me in the schools, I felt this constricting atmosphere less than I had done on the ship, but it was sufficiently powerful to force me to conform outwardly to its rhythm. I made no more effort to break through that circle that enclosed me or to detach any other from its influence, but finished my meal in silence.

When I had finished, my guide got up and motioned me to follow him out. We came on to the paths between the enclosures again, and, keeping to the right, arrived in a short time at a very large enclosure from which a soft music was coming.

We passed through an opening and found ourselves in a very large space, paved with stone and with baths let into the floor, and basins, with running water, along the walls.

Immediately my spirits arose. This was the first instance where I had met modern appliances and anything approaching a house. It is true there was no roof, and the walls were not high, but the space was a room excellently floored, and furnished with all bathroom necessities, and the sight of these familiar things had a healing and restoring effect on my mind.

There were only men in the room, and several of them were lying naked in the baths. I went over to one that was empty and, on turning a sort of metal tap, water gushed forth.

I looked at my guide. He motioned towards a little cubicle at the end of the bath. I went to it, and found a mixture of dressing-room and lavatory such as I had found on the ship.

I noticed that here, too, everything was scrupulously clean, and, indeed, under the soft greenish light, the room looked like a scene in fairyland.

To me, whose whole associational self was longing for something like the dwellings of men on the upper earth, it was an unexpected relief to be back again in rooms with floors and walls and baths. The music that I had heard outside the enclosure filled the air with a dreamy softness. My mind, exhausted by the emotions of the day, had fallen into itself. It was becoming numbed into calmness, and an impelling desire to sleep was coming over me.

At the back of the cubicle there was an opening, and, when I looked through this, I saw a very big enclosure with couches, on which men were sleeping.

A man came up and motioned me to a low bed with some silken stuff over it. I went to it and lay down.

So ended my first day in that strange city where there were neither streets nor houses nor buying nor selling nor transport of any sort, nor any animals except human beings, nor indeed any human beings in our sense of the word. Yet in it there were government and education so fundamental that they had seized on profound abysses of the mind and drawn forth from them forces that remain hidden in men of the upper earth.

I was surrounded now by its silence, its extinguishing silence, which made the life of men on earth seem a noisy heap of selfishness and absurdities and vulgarities, without manners or meaning.

Those were two of the menacing things about it, that stillness—a quietness such as humanity has never known—and the forces that lurked in the silence, like wild beasts in the darkness. I could feel it all round me, encompassing me, compelling me. I felt as a creature of the upper earth might feel in the depths of the ocean, and, under the pressure of these depths, subjected to a calm that was more violent than the worst storm. It was through the silence that they were invading me and shaking my mind.

The thing was so preposterous that I felt easier. The idea that this dumb show, or the silent depths that lay beneath— whatever powers they had dragged up from the primordial abysses—could draw me away from the life of men, the multitudinous sunlit life of humanity that was racing through my body, was so preposterous that it could not trouble me.

But they had seized my father. If what they had told me was true, he had willingly allowed himself to be sucked into the depths of this human swamp, and, if I yielded, they would overpower me and drag me down into it with them. Whether I yielded or not, they would try to drag me down. I must keep calm. There was only one way in which I could defeat them—by knowledge. There was no other way of escape. No use dashing myself against the hard fact that they had me, and they would hold me, unless I could get enough of their own knowledge to use against them.

They were giving me a chance to get this knowledge, because they were so circumscribed by their own feelings that they could not imagine their hypnotic tentacles failing to get me if I were long enough under the influence of their powers.

They would prefer me to come in of myself, the Master of Knowledge had told me. That was why I had been sent to the schools. These were the shapers, the creators of desires. It was in them that the atmosphere which was to destroy and remake me was stored. I had felt its powers and had barely escaped....

Should I be able to escape the second time? I thought it likely. I had already escaped when I had been taken unawares. That was a thing to hearten me. They had failed to gauge my full powers. That should be a help to me. It betrayed a weakness in their strength. If I got to know more about them, I might find other weaknesses. They might not be as formidable as I had assumed from their silence and calm. They had penetrated to depths of which I knew nothing, but there were resources in the individual mind of which they were not aware, or which they had forgotten.

I must crush down my feelings. That was the mood through which they would try to get me, if I gave way to feeling. I must keep away from feeling and try to get knowledge, see everything I could, learn everything.

I was again staggered to think that only a week ago I had been living the life of earth. It seemed unbelievable that, above that dome of darkness over my head, men and women of my own race were still living in the sunlight, working and playing, travelling in trains, reading newspapers!

Perhaps it was night-time, and they were hurrying to dances, to theatres, or sitting happily round their own firesides, while I, who had been one of them, was now lying in the grip of this monstrous thing bred of the primeval darkness and the dreadful abysses of the human mind.

CHAPTER ELEVEN

I Resist Invasion

I THINK that I must have lain on that bed for a long time, for, when I awoke, I felt as if many days had passed. Also I felt extraordinarily refreshed. There was that same electric quality in the air of the underworld which had a most bracing effect on my nerves, whenever I could fling off the trouble and fears produced by my situation.

When I awoke now I felt this stimulation. I did not awake, as on other "mornings," to a dream of the upper earth from which my mind had to be translated into a very different reality. I woke to an immediate realisation of my position. I remembered my experience of the previous day. In my present calmer mood I could hardly believe that it had been real. It seemed strange that I should have felt such panic or experienced such a craving to give myself up to these people. Yet my whole experience of them hitherto was so fantastically unlike all other experience that nothing was incredible.

One thing was certain—I must be constantly on my guard. If I allowed myself to be shaken, to be hypnotised into panic or hysteria, they would have me at their mercy. I must keep calm, guard myself against their atmosphere, but not allow myself to be frightened by it. I must avoid emotion, gather knowledge as to the extent of their powers and their resources, try to get some clue to the whereabouts of my father.

I had already learned that he was still alive—changed, according to them; transformed in such a way that he had lost his identity, but still alive. If I could only find him, I might re-awaken his memories, re-create his individuality, if indeed it were lost. But it might not be lost. He might have merely taken refuge in pretence. If that were so and I could find him, he might have knowledge that would enable both of us to escape.

Perhaps he was quite near me, waiting for me. He would know that I would not have left him to his fate.

But how to go about finding him? I must tackle that problem at once. I must put away all fear. I must learn at once everything that I could about this new world and its people, in order that I might start my quest. Every day lost might prove an irreparable loss, since I was only on respite, and I was up against an undefined time-limit which might be near or distant.

So far, I had not only got no clue as to how I might start my search for my father, but I had not got even an inkling as to how I could get such a clue. I had let my emotions get the better of me and had allowed the atmosphere of the schools to produce such a state of fear and confusion in my mind that I had learned nothing.

They would certainly send me to the schools again, in order to expose me to their atmosphere. I should get no choice in that, but, if I kept cool, there was no reason why I should not turn the visits to my own advantage.

The teachers were the only persons with whom I had been able to communicate, and they were more likely to supply me with information than anybody else. The imparting of knowledge was their province, and, in giving it, they might possibly drop some hint that might set me on the right track. I must face their atmosphere and overcome it, so as to get all the information that I could get from them and learn everything that I could about the system and the powers of their people.

I sat up and looked round me. For a moment the hope came

to me that my father might also be in this enclosure. Then
the absurdity of the thought was clear to me. They would not
have brought me to any place where he was, since they did
not wish me to meet him.

Still, I looked round eagerly. The place was full of sleeping
men. Others were getting up or lying down. No one that I
could see could possibly be my father. He would have towered
over them. I put the hope of seeing him resolutely from my
mind. My task would not be as simple as all that, and the
fostering of foolish illusions would not help me.

I got up, made for the washing-room through which I had
come before my sleep, and, finding a place vacant, had a bath.
The room was full, but no one appeared to take the slightest
notice of me. They could not have been entirely unobservant
of my movements, however, for, while I was taking my bath,
my guide appeared, as if he had been informed of my being
awake. He made no sign of recognition beyond standing near
me while I dressed, but, when I was ready, he led me to the
eating-place in which I had eaten before. There we got somewhat similar food to that of the previous day, and, after the
meal, we set out again.

When we left the eating enclosure, I stopped and asked my
guide where he was taking me. If he had answered that he
was taking me to some place other than the schools, I think
that I would have tried to change his plans, so keyed up was
I in my resolution, but his message came at once:

"To the higher schools."

I had little hope that I could get any more information
from him, since I had already had experience of his refusal
to have any communication with me, except the minimum
needed for his task as guide. In spite of this, I asked him what
they did in these schools. As I expected, he made no answer.

It was as if he was aware of me to the extent of the circle
of his particular task as guide, and had answers given him to

that extent for me, but that, the moment I went beyond the radius of that circle, he ceased to be aware of me or of my questioning.

It was his business to take me to certain places. He was in contact with me to that extent only.

However, I did not trouble myself about this, as I had had little hope of getting any information from him. My hopes in this respect were now all centred on the schools.

As it happened, the very first school that I visited on that second day supplied me with information about the geographical framework of their country.

We reached this school after about ten minutes' walk between silent enclosures along paths that were empty except for occasional automatons. It was a dreary city to traverse, but my mind was now busy with other matters besides its longings for the noise and traffic of ordinary humanity. It was nerving itself up to meet the impact of the atmosphere that I expected to find in the schools.

I was perfectly calm, ready to resist with all my strength, but quite cool and collected. Then we went into the school, and I felt like a man who expects another step of a stairs in the darkness and finds none.

There was no atmosphere beyond that to which I had by now become accustomed in all the gatherings of that people, certainly nothing special that I needed to draw upon special resources to meet.

I felt relieved and more confident.

Then I remembered that, in the schools that I had already seen, as well as on the ship, the influence that I feared had made itself felt very gradually, only after I had been some time in the midst of the people. I determined to watch closely for its first appearance now.

The school itself was the usual type of enclosure, and, when we went in, there was, in the first section of it, a group of pupils of about sixteen years of age standing round a teacher.

When my guide brought me up to the group, I noticed that, compared with the faces of the children I had seen on the previous day, the faces of these pupils had been dehumanised. They were more concentrated, but they were emptier, less aware of me, more vacuous in expression and yet more definitely powerful in a fixed, staring sort of way.

The teacher was of the same type as those I had seen in the other schools, but perhaps more concentrated in expression. When I came up to the group, he was at once aware of me, as if he had been informed that I was to be shown his methods, for he immediately sent me a silent message that this was a class of pupils who were later intended to be in charge of food distribution throughout the country, and who were now being trained in the knowledge needed for that particular task, as well as in the conveying of thought without speech. He then turned away from me and evidently required one of the pupils to use me as the object of his efforts.

The lad, a boy of about fourteen or fifteen, came near me, fixed me with his eyes, and tried to communicate with me. Still there was no sign of any crowd-influence emanating from the group. I decided, therefore, to let my mind lie as open and passive as possible, so as to receive the boy's message, while at the same time watching for other influences that might be lurking around me. The message began to come through to me, but only in fragments.

It was a description of the land, the shape and size of it— the things that, as an officer engaged in the transport of supplies, the boy would need to know in order to perform his task properly. It was also one of the things that I most wanted to know, since information as to the shape and size of the country, and the extent of its population, would be most important to me, both in my effort to find my father and my plans for escape. I was, therefore, very anxious to aid the pupil as far as possible in the conveying of his knowledge to me, but, in spite of all my efforts to make my mind passive and receptive, I was still too wary of the atmosphere to offer a free passage to his thoughts. The result was that, for a while, I got little of his message, until at length the teacher intervened and began to help him, by reinforcing his powers of transmission in some way through the addition of his own. It is possible also that the passive resistance that my mind had been keeping up may have lessened. Whatever the reason, the message began to come through more clearly, and, in a short time, I gained geographical information that I could not have gathered in any other way.

The sum of it was that their country is a deep valley that lies between mountains which support the roof of the land on all sides. In the middle of the valley the Central Sea runs along its whole length, until at this end of the valley it narrows into a great river that flows under the mountains behind the city. This Central Sea is salt water, and the main source of their food, since in it live most of the creatures from which they get meat and fish, and also most of the edible plants. On the land, fungi grow, which are also used as food, and some plants that have come up from the sea to the land and now can live wherever there is sufficient water.

Their settlements are all placed on the western shores of the Central Sea, and occur, at intervals where there is fresh water all along that shore, up as far as the great cliff that bounds the sea to the north.

All transport between these settlements is done by water, and it is the business of the directors of transport to see that each settlement has sufficient supplies of all necessaries, and that its surplus in any stuff is transferred to other settlements that need it. It is also their task to keep an exact census of the supplies available, and to inform the Masters of Knowledge, so that they may adjust the population of children in such a way that there may not be more population than the valley could feed.

There was much similar information of a more detailed type. The city itself is ringed round with food supplies from the great snake compounds, the waters of the Central Sea, and the big fungus farms. The other settlements had, in general, food supplies in their own neighbourhood, but the region along the great Wall that guards the gap between the northern cliff and the eastern mountains was a barren one, for which a supply of food had always to be arranged.

I have given the summary of this lesson, partly to show the manner in which the pupils were trained in the schools for their particular avocations, but partly also because of the information contained in it.

I was particularly interested in the existence of a Wall that guarded a pass in the north, but, though I wished to get more information about it, I thought it better at the moment not to ask questions that might show my mind, even though I thought it quite probable that the teacher was reading it like an open book.

I left the school in a more confident mood.

The next school to which I was brought was one of a similar type, but, as it was one for the training of higher workers in the great woodwork compounds, there was little information given in it that was of any use to me or that would be worth giving in detail. Neither was there any serious interference with me from the group magnetism.

It was the same in most of the other schools that I saw on that second day.

I was extremely anxious to get some knowledge of the methods of shaping the minds of the pupils, but I found them difficult to grasp owing to the fact that all the work was done in silence, through thought transmission.

I was able to get a certain amount of information, through

the interception of the silent messages, but it was detailed
instruction in the direction of various crafts—of considerable
interest to a person in a normal condition, but of little use
to me.

The last school that I visited was, however, of a different
type, and in it I not only got information about their system,
but felt once again, very strongly, the mysterious force that I
had learned to fear.

This school was one for the shaping of teachers, and, when
I went into it, I found four young men and three young
women seated round a man with a face of such concentrated
power and intelligence that I thought at first that I was in
the presence of a Master of Knowledge, or of one very close
to the Masters in power.

The group seemed to be doing nothing, but, when I came
near, the man's mind suddenly swept on to mine, like a searchlight, and the next moment I was aware that I had come inside
the radius of an intense discharge of thought. So great was
the power with which the thought was transmitted that it
seemed to me that not merely was I receiving it, but that I had
entered into the man's mind and was myself thinking the
thoughts that were being created in it, as they were being
shaped. There was no question here of my letting myself
become completely passive and receptive in order to receive
his message. It was impregnating my mind with such force
that it seemed to me that, even if I wished, I could not
resist it.

If I had been in the mood of the previous day, I believe that
I should have taken fright, because of the power of the man,
but my mind had by now settled down to measure everything
calmly, and it received his thoughts willingly and clearly, con-
tenting itself with watching their effects and holding itself
ready to resist any invasion of my personality.

At first I felt no sense of intrusion, nothing but a stream of
clear message, though I realised that the message was being

especially directed towards me, and saw that the purpose was the impregnation of my mind with their point of view.

"No man now can know," his thoughts ran, "the things that men suffer, when each man has to face alone the forces of darkness. We can have no experience that could give us such knowledge, since we are all one—a great body of life surrounded by a deep unchanging situation, through which the forces of darkness cannot penetrate to us.

"We have been able to unite and to build this shelter round our people, because each man and woman has been willing to shed the outer shell of individual feelings and behaviour that would otherwise separate him from his fellows and make it impossible for him or her to become at one with all others.

"Feeling and thought flow freely between us, as the blood flows through the body. We cannot be shaken by dark outer forces, because we are one great body, fused by one emotion, directed by one thought.

"Our fathers had no such protection. They had no great emotion to bind them together, nothing but a multiplicity of conflicting thoughts and feelings. Instead of combining into one body against the forces that destroy man, they spent their days in attempts to face the great evils alone, and so perished."

He paused and stared into my eyes. I watched him closely. He was, I knew, reading my mind like an open book. I could not help that. He was not at the moment trying to enforce his will on me. Of that I was equally sure. I had no fear of him, but I was watchful and wary of attack.

His message began to come through to me again:

"There is a man amongst us whose life is in the same defenceless state as the lives of our fathers. His mind is in the same stage of ignorance and confusion. It is watching us, lest we should deprive it of that outer shell of individual feelings and behaviour that we have stripped from ourselves and which it calls its personality.

"Our fathers had the same sort of belief, the same sort of

confusion and fear. They too treasured something that they called their 'individuality,' although it consisted of nothing but a heap of different behaviours and attitudes. They valued their 'individuality' so much that many of them spent almost the whole of their lives trying to assert it, by taking on and putting off attitudes and behaviours."

Again he paused and watched me. I felt that he was reconstructing his vision of the past from the pictures that he saw in my mind. It was a strange experience to stand in front of this alien creature and have him construct what was to him a prehistoric world from my thoughts and feelings. His message was coming to me again:

"The great destroying forces were around them and upon them, and they thought they could meet them alone, each man encased in his own little set of attitudes.

"The powers of fear and loneliness and decay bore them down, and, in their blindness, they tried to meet them, not by fusing together into one great community, protected by a great emotion, but by occupying themselves with a heap of petty emotions and actions—things that had no real existence, obsessions about their individuality and the attitudes of other people to them.

"In doing this, they were moved by a partial grasp of the truth. They knew that without emotion a man cannot live and face the great fear, but, having no leaders to direct their emotion, they did not know how to use it so as to attain to depth and security of life.

"Instead, they squandered it in a variety of little ways that could only bring them sorrow and defeat in the end. So they suffered and died, having attained to nothing, some of them spending their lives in the amassing of material things, most of which they could never use; others giving themselves up to a quest of complete personal union with some friend or lover, an association which is entirely impossible between two persons.

"The man who is with us is still in the stage in which they were. He has come to us from his own people because of such a relationship and such a quest."

At his last words a surge of feeling rose in me. At once he stopped.

Knowing the incapacity of that people to get any personal reaction from the feelings of others, I knew that he was not moved in any way by the sudden effect that his message had produced on me. His purpose was a purely practical one. He had been holding up to me a mirror of my own thoughts and feelings as he read them, so as to show me how futile and useless they were. That there could be any other point of view he could not understand. Yet, now that he saw that he was producing resistance, he turned aside at once from the question of personal relationships.

"If," he went on, "men are allowed to remain in their primitive condition, with all the thoughts and feelings that are inherited by them from their ancestors, they can never be fused together into one body that will be powerful enough to save them from disaster. It is not merely that they will remain separate, but that inevitably they will be in conflict.

"If men are not remade in their minds, each man will think that he is the best judge of his own value and will try to enforce his judgment. The community will be torn by a crowd of petty conflicts. It cannot save itself, because in the tumult of little motives, and the jostling of little ambitions, it cannot even create itself."

It was strange to hear this man discussing our motives and ambitions, who himself was so devoid of personal motive and ambition that he could have no real knowledge of what he was talking about. I knew, however, what was happening. He was reading my mind, gathering knowledge of its motives and tendencies, as I might read a book, and condemning what he found in it, in his empty, indifferent way, which contained neither anger nor contempt, but was more searing than the worst form of either.

My bitterness had not gone. Now it welled up in me again at this new revelation of my impotence, and I interrupted him.

"You have forgotten many things," I cried, "that your fathers knew, about the significance of the individual. Individuality does not consist of a heap of behaviours, but of a deep unity of qualities. The men of the upper earth still remember these things, and are still too significant to themselves to allow themselves to be deprived of all the things that make life worth living, in order to avoid its tumults and risks."

He paused, when I had finished, as if he were trying to grasp the feelings that lay behind my words. Then his message came clearly again:

"The significance of even the finest individual is slight, that of the poorer individuals slighter still, compared to the significance of the people as a whole. We could not allow the continued existence of our people to be jeopardised and destroyed for the sake of the petty significance of individuals, each trying to express his own importance, as our fathers did.

"Even if their acts had been based on proper motives instead of the improper ones that moved them, we could not have permitted that. But their motives were petty ones, like the motive that has caused you to speak in that fashion—mere desires to exhibit their individuality, to show their freedom, to avoid humiliation, to produce love, fear, and other little results, so that they were always driven by a morbid impulse to effort, a mania of effort which was exhausting for themselves and others.

"Now we give each individual his proper significance from the early stages, by assigning to him definitely the task that he has to perform, enabling him to perform it, and not only preventing any other persons from interfering with him, but pooling the competence of all in one co-operative mind."

He paused again, reading my thoughts, then went on:

"If you become one with us, you will not be, as you are now, a prey to every evil force that surrounds you. You will gain the fullest community with people of the highest powers. You have come here because you need such community, the life and protection it gives those who are in it."

"No! No!" I cried. "I have come here for one thing alone— because I want to find my father."

"Why do you want to find him," came the answer, "except because you are seeking for depth of life and emotion? He cannot give it to you. No one person can give it to you. If you remain as you are, you will always be a prey to fear and loss, baffled and beaten by your own insignificance.

"Like most human beings, you need depth of emotion to give your life a meaning. Like most human beings, you have not sufficient power to enable you to draw on it by yourself or to concentrate it on an object that will not fail you in the end."

His message grew faint, died away. My mind was ceasing to receive it.

It needed to receive it no longer. It knew that it was true.

It was no longer recording it, because it was itself producing the same thoughts, feeling the same feelings. I could not do without these people. I could not live alone, unfulfilled, unprotected.

I saw my life as something miserably petty and empty, a little thing surrounded by great powers of evil, from which it must be protected. I must become one with them.

I was trembling with dread.

His message was coming to me now, not through thought, but through feeling.

"We will save you. We will take you into the shelter of our deep, unchanging situation, through which no fear, no loss can come to you. We will absorb you into our unity——"

Suddenly my mind recoiled.

Absorb me! No! Never! What was that dreadful thing that

came with that thought? Ah! It was the faces, the dead eyes, the other eyes empty of everything too. No! That way was death.

I drew myself upward. I had been crouching, cowering under the fear that was coming to me. What was this dread that was oppressing me? They were hypnotising me, frightening me. There was nothing to be afraid of, nothing but themselves. They were the thing to fear.

I flung my head back and stared at the teacher.

He was staring at me fixedly, but I could feel no power coming to me from him, no feeling.

A wave of fear seemed to be throbbing through me, but it was not coming from him. He was staring at me, but he was only reading my thoughts.

My mind was under the scrutiny of his mind, but not under the influence of his will. He had no grip over it. As far as he was concerned, it might as well have been in contact with a sort of mental X-ray, and yet there was something that was filling me with a deep dread. He was offering me help, protection against the thing that was threatening me. That was all. He was not causing it.

I looked round at the faces of the others. They were not doing it either. They were all concentrated, but they were concentrated in an empty, impassive way. My mind was not even within range of their thoughts.

As far as I was concerned, they were non-existent, not expressing in the slightest way any intentness, yet I was in the midst of a storm of disturbance.

Then I understood. Whatever it was that was perturbing me was not coming from any one of them, but from them all as a group.

Their emotion was seizing me, compelling me to be one with it, to be possessed by it.

I put forth the strongest effort of my will. But what was there to resist? Nothing.

Yes! This dread, this deep fear.

I struggled against it. It was as if I were dragging myself physically from a wave that was engulfing me; only the drag and pull of this wave was not on my body, but on my emotion.

I glared round at them in a sudden rage. Then, as suddenly, I realised the futility of my anger. Not one of them existed as a live force, as far as I was concerned. Each was nothing in himself or herself—a mere nullity, stripped naked, cleared of all individual life, of all intentions, of every shred and vestige of attitude or behaviour to me. This dread that was engulfing me was a wave of hysteria welling up in myself, generated in me by some deep feeling that was coming to me from them, like the hysteria of an angry mob.

But how could such a wave of hysteria come from that group that had no feelings, not even the shadow of feeling, nothing but the frozen calm of total immobility?

Suddenly I understood. This hypnotic calm was the result of the most profound form of hysteria, a hysteria so deep and compelling that it had drowned the personality. This thing that was invading me and oppressing me, compelling me to conform to it—this force that was emanating from the group— was a wave of feeling that was welling up from depths of fear; the panic, not of an individual, but of a whole race, a permanent dread that had seized the depths of its life. It was through this that rulers, driven mad by it themselves, had been able to hypnotise a nation.

Now it was beating on me, calling upon that hidden fear that lies in the depths of the mind of every man, and of which most men, happily, never become aware. It was calling this nameless dread from the depths of my own mind. It was a mass-agony that was encompassing me, engulfing me, drowning my personality in its waves.

I pulled myself together. Already I felt freer. It was receding.

Now that I understood it, I would not give way. It would

not get me, any more than the impact of one of their single master-minds would hypnotise me. They would not get me either way.

I kept on affirming this to myself. If it got me, I should be like a man engulfing in a marsh.

Even though I might escape in the end, I should be maimed —distorted.

I called on all my memories and my associations to help me. I must get back to my mother, to the sunlight.

I recalled the story of the man who had found himself in a mob that had lynched a negro and who had never recovered from it, remaining insane—permanently contorted in his mind —not by reason of the fact that he had been swept into some sort of complicity with a deed that he loathed, but because the pulsation of feeling that had come from the mob, and had struck him like a wave, had permanently twisted his mind.

I wrenched my body round with an effort towards the opening of the enclosure and began to walk towards it.

Immediately I felt free—physically free, and almost free of fear.

At the opening I turned and looked back. Neither the teacher nor the class seemed aware of my going.

I walked out. My guide appeared beside me and led me away.

I was panting like a quarry that has just escaped from the hounds, but my breath was coming easier with every step.

We were going into an enclosure for eating.

I breathed more freely. Once again they had almost got me, but I understood them now. I understood and I pitied them. It was not they that had oppressed me. It was their pitiful fear.

They had no powers over me, if I could only hold down the fear that lay in the depths of my own mind.

CHAPTER TWELVE

Mind-Murder

FOR FIVE MORE of their days they brought me around the schools, but the critical period had passed. Fear encompassed me, pressed in on me, but I was not at any time in serious danger of being overcome by it.

The understanding that had come to me on the second day had given me a psychological strength to meet it, and I walked amongst them much more securely.

It was clear now that their system had arisen from the deep fear of the darkness, and the forces of destruction and death that they dreaded in the darkness. Under the pressure of this fear they had gradually withdrawn themselves from ordinary life by putting away all thought and feeling about everything except the things that were needed to protect them.

When they had once entered on this downward course, the rest of their story was easy to understand. The system that had been created by their fear grew, until, in the end, it began to function for its own sake and to suppress, not merely irrelevant or unnecessary things, but all tendencies, emotions, actions, whether essential or not, so that it might control completely the social, mental, and emotional life of its people.

The driving-force behind it was the throb of this dread, the mass-hysteria of the race, that kept welling up through the ever-present darkness. It was that fear that had been encompassing me in the schools and in all their gatherings, calling to the dread and the hysteria that lay deep in the abysses of my subconscious mind, urging, compelling me to come into this shelter they had built, away from the storms and agonies of individuality.

This was the force on which the Master of Knowledge had counted to draw me into their orbit. It might have done so if I had been of a more sensitive, a less tough and resistant, fibre. It had failed, and, now that I had a rational attitude to it, as well as experience of its effects, it would have little chance of succeeding, unless other forces, of which I knew nothing, were brought into action.

If they were to get me, they would have to seize me through the attack of a powerful individual mind—a mind, like that of the Master of Knowledge, so overwhelming in its powers of concentration that I should not be able to resist.

That attack was coming. The Master had left me in little doubt about it.

At the end of my respite I should have to meet the assault of his mind, and that might mean either madness or death.

The alternative was absorption, and I felt that, if I were driven to it, I should certainly choose death rather than live as an automaton.

If only I could find my father, I felt that I should make some headway in my struggle to rescue him and myself from this peril, but, although every hour that passed was bringing the end of my respite nearer, I was making no progress in my quest.

During the days I spent in the schools I had not succeeded in finding the slightest clue that could help me to trace him. In that, the chief thing that I had hoped to gain from my visits, they were yielding me nothing, and, before the end even of the third day, it became obvious to me that they could never yield me anything.

Even if the teachers had known something about my father, they could not have given me the information, since they had no volition other than that supplied them by the State. But, even if they had volition of their own, they had not, and could not have, any knowledge of him, since he did not come within the radius of their particular task.

Even if they had ever met him, they would have been aware of him only to the extent required for the explanation of their work to him. Any memory or knowledge of him would have been sectional, and my attempts to get information from them about him or any other matter unrelated to their task could, therefore, have no result.

So I went my round in a cold waiting mood, with the end drawing in on me.

If it were not that I knew that my father was somewhere amongst them, I should have tried to escape and face whatever ordeals my attempts might bring upon me, whether it succeeded or failed. But, with my father in their clutches, any attempt to escape was out of the question. It would be too great a desertion and betrayal. It might even worsen his fate, whatever that was. That was no way out. I must remain, and await whatever was in store for me.

Had I, while waiting and watching, been able to learn something of the methods by which the Masters seized domination over the minds of men, it would have given me some hope. The higher schools were the places where I could see these methods at work, but, even where the teachers could give me some aid, I had made no progress.

I saw clearly the importance of trying to get an insight into their methods. I realised that, if I could do so, it might enable me to offer a better resistance when they turned these methods against myself. With this in my mind, I applied myself as best I could during the last five days in the schools to discover the actual manner in which they obtained such power over others, but, in spite of all my efforts, I failed to grasp their processes.

Not that they made any attempt to conceal them from me. On the contrary, they answered all my questions, in so far

as they could understand them, but their explanations were
of little use, since I could not see their processes in operation
owing to the fact that, at this stage of the training, the directions and the work were done without words.

There were, they told me, exercises in isolating the attention, checking and controlling tendencies and holding them in
suspense, atrophying and destroying thought and emotion,
developing selected powers, receiving or conveying thoughts,
focusing the will on the minds and wills of others. Their information stopped at that.

If I had been willing to submit myself to their operations
I should have some experience of how they translated their
methods into acts. Otherwise I could obtain no real knowledge
of them.

I could see that their knowledge of tendencies, psychic re-
flexes, and the various automatic reactions of the mind, made
it possible for them to turn into account the different forms
of suggestion which produce an automatic functioning of this
or that tendency. The power they showed in handling these
automatisms of the mind deepened my apprehensions, but of
its secrets I could learn nothing.

In the schools for the workers I saw them take control of
the mind of the victim as a surgeon takes control of a body
under an anæsthetic, and remove or atrophy every capacity,
tendency, interest, or emotion that was not necessary for the
work that he or she had to do.

In the higher-grade schools I saw them isolating the will,
and developing it to a remarkable degree by the destruction
of all those individual reactions and collateral thoughts and
feelings that the events of life call up in normal human beings,
and that make life so rich and complex. In these latter schools
also I saw the pupils being trained to focus their will on the
wills of lower-grade pupils, who were brought there specially
to be experimented on and have their minds vivisected.

In both schools there were lessons of the most profound importance to me, if I could have learned them, but I could not learn without submitting myself to the processes, and I did not dare to do so.

The result was that, even from the point of view of discovering the secret of their powers, I learned nothing in the schools that I could have turned to the slightest use as a protection. I learned enough merely to realise the thoroughness and effectiveness of their methods, and to marvel that such efficiency and such slavery could be produced in man even by the hysteria of overwhelming fear.

Their calm was for me no longer a sinister symbol of their power, but a warning as to the depths of flight into which panic can drive the mind of man. It made me long, while I was in those silent schools, for anything that would express the protest of individual life. Better the most senseless form of life than that flight from it.

It was in those schools that I first began to understand, with sympathy, the aspects of our social life that had seemed to me most absurd on earth—our noisy clamour, our need for the sensational, all those pathetic attempts of ours to obtain stimulation to face life and its end, by social gatherings, gambling, drink, love-making, games, competition in work and play; our mania for making ourselves prominent, for producing melodramatic outbursts, for society taboos, for belonging to something exclusive or secret or mysterious.

All such attempts of our humanity to strengthen and emphasise our individual position, and to call up latent powers in ourselves to ward off the forces of destruction and darkness —all these now became dear and significant to me, as I stared into the abyss into which those men had fallen, through taking the opposite road. That, indeed, was one of the chief things that I learned in those extraordinary schools.

CHAPTER THIRTEEN

Fuel Supply

TOWARDS THE END of my visit to the schools I had begun to feel that my respite was drawing to a close.

Though nobody that I had met had seemed to watch me, I had little doubt that the Masters of Knowledge would by now have come to the conclusion that their plans for drawing me into their system, through the atmosphere of the schools, had failed; and, since the schools were their most potent centres of influence, I felt that they would hardly trouble to show me any other part of their system before dealing in other ways with my resistance.

I almost hoped that this would be the case. I had by now realised fully that I had no chance of getting any information about my father, and very little chance of getting any other sort of information of any practical value, and when, on the sixth day, I was told that I was to be brought to see the industrial quarters, the news aroused little hope and little interest.

It meant that I was to have a further respite, but, in the circumstances, a further respite merely meant further suspense.

If the teachers could not give me any information about my father, what possibility was there of my being able to get it from the industrial grades, who were bound to be much more circumscribed in their knowledge than the teachers, and of much lower grade of intelligence? And, if I could get no information and make no progress, what was the use of the postponement of that final struggle that was coming upon me?

The hopelessness of my position and of my search was becoming so clear that my mind began to evolve plans of escape.

The thinking out of these plans was probably of some help as an outlet for my thoughts, but it brought little real relief to my mind, since I could not imagine any scheme that would have the remotest chance of success.

The more I considered my position, the more it seemed to be that of a rat caught in a trap—the only possible action being to dash myself against the bars, with the chance that, if I did so, I should be worsening my father's position, if it was one that could be worsened.

It might be thought that, the longer I was free to go round the city, the better chance there was that my presence there might, in some way, come to the knowledge of my father, and enable him to come to me or communicate with me. But the more I had seen of these people, the more clearly I knew that there could be no foundation for such a hope, since no one could convey any knowledge to my father without the will of the State, and the chances of his coming across any traces of me, even if he were in a condition to do so, were practically non-existent.

Such was the mood in which I began my visits to the industrial compounds, a mood of cold despair which was justified by events, since during all my visits to these compounds I learned, as I had expected, nothing that was of the slightest use to me.

If they had had anything new or striking to show, it might, by rousing my professional curiosity, have afforded me some relief of mind by taking my thoughts off my position. But my first sight of their works showed me that, unlike the schools, they had nothing that could interest a modern scientific worker.

Not that there were not things in them that might have interested a man in a normal mood. There were, in fact, such sights and occurrences, some of them most poignant in their appeal to the common feelings of humanity.

One of these pathetic things was the attention and care lavished on the waterclocks—those relics of ancient days, by which, though they have lost the alternating rhythm of night and day, these people still measure time, after the Roman mode, spacing it into periods of twenty-four hours' duration and combining these units of "days" into months and years, on the model of the Julian calendar. In this way the Masters of Knowledge have attempted to set some sort of ebb and flow in the continuity of a tideless time which would have been insufferable, even to minds such as theirs, if it had not been divided up and made bearable by a series of marks and limits, such as are supplied by the ebb and flow of diurnal, seasonal, and annual rebirths of nature on earth.

While, however, such pitiful human relics were still existent here and there amongst them, there was little else that could stir me to a feeling of our common humanity, or make it worth my while to chronicle the details of the days I spent in visiting the different parts of their settlement.

Compared to the occupations of people on the upper earth, the occupations of these people are few, and their range of tools correspondingly small. In that city, for instance, although it was, I understood, the chief centre of population of the country, the only large industries that I saw were woodwork, metalwork, the weaving of cloth, the making of earthenware, the preparations of the various oils and fats, and other essential industries such as the building of boats and ships. Everything was done in an elementary way with the tools and methods used by the Romans on the upper earth two thousand years ago. They have still no power other than that supplied by mechanics, and their mechanics are of the most elementary type.

Their appliances may be summed up as the lever, the inclined plane, the wedge, the pulley, and simple combinations of these. Beyond that they have not gone, and every process that I saw in their factory compounds and industrial enclosures was carried out solely with tools based on such combinations, without any development on the type of tool used for similar purposes in Ancient Rome.

The contrast between the primitive nature of their work here and the remarkable developments I had seen in the schools was astonishing. There, I had been as completely out-ranged in power as they would be if they could be introduced to the works of one of our great industrial concerns on earth. Here, there was so little of note that the only value my visits to their compounds had for me was that they gave me information as to the lay-out of the city, which I thought might possibly be of use if I should attempt to escape.

I discovered that it was divided into half a dozen great compounds, each of which was assigned to a particular trade, and was a separate unit, to the extent that it supplied all the needs of its group of workers in so far as these could be supplied from its area.

The distributive group, for instance, is placed in the neighbourhood of the harbours, and occupies all that quarter, with the exception of a small quarter near the great harbour set aside for the governing class.

The woodworkers are grouped in a series of compounds along the shores of the Central Sea, since the wood on which they work is rafted down by water from the forests along the shores of the lake.

The groups that make cloth and earthenware, and articles made from these, are situated in the centre of the city, as are the groups that deal with preparations for food-stuffs. The compounds of the ironworkers, on the other hand, are situated some distance behind the other settlements, in the neighbourhood of the coal- and iron-mines that lie at the foot of the range of mountains that forms the southern barrier of that land.

In all cases the compounds contain not only separate sections for the various types of processes needed to work up the raw material, but also full accommodation of communal kitchens, eating-places, sleeping-places, baths, and gymnastic fittings for the whole of the staff.

Each of the great compounds is under the control of a manager, who is at once an expert in the particular industry and a man with a controlling will, and under him or her there are subordinate officers of a similar type in charge of each section.

All these officers evidently had orders to show me everything, for they gave me free access to their works, and answered my questions in so far as they grasped them. In most cases, however, they were so restricted in their radius of thought that they could have little communication with me.

In the very first industrial compound I visited I had experience of this. It was a woodworking compound, and, when I went into the first section of it, I found men sawing logs with a most elementary type of saw—a thing with straight teeth stretched in a curved frame, to which it was attached like a string to a bow.

The commandant who was in charge of the section was standing beside me, and, in order to try to get into some sort of contact with him, I began to explain to him that, if the men used saws with cross teeth, instead of the ones with straight teeth that they were using, the blades would not get stuck constantly, as theirs were doing. He stared in front of him with a fixed stare, as if he hadn't heard me. I began all over again, more slowly, but my second attempt to get his attention for my explanation was no more successful than the first. He was there merely to get the work done, and any discussion about the improvement of the tools was outside the range of his attention

It was the same in most of the other cases where I tried to discuss tools or methods.

It is possible, of course, that in the case of these industrial foremen, with whom I failed to establish contact, one reason, at least, for their lack of understanding of me was that their minds could not grasp my method of speech and were themselves too feeble to communicate with me by thought-transference, except in the simplest matters closely affecting their work. Whatever the reason was, I could make little contact with them—not even as much as I had made with the teachers, who were at least able to communicate to me views of the State, and meet my answers and objections.

The only gain, indeed, in my change of centres, was that the atmosphere which I had found so perturbing in the schools was not as powerful in the industrial compounds, as if the higher grades felt the urge of that primeval fear more poignantly than the less vital types.

In all other respects the workers were on an entirely lower plane, as regards either interest or information, than the teachers.

The sight of the craft-workers in the first industrial works, indeed, gave the last blow to any faint hope I might have retained of being able to use my further respite to obtain any information that could be of use to me.

One result of this complete destruction of my hopes was that my mind settled down still more to its fatalist calm. Since there was nothing else to do, I forced myself to take an interest in their works and processes, and, although they were of an elementary type, I succeeded, to some extent, in doing so.

When, for instance, after my visits to the woodworking compounds, they brought me to the compounds for the working of metals, I found myself sufficiently interested to occupy myself with an objective examination of their machines and processes.

One reason, perhaps, was that these compounds resemble more closely our ironworks, since they have large blast-furnaces for the reduction of the various ores, and these gave me an illusion of home associations.

Apart from this, however, the sight of the automaton workers carrying out their various tasks in the glare of the great furnaces had a horrible grandeur of its own, with its suggestion of damned souls working in a state of stupefaction in the glare of penal fires, and I have still a vivid memory of that strange sight.

I will not trouble the reader with the details of their metal-work, since these could be of interest only to specialists.

There was, however, one incident that impressed me profoundly during my first visit to these latter works.

I was examining one of the larger furnaces in the iron-workers' compound when two automatons came in with the dead body of a woman. It was the first dead body I had seen, and the sight of it in the works surprised me. Then they fed it into the furnace, and I realised that they were using it for fuel as if it were a barrow of lignite!

I should have been sufficiently hardened by now, but I confess that this sudden revelation of the lack of respect of these people for the last remains of their dead came as a shock to me. It was as if the desecration of the body that had been carried out in life had been perpetuated in death.

When I spoke to the foreman about it, however, he did not understand what I was trying to convey to him, and, thinking that I was merely asking for information about fuel supplies, he informed me that all the workers in a compound, from the highest to the lowest, served, on death, as fuel for the furnaces of the compound, if it had furnaces, and that all furnaces had, as part of their fuel supplies, the dead bodies of its people who lived within a fixed radius of their site, so that in this way the dead of the whole city and its neighbourhood were apportioned out in death, as in life, to the service of the State.

As I listened to him explaining how the slavery of this people is continued on into death, I saw that it was no use trying to get him to understand the feelings which his words were producing in me, and, instead, I fell to wondering whether, under the profound crisis of death, and the pangs that some people suffer when dying, there is not, between the two slaveries which this race has to undergo, a moment before death in which some of them, at least, wake up from the hypnotic sleep in which they have spent their lives, and for a brief interval revert to normal human beings. Does the deep unchanging situation, inside which they shelter themselves, fall away from them at death? Do they stare, with feelings similar to those I felt, at the empty masks round them? Do they call out against the isolation in which they find themselves, or try miserably to remember what had become of their lives since last they had individual consciousness as little children?

If there is such an interval under the pangs of death for these people, the ordeal of dying must be greater than on earth. I was never able to discover whether this is so or not, for, although there are special enclosures for the sick in each compound, and I was shown through these, I never saw anybody dying, and the patients I saw in the sick-wards differed in no respect in appearance or look from the others.

As hypnotic treatment and suggestion play a most important part in their curative processes, it is probable that, in the great majority of cases, they are able to drug the dying into a hypnotic state deep enough to prevent their awaking to individual life, even under the pangs of death.

CHAPTER FOURTEEN

The Battle Without a Morrow

AFTER I had visited the wood and metal enclosures, I was brought to a variety of other industrial compounds which it would be tedious to describe in detail, since there was no scientific interest to be found in them.

In pottery, for instance, in which one might have expected these people to excel, since the Roman pottery of the Empire was excellent, I could not see that they had even been able to retain the competence of their ancestors.

It was the same in other branches akin to this. If, for instance, they ever knew how to make glass, they must have forgotten the art, for I saw no sign of any glass, either in use or in the making. Spectacles are, of course, unknown to them as they were to the ancient Romans.

Their cloth-making I found somewhat more interesting, mainly because the material from which they make cloth is necessarily different from ours, and the processes by which they make it had therefore some novelty.

The material from which they make their very fine cloth is the silk stuff spun by great spiders of the same size and type as the lassoing brutes that I had met in the higher lands. They breed these in captivity for this purpose, and keep them in enormous iron enclosures.

Their coarser cloth is made from two types of fibre, one got from the bark of a certain bush that grows freely there, and the other from long stalks, like seaweed rods, that grow in marshy ground. The latter are the chief source of their coarser cloth, and are treated somewhat like flax with us, being pulled up by the roots, then steeped in water, dried on hot stones, beaten heavily with clubs, loosened into fibres, and combed.

The spinning of the fibre is entirely in the hands of women, and the sight of the work in the spinning compounds affected me strangely. Like all the other industrial processes of these people, it is done in an elementary way, by hand. The women use a cane distaff and a wood spindle, so that, from the point of view of processes, there is little difference between their method and that of our own women spinners in the "out-by" farms.

It was the combination of this resemblance in working methods with the difference of expression and atmosphere in these under-earth women that moved me.

One of the most joyous memories of my childhood had been the sight of the women in the "out-by" farms chatting and laughing so merrily at their work that it was an intense joy to watch them, and the sight of these female automatons, with their dead faces, drawing down the raw material from the distaff, jamming it into the notch of the spindle, and turning the spindle, hurt sharply, through the contrast between their inhuman mechanism of movement and expression and the joyous associations I had with spinning at home.

It was the same with the weaving. Here again I found that the work was entirely in the hands of women, and was done in a primitive way, with simple hand-looms, as I had seen it done in far-out villages of the North Country. There were differences, since the weaving of these underground women is carried out from below upwards and their shuttles are not two-sided, with the result that they have to be turned round each time, so that the point may come in the direction of the throw, but the close resemblance of the work to that which I knew as a boy was sufficient to rack my mind through its associations.

For some reason or other the sight of these women seemed to bring closer to me the doom that had fallen on that race than the sight of the men automatons had done in the other enclosures.

When I left the compounds of the cloth-making industry, I felt as a man might feel who had been shown some peculiar form of madness into which he himself would soon be thrust.

Next to the compounds of the cloth-makers I found those for the making up of the materials into garments.

There is little for me to record of these enclosures, as the garments of these people are of the simplest type, and the pieces of cloth are woven to the right size at the beginning, so that they can be worn with small alteration; but, again, the associations were painful, since the women were working with thimbles, scissors, and needles that differed little from those used by my mother, and the sight of these beings, with their blind, unseeing faces, working with these familiar things, brought back a flood of memories.

One would have expected that, since all the rest of their humanity had been sacrificed to their work, the women would be absorbed in it. The contrary was the case.

They have been so completely sacrificed to their work that they are in a profound sense non-existent apart from it, since their active existence is in evidence only through their act of work, yet the effect produced by the individual workers on the onlooker is that they have no more contact with the work, or awareness of it, than they have with the other human beings round them.

It was not that they did not perform their various tasks with thoroughness and efficiency. In that respect, I could not see any sign of defect or unevenness such as one finds amongst workers with us. It was rather that in their work, as in their life, there was no connection between themselves and their task, as if they are unaware of it, unaware of effort, unaware of their own action or of any process arising from themselves.

This double isolation made me realise more fully than before the gulf into which they had fallen, and to realise it all the more because I had been under the illusion that, in the case of the skilled workers, the concentration on their work, aroused by their absorption in it, would take the place, to some extent at least, of the individuality and human joy that they had lost.

The destruction of this illusion, by removing the last barrier of preconceived ideas about their lives, gave me a much clearer view of the state of these people than that which I had got at the beginning, and this insight reached backwards to a new understanding of the other things that I had seen.

I saw now that even the teachers in the highest schools, the commanders of the highest grade—all were in the same gulf of emptiness; not merely in a state of isolation from all other things, outside their particular task, but in a similar state of isolation from the task itself. Not one of them, from the highest to the lowest, lived even in the work to which he or she had been sacrificed.

I have since discovered that this is a condition which is common to all people under the influence of hypnotism, even on the upper earth. The hypnotic subject is not aware of his task, but is aware only of his emotional state towards the master who controls him and makes him perform it.

At that time, however, I looked upon this evident lack of awareness of their work as the final proof of the total enslavement of the people, and it made me long still more poignantly for that other protection that life has built up round itself on the earth—the music of humanity, its rush and its tumult, above all things that joyous, casual laughter of man which is the sunlight of the mind.

Never before had I grasped the deep need that every man has for man's company, his humour, his rages, his love, and his laughter, all that collection of individual feelings, tendencies, reactions, ideas, that constitute the consciousness of men like us, and is our home as well as our very self, at once our ego and the sheltering circumstances that enfold it.

The sense of brotherhood was being developed in me by the sight of those unfortunate kinsmen of ours who had striven to protect themselves in the opposite way—by retreat from individual life and its tumultuous reactions—but it was being developed in me by an extreme revulsion.

By the time that I had finished my round of visits to their industrial compounds, I was reduced to such a state of mind that I looked on the lassoing brutes, that I had met on the downward journey, as fellow-creatures, in comparison with the human beings who surrounded me.

The industrial compound that had the most real interest for me was, in fact, that in which the enormous spiders had been trained to spin silken webs by a supply of chunks of meat at the end of each task.

How the men had managed to train them to produce their lovely silk webs in captivity I don't know, but it was certainly not through inducing in them a hypnotic love and submission, for their masters did not dare to go into the big enclosures in which the spiders were working while the brutes were there, and, if anybody approached the iron bars behind which they worked, they showed all the savage ferocity of newly caged tigers. The fact that the sight of their savagery gave me a feeling of joy will be some measure of my dread of the slavery that they, unlike their masters in this lower world, had refused to accept.

The great spiders were indeed the only creatures within the reach of that state that it had not enslaved.

In the snake farms, for instance, that lay behind the city, the dominance of man has been completely established, and, when I was brought there, I was fascinated by the control exercised over these creatures by their keepers, a control so complete that it would make the control of the snake-charmers of India seem feeble and superficial.

The snakes appeared to love their masters; and the long lines of them rolling forward on command was one of the most impressive scenes that I have ever witnessed. The relations between them and their keepers almost gave me the illusion that they were pets, but it was only an illusion, produced by my own associations, for these people are as incapable of having the individual contact with other creatures which creates pets as they are of emotional relations between human individuals.

The sight, however, of the moving coils of green phosphorescent light was a marvellous one, not easily forgotten. For me, at that time, it was an additional revelation, if I needed one, of the strength of the forces that I was up against, but, now that the menace has passed, the memory of its beauty still remains with me.

Another vision that comes to me, as I write, is that of the great fungus farms in which the various forms of edible fungi glowed with green and blue glimmerings, while the dark shapes of the workers gliding amongst them gave an impression of ghosts floating through veils of dim fire.

To the left, as one looked up the lake, the city was surrounded by these fungus farms, as far as the eye could reach, and the effect of their sheets of soft glowing lights, when seen from a hillock beside the city, was extraordinarily beautiful.

These and similar things I saw during my short stay in that underworld city—the capital of a people that has been permanently defeated, a people sprung from a sunlight race that has been permanently deprived of the sunlight, and of all the ardours and ecstasies it brings.

While I moved amongst them, under the shadow of a fate that seemed to me worse than death, their life and all its accompaniments excited in me no feelings but those of fear and repulsion.

Looking back now in calmer mood, I am willing to acknowledge that I may have been unfair and unjust in much of my judgment of them.

Even on earth, under the influence of overwhelming defeat and the panic and hysteria that it brings, nations have been known to hand themselves over to the hypnotic suggestion of their leaders, and, under that hypnotic subjection, to take courses that are abhorrent to the normal instincts of humanity. But no race on earth has ever suffered a defeat as deep as that which has been suffered by these people, a defeat in many ways more dreadful than total annihilation.

With them the dread thing has literally happened, the *schlacht ohne morgen,* the battle without a morrow—that last and irreparable disaster from which there can be no recovery, no emergence. Yet they live to endure it.

How can a man of the upper earth plumb the depths of emotional hunger of such a people, their craving for consolation, their need to give themselves up to any leader, any system, that could promise relief or refuge from so dreadful a deprivation?

Yet what leader or what system devised on earth could supply such refuge or consolation?

They had abandoned religion. Deprived of that salvation, their leaders, as well as themselves, were emotionally as well as spiritually destitute. What could such leaders give their people, when they cried for life, but a drug that would be potent enough to give them oblivion?

Hypnotic suggestion, which is rooted in the passionate side of human nature, has always been the substitute that such barren leaders have offered.

Those leaders below have merely done to an extreme degree, proportioned to their great need, what similar leaders have done in a small way on earth.

That their achievement is almost an incredible one I cannot deny. Nor can I deny that, as they claim, they may have attained peace—a dreadful peace, passing the understanding of any men on earth in the depth of its withdrawal from the conflict of the emotional storms and tides which are the life of man.

There were times when, under the impact of the mysterious force that emanated from them, I, too, fell under the influence of that peace, and almost believed in it.

There were even times, during my wanderings through that incredible city, with its incredible people, when I felt tempted to yield myself up to the peace to which they seemed to have attained, or to ask to have my will concentrated to such an intensity of life that I might draw into myself all other life in that world below, as the higher grades have done.

But I knew that such a solution could give me no peace or rest. It would be a denial of all my hopes and beliefs in this world and the next. I must go on struggling till I died.

If my father, caught in the web of his own dreams, had surrendered himself totally, I could not save him, but, if he had only surrendered part of his mind, I might yet save him, or, if I could not save him, I might yet touch him before he and I died.

If only I could find him! During all my peregrinations—on roads, in enclosures, in schools, working-places, eating-places, all their gatherings—I had been watching for him. With his stature he would have been very noticeable amongst them, but I never saw anybody who was in the remotest degree like him —none that could, by the wildest flight of fancy, be imagined even to be such a person as they could have transformed him into. Nor did I come upon any trace of him whatever in any other way.

Whenever I asked about him, I got always the same answer —there could be no such person.

As far as information about him was concerned, I was, at

the end of my time in the city, exactly where I had been on the first day I started, with this difference—that, in the end, I realised better how little chance he or I had of rescue or escape.

I was like a trapped wild creature. I could not surrender and I could not escape.

I thought of my pet rabbit that I had found being killed by a stoat when I was a child of three—my first vision of the deadliness of life.

The memory came back to me vividly when, at the end of my wanderings through the city, I received my second call to appear before the Master of Knowledge.

I had blundered after my father into the most ghastly prison-house ever devised by the human mind for humanity, and now, after I had been shown round its cells, I was being called to hear my sentence.

The patient, frightened face of the rabbit as it lay under the stoat came to me, my own screams as I ran to save it, the rush of the stoat at me, and its hiss as my father's stick broke its back.

Now it was he who was lying under the stoat.

CHAPTER FIFTEEN

The Master of Knowledge

WHEN I WAS brought before the Master of Knowledge the second time my mind was in a state of frozen calm.

The Master was sitting under the same globes of phosphorus light in the same enclosure, or a similar one. When I was brought before him, he looked at me for a few moments without communicating with me.

I let him read my thoughts. The sooner my fate was settled the better.

Almost immediately his message came:

"You have learned nothing from what you have received from our people. You are still unwilling to become one with us."

"I could not become one with you," I answered, "without losing all that makes life worth living."

"You have nothing to lose," came his answer, "that can make life worth living. There is only one thing that can do that, and that is love of something so great and permanent that you cannot lose it. You have not got that."

I made no answer. He watched me for a while—then his message came again:

"That is what you also desire, but, having lived your life on the surface of things, you do not even know your own desires.

"I see deep in your mind a need that you are only dimly conscious of, a hunger for depth of life. You are desolated by your own emptiness, starving for something that flows deeply below the surface on which you are floating."

Again he paused, watching me. I watched him steadily. I had no fear of him. My mind was made up. He could kill me or drive me mad, but, if he was looking into my mind, he would not see fear of his power.

I heard myself speaking in answer to his thoughts.

"It is true that I am starving," I said, "but it is starvation from lack of the sunlight, and the richness of life of men who live in the sunlight. I loathe the life lived by your people, and I will not share it."

"You have no understanding of our life," came his answer, "because it is lived in those depths to which your vision cannot penetrate.

"You have been shown a life deeper than any that you have ever known, and you have seen in it only darkness and silence, austerity and terror. All these I see reflected in your mind, and only these; no glimpse of its richness, its fulfillment. Until you have plumbed the depths, you can know nothing."

"I do not want to plumb the depths of your life," I said. "I want to go back to the brightness and joy of my own. Will you let me go?"

He made no answer, but his stare swept my mind like a searchlight. I feared that, if I kept quiet under his gaze, he would hypnotise me.

"What do you want to do?" I cried. "Do you think that you can hypnotise me, with your eyes, or your incantations, into believing what I do not believe? If you cannot do that, what good can it do you to hold me here? If you can read my mind, you must know that, whatever you do or think or send into it, I will never become as one with you."

"You understand nothing," came his answer. "Faith and love and joy are all round you, and you cannot see them."

"And I will not see them," I said, "not even if they are

there. I do not need your faith or love or joy. I have a deeper faith, and I will not give up my individual life in order to see or to possess yours. My life was full of faith and love and joy before I came to your land, and if I could find my father, and he could once again see the sun and feel the rain and tread green grass, I should be infinitely happier than all your automatons, who know no god but fear."

"Your life," came his message, "could not have been full of faith before you came to us. If it had been, you would not have left all these things to come here.

"You came here because your life was empty and meaningless as the life of no man or woman can be with us, since they share in all the greatest life there is, and it cannot be taken from them."

"I came here," I answered, "because I loved my father and wanted to find him."

"Such love of little things is meaningless," came his answer. "Even if the things you love were greater and better than yourselves, and worthy of love, they die and leave you, or you die and leave them desolate. Therefore your lives are empty and miserable.

"Here no man can be left desolate, because each man here loves a thing that cannot die; not himself, nor little men like himself, but something great and permanent that he shares with all. So, in no way can death destroy his peace or leave him empty.

"No one man matters. All the selfishness, vanity, egotism, that wrecked our fathers of old, and that is still in your mind —all that is gone. Our knowledge and our wills are now at one, and we are one through our emotion."

"Yes," I cried, "you who are the wills, have seized the power and made the others love you, by emptying their souls and their minds of everything else. You have all the intensity of life. You have robbed them of it and gathered it to yourselves, as our capitalists have gathered the goods of the earth; but the stealing of the goods of the earth from others is a small matter compared to the stealing of the intensities of the soul. No, no, I will never take part in what you are doing. I will neither rob others of their inner life and fire, nor allow others to rob me and call it 'faith' and 'joy.'"

He looked at me for a while, as if digesting my thoughts, then he began to send his message again:

"You understand so little that it seems useless to try to get you to grasp things. Yet it is not right to abandon you without attempting to save you, since you are a human being.

"No man here robs another. No man can rob another, since all men share equally. Those who have a deeper intensity of life give it to the others. Those who have a deeper intensity of knowledge direct the others, not in their work only, since that is but a surface thing, but in their emotion, which is the source of all life.

"That is where your life has gone wrong. You have deep feeling, but you have wasted it on little passing things, because there was no one to direct you, and you are not great enough to direct yourself.

"Man cannot direct himself unless he is at the creative stage, when emotion and mind combine to discover an object of emotion great enough and permanent enough to give full content and direction to the human soul.

"Few men are at that stage, and these few alone can produce that act of will which can save themselves and others. Without such men our people would have perished, as you will perish if you do not become one with us, who have vision and the will that springs from the fusing of vision and emotion."

"I will not become one with you," I said quietly. "I will not give my soul into the hands of any leader, however great.

"You may have descended to depths of feeling of which I know nothing. The darkness that surrounds you is so great that, in your efforts to escape from the surface of your life, over which it broods, you may have won to unknown depths of thought and feeling.

"You have risked everything in your effort to escape. You have given everything that is dear to man. To me it seems the last surrender. But I do not judge you. I cannot judge you. I have not been born to your darkness and despair. I am a child of the sunlight of the upper earth. I will not surrender to the darkness. I will not be one with you. We are playing for the greatest stakes that man can play for in this life. You say that you have won. I think that you have lost everything. Only God can judge. But, even if you have won, I would not give up the agonies and exultations and faith of individual life for any peace that you may have reached in the depths to which you have plunged or sunk."

For a while we stayed without further contact of thoughts; then his message came to me again:

"Your thought of darkness is, like all your other thoughts, superficial.

"You think only of the outer darkness, which matters little.

"The inner darkness that destroys is common to all men, whether they are born here or under the light. No sunlight of the upper earth can save you from that.

"I see the depths of your mind, and they are full of the dread of it."

"No, no," I cried, "I am not afraid of it. I will not fly to your refuge from that inner darkness. When the last defeat comes, I shall take it, with God's help, but I will not defeat myself.

"You shall not drag up that fear again from the depths of my life.

"I will not plunge down with you into the primeval darkness because you have gone mad through fear of it. Now put me to death or let me go."

"Then go," he answered. "Go forth to a deeper experience—the experience of the darkness from which we have learned our wisdom."

He paused, watching me.

My calm was gone. I was to get another respite, another chance of regaining life. My heart was thumping.

He read my thoughts, and began to answer them.

"No," came his message, "do not think that you can escape, or that you can stay away from us and live.

"No man can escape from the territory of our State without our sanction, and no man of human breed can live permanently alone in the darkness and remain as you are. Such a man must either die in madness or seek refuge in the depths of life, as we have done.

"Under that sun, of which your mind is so full, men may live as you do. Here in the darkness men cannot do it. Your sun may give some sort of fusion to the shifting mass of little tendencies which you call emotions, feelings, thoughts. The darkness will not do so. It will disintegrate the man who cannot fuse himself into a unity. All that you will learn from the outer darkness and the inner darkness that it releases."

He paused, staring at me, then went on:

"Perhaps you will choose to die in the darkness rather than reintegrate.

"Perhaps you will merely disintegrate. Then we shall reintegrate you, if we can find you.

"Sheltered by our civilisation, you have seen nothing of the causes of it, only the results, which you do not yet understand. Go, therefore, and discover, through your own experiences, why you must be as we are."

"That I will never discover," I said. "I will never come back to be absorbed."

"You will be forced to, but not by us. You will be absorbed, whether you come back or not.

"If you do not return to us, the forces of darkness will absorb you—disintegrate you and absorb you.

"Do not think that you are to be left to die—thrown to the powers of darkness.

"Whenever you come to a settlement of the people, they will supply you with the necessaries of life, but they cannot supply you with more than that. They can only help you with external things. They cannot help you to face the powers of darkness, since you are not one of them. That struggle is a struggle of the soul that you must wage alone.

"No other man can help an isolated soul. Now, go."

CHAPTER SIXTEEN

The Search Begins

I LEFT THE ENCLOSURE of the Master of Knowledge with a feeling of liberation and exhilaration that seems pathetically ludicrous to me now, when I remember the slightness of the grounds I had for it and the experiences that followed. Yet it was natural at the time that there should have been a great swing round, in my mind, from fear to relief.

Before my visit to the Master I had been a prisoner, with a sentence of madness or death not merely hanging over me, but about to fall. Now I had got another respite. The doom had not been averted, but it had been postponed. Not merely that, but I was free to go through the land and use my own efforts to try to attain my two objectives—the discovery of my father and the finding of some exit by which he and I could escape.

What if my respite arose from the belief of the leaders of the people that I had no chance whatever of gaining my ends?

They were the masters of all the knowledge or wisdom that had been accumulated to deal with the problems of their land, and they must be in a good position to judge of my chances of success. But even they could not be sure. They understood the difficulties and risks of my task, but how could they understand fully the resources that an individual man, brought up to rely on his own powers, could draw upon to overcome obstacles and attain his ends?

In any case, my task was there to be tackled, clear and

straight in front of me. I had no choice. I had come down to this world to rescue my father, and I was at last getting a chance to begin my attempt.

I could not complain of my luck so far. I was, indeed, luckier than my foolhardiness had deserved. I might have met with any fate. I might have found a people who would have murdered or enslaved me. I might have succumbed to any of the other dangers that beset me. I had come through all that without loss or maiming so far, and now, even though the knowledge of the country and the people that I had gained was not such as to aid me materially in my search, I had, nevertheless, some conception of the nature of my task.

It is true that that knowledge was, in a sense, perhaps more paralysing than ignorance. At least, it might have been so to a mind differently constituted from mine. The people that I had to deal with were as monstrous as the land they dwelt in. Even though I had received gentle treatment from them, it would in one sense, and that a very profound one, have been less desolating for me to have fallen into the hands of the lowest and most ferocious type of savage.

No horror of torture or ill treatment, short of death itself, could be as disastrous to the mind of a man of the upper earth as the environment in which I found myself; and on the upper earth there is always hope of rescue, of the arrival of help, of some normal means of escape. Here there was no contact with another human being, no hope of rescue, little chance of escape, unless, by a miracle, I could find some exit other than the river by which I had been carried into the Central Sea.

I knew that looking for such an exit in so great a space was like looking for a needle in a bundle of straw. I might go on until the end of my life, if they allowed me, or for centuries, if I had them, without finding any such exit, even if one existed. Nevertheless, the rebound had come in my heart.

As I walked out of the enclosure I was full of hope. I was

at least free to try, to use my own powers, to see what I was up against and measure my strength with the strength of the forces of darkness. My own initiative was back with me again. That absence had been heavy on my spirit, making heavier still the fate that had been coming towards me—that absence of all power of action.

I was not like my mother; that smile of hers on the evening of my father's disappearance—it had wrung my heart, the patience of it. I was different. I must go out into the open, on my own, spend my trouble in action, even if the action led nowhere in the end—die in action, if it failed.

But it might at least lead somewhere. I had got into their land without their knowledge. Where a man could get in, he might get out, even if, in the end, my way led up that tunnel, against the torrent. There might be a way over the mountain it ran under—over some mountain. There must be some way round the land beyond the cliff through which I had come down.

When I left the Master of Knowledge, the guide took me to the bathing-enclosure and, after that, to the eating-room. When I had eaten and was ready to go, he brought me into a little cell off the bathing-chamber and there, to my joy, I found my clothes and my outfit complete. Nothing had been taken away or injured. They were giving me back all my own things.

My joy at seeing and touching them would hardly be credible to a man living under normal conditions on the upper earth. It was as if I had suddenly made contact with human life again.

I took up each article of clothing and fingered it with delight. I took the things out of the knapsack, every one of them, and handled them as a miser might handle his gold. A flood of memories and associations poured over me. I felt my hands trembling.

I saw the Wall again in the May sunlight, the masses of flowers, the country lying below, the little farms under the haze of heat. I heard the barking of dogs, the lowing of cattle, the cries of the children at play, the sound of the carts on the country roads. They were all in my own clothes, in my knapsack, in the absurd little things that it held, and the courage that came back to me at the sight and the touch of these familiar things—how could it be credible to a man on the upper earth?

Immediately I began to lay my plans for escape. My head was suddenly full of them.

First to be considered was the circumstance in which I would have to work—the fact that the life of this people was a coastal one based on the Central Sea, and that that sea was not fresh water but salt water. As it was formed by the great river that had carried me through the tunnel under the northern cliff, it looked as if that river must itself be merely an underground branch of the seas of the upper earth. That might be an important factor or it might not, but it was in some way encouraging to the mind to think that the Central Sea was fed from the upper earth. If its waters did not come from some leakage in the ocean floor on earth, it would be difficult to account for its two characteristics—namely, that it was flowing salt water and that it supported life abundantly. Water that has not had some sort of contact with the sun, and been vitalised even indirectly by its rays, could hardly support life. At least it could hardly produce life with the fertility with which that great water produced and sustained it.

It is true that, in the higher ranges of the mountains down which I had descended, I had found a rich vegetable life and some forms of higher life, but these regions are apparently watered by rain that comes through the upper surface and vitalised by some rays of a nature not known to me—rays probably generated by the sunlight, and so strong that they can pierce through the upper crust of the earth.

. The same forces to a lesser extent sustained vegetable life on the lower lands. But the main body of life existed in the Central Sea and on its shores. Its abundance of fish was the chief food-supply of the people. The serpents and lizards that lived on its shores and swamps formed a large part of the remainder, and the people cultivated the fungi and the various sea-weedy vegetables to give variety to their dishes and counteract the effects of a preponderant fish diet.

This, then, was the geographical framework in which I had to work.

The eastern shores, as far as I could gather during my visits to the schools, were, except at their southern end, a tumble of precipitous rocks and mountains, with little food-supply and only a sparse population of fishermen and snake-hunters. On the western shore, however, there was a fairly broad strip of land between the lake and the impassable cliffs that, they had said, bar all exit to the west. Along this, the settlements of the people were scattered, wherever there was a sufficient supply of fresh water from the hill-streams, and a sufficient food-supply to make each group self-supporting and at the same time capable of exporting its quota to the chief settlement.

All of this I had gathered in a variety of ways during my stay in the city. Now, as I was getting ready for my journey, I kept turning it over and over in my mind.

When I had bathed, eaten, and dressed in my own clothes, I came out of the eating-house with the guide, along a road that led through the enclosures of the distributing grades, and so past the outer settlements to the north-western boundary of the "city." There we stood on the edge of a plateau looking out on dark lands that stretched away to the west and north.

For a few moments we stood there. Then he pointed to the

northward and turned and left me. Once again I was alone. "Again alone!" The thought seemed an absurdity. I had never been anything else. Ever since I came, he, or someone exactly like him, had been with me at all times, except when I slept, yet I had never had the slightest contact with him or them. I didn't even know whether the man who brought me to the boundary of the city was the same man or one of many that had guided me before, so similar are all these people to one another in shape, size, and lack of all distinguishing mark either in body or personality. When he left me, I felt no loss of companionship, since there had been none, not even such as the lowest form of animal would have given. An insect or some other entirely alien creature might possibly have given me as little. It could certainly not have given me less, and, though I was now leaving the chief human settlement of that land to go out into the darkness of the empty spaces, I believed that I could experience scarcely worse effects from the most appalling loneliness of its barren lands than I had done from the total lack of all contact amongst its people. I had, indeed, very little understanding of what confronted me.

I stood and looked round. Behind me the "city" lay silent, inconspicuous, invisible, except for the dim lights that glimmered faintly behind the nearest enclosures. In front of me the land stretched dim and mysterious, with dots of phosphorescent growths glimmering here and there through the darkness. On my right I knew that the waters of the Central Sea stretched away to the northward, but there were no gleams of light in the vault above me, and I could only guess that the sea was there, and that the three dim lights that moved over it were the lights of vessels. To the left a space of dim luminosity, that I guessed to be a cultivated field of fungi, broke the darkness at some distance away. Otherwise I could see nothing.

I stood peering into the darkness and thinking out the best

way of tackling the job that lay before me. My mind was full
of concentration and yet full of irrelevancies. I thought
absurdly of Tom, the owl that my father had given me for a
present on my sixth birthday, and that used to come to him
when he hooted. If Tom were here now, he could help me to
track him in the darkness. The absurd idea made the darkness
feel familiar, the problem not much more difficult than a
similar task on earth. My father was in this land. That was
certain. He was somewhere—perhaps quite near me. How to
find him? That was the first problem. How to begin? If I
could only have discovered what was his grade or condition!
But they had told me nothing, except that they had "transformed" him and "absorbed" him. The Master of Knowledge
had said that he was willing to be absorbed, happy. If that
were so, I felt that I could safely assume that they were using
him in some condition where his will could be exercised. What
such a condition might be, it was not so easy to guess. They
would hardly make a stranger the head of one of their settlements, or put him in command of a ship. He would have been
useless in a factory or farm, and it was unlikely that they
would entrust an outsider with the post of teacher, no matter
how completely he had given himself up to them. What, then,
could he be?

Unless I could get some clue to the question of my father's
probable position, it would be difficult to imagine where he
would be likely to be found. Possibly in the city which I was
leaving; but, if he were in the city, I should have little chance
of ever finding him. They would make sure of that. Nor would
there be any chance of his becoming aware of my presence.
I knew that also. I had ceased to import into their world the
circumstance of the upper earth. The city was so great an
assemblage of people that, even if I had been allowed to
search it for him, I should have had little chance of finding
him, unless I had most unlikely luck in my search. In any

case, all that was over and done with. It was clear that I had no longer the liberty to look for him in the city. I was being sent out of it because these people believed that, in the shelter of its comforts, I would never learn to understand the need for their system. I was not free to return to the city. I was only free to wander through the country and the smaller settlements of their people. It was quite possible that my father was in one of these smaller settlements, and, if he were, there would certainly be a much better chance of my meeting him, or of his meeting me, during my visit to such a settlement, than of our meeting in the chief town.

My best plan, therefore, seemed to be to go along the shores of the lake, from colony to colony of this people, to search each settlement for my father and also to use each settlement as a centre from which to explore the country at the back and the possibility of finding some way out over the cliffs or the mountains.

With these plans, I started on the second stage of my wanderings with a feeling that was almost one of gaiety. The making of definite plans again, the feeling of my own clothes and my own knapsack, the sense of freedom, all gave me a confidence which was as unfounded as it was short-lasting. I had not gone half a mile before I discovered this.

The ground on which the city stands is a wide, low plateau of firm, dry land that came to an end a short distance from the point where I started on my journey. When I descended from this plateau I found the ground slimy and slippery underfoot, and almost completely dark. There were few fungoid growths, and, apart from these, no phosphorescence, and, although I had my electric torch, I found the going slow and difficult. In a little while my torch went out and I had to stumble on, in a darkness that was almost complete, over ground that would not have been easy even under a good light.

They had put into my knapsack some phosphorescent balls,

of the type they use as lanterns on dark paths. I took one of these and held it in front, but, in that darkness, its light was too feeble to do more than prevent my falling over obstacles that lay in my path. There was an occasional fungoid growth that lit the way with a dim point of light, but I began at last to realise the conditions that I was going to be up against as I went forward, groping, my phosphorus ball held in front and my feet dragging through invisible slime.

Before I had been an hour on the journey I understood still better the nature of the ordeal to which I was being subjected. In this darkness I could see nothing, discover nothing, learn nothing, except the one thing that the Master wanted me to learn, namely, that I could not do without the help of the people. If I reached a settlement, they would supply me with food and other necessaries whenever I needed them, but these things were to be supplied to me only so that I might be enabled to live through such suffering as would hand me over to them, broken and defeated, to do with as they wished. Perhaps they had treated my father to the same lesson before they had absorbed him. Again I began to think of the eyes of my white rabbit as it lay under the stoat.

Before my guide had left me I had asked him how far it was to the nearest human habitations, but he had, as usual, made no answer. I began to wonder how far it could be. A long way off, probably, and all the time spent in travelling to it would be mere waste—waste of time and strength, since my father would not be anywhere in this outer darkness, and, if he were, I could not find him. And there could be no exit here on these barren lowlands, only up in the mountains— wherever they were.

Unless my father were a fugitive, he could not be here. He could only be in one of the settlements. I had fully understood all that before. I must hurry on to the nearest settlement. This people always travelled by water, except in the settlements themselves or their immediate neighbourhood, where they had to go to their fungi farms or spider compounds, or where they had well defined paths lit by phosphorus. The difficulty of travelling by land did not arise for them. There was no need for them to keep the settlements near one another. But they were making me travel by land where there were no paths, nothing but sticky, invisible slime, with a sparse covering of some sort of trailing growth that impeded me even more than did the slime. They were going to show me what it was like to live without them in the darkness.

I went on, wondering when I should get to a settlement. Luckily the ground, though slimy, was not much encumbered. Twice snakes slid from my feet in curves of greenish light. Otherwise there was no sight or sound. The travelling here was of another sort altogether from my journey through the higher lands beyond the great cliff and the river. There the lands had been lit up everywhere by phosphorescent growths—countless ground fungi, big phosphorescent trees. Here there was nothing of that. Either the fungi hadn't been there, or they had used them up, made the land a desert and never replanted it.

Up above, also, the sky-lights had been vivid and frequent. Here there were none.

My watch had been returned to me with my other property. It had run down, and I had no idea what the time would have been on the earth above me, but, when I was dressing, I had set it going at 2.26, the point where it had stopped, partly for the mere pleasure of hearing and seeing it going again, but partly also because it would supply me with a measure of time. For a long time, after I had begun my journey, I didn't think of looking at it, but after I had been going, as I thought, for many hours, I remembered it. I looked by the light of the phosphorescent ball. It was 4.38. Making allowance for the time I had taken to come through the city to the verge of the dark lands, I had not yet been two full hours on the journey!

I couldn't believe it. I put the watch to my ear in the belief that it had stopped, but its ticking came to me loud and insistent. It was working properly. It was then that I first realised how timeless is the thing that we call Time—that purely relative mode—a matter of feeling and not of spatial or temporal divisions. Taken away from the motions of the earth and the moon and the sun, it loses all external reality, and takes on something dreadful in its stead. That was the discovery that began to seize me—the thought that one moment of the so-called time of earth can hold for the individual the whole of eternity, if his feeling is infinite enough to produce it.

According to my watch, it took me something over eighteen hours from the beginning of my journey to reach the nearest settlement. In fact, it took me so long a time, in intensity of endurance and the despair that arose from the realisation of the hopelessness of my task, that I was many years older by the time I saw the first signs of human habitation. It was a fungus farm, and, when I saw the luminous space made by it, my heart began to pound against my ribs with excitement. There were two men working among the fungi, and, when I saw them, I began to cry out to them, as if they were ordinary men. In my misery I had forgotten. They must have heard me, for, in that silent world, the noise of my shouting sounded like the hooting of a siren, but, if they did, they made no sign, but went on with their work mechanically.

I didn't waste any more time on them, but hurried on. I was on a firm piece of ground now, and in front of me a path began, lit by phosphorus. I turned to it, and ran along it towards the cluster of enclosures, the lights of which showed in front of me.

There was a man standing in the middle of the path with a globe of phosphorus in his hand. When I came up to him, he looked at me with empty eyes, as if he didn't see me, but he turned and walked beside me when I went on. I was worn out with fatigue and hunger and thirst, and I hoped that he was a guide to bring me to a place of food and rest. He led me into an enclosure where a man of a higher grade sat under two soft globes of light. I went forward, and stood staring at him with eyes that blinked under the unaccustomed light. He stared at me, reading my thoughts. Then, as if to satisfy himself that he had read them aright, he sent his message: "Why have you come here?"

"I need food and rest," I answered wearily.

"You cannot have used up all your food," came the answer. "You got food supplies for a long time when you were leaving the city. Also, you cannot need so soon to come to a settlement to rest. You could rest anywhere. Why, then, have you come here?"

I made no answer. There was no answer to make. Even if I could explain my feelings to him, it would be useless to do so. At last I understood fully the sentence that had been passed on me. I had been outlawed; deeper still, I had been excommunicated. I was to be kept alive, so that I might be shaped by the darkness, as they had been shaped by it. I thought that they had given me no contact, no communion. Now I knew that they had given me much communion, the shelter of their civilisation, of the circle of light and comfort that they had made against the darkness. The giving of their dress to me had been a symbol of their acceptance of me. The return of my own clothes and all my belongings had been their formal act of withdrawal of recognition. I had refused to come into communion, as they understood it. I had wanted to have the advantage of what they had won for men here below, without paying the price they had paid. They would not allow me to do that. I could either remain myself or become one with them, but I could not do both. I had chosen to remain alone, and they had taken away their contact with me and given me back all that I had when I came to them.

I turned and left the enclosure and went into the darkness. I was alone. I had left my own people on the earth. I had refused to be one with these people on whom I had intruded. Now I was alone, alone without vision or sound or touch with anything that lived and moved, alone in the darkness.

Suddenly I knew what it meant to be alone—the thing that I had never really known. I was looking down into a bottom-less gulf. My head was reeling. I musn't look down into those depths. It was like the dreams in which I used to find myself suddenly standing on ropes that led across vast gulfs, staring, paralysed, downward, unable to move backward or forward.

I must pull myself together. Even on the earth, I had heard of people who had gone mad the moment they realised that they were lost—irretrievably lost.

I must not do that. I had been living on the surface, in the skin, without knowledge or understanding—pitting myself against things that I didn't understand. I began to hurry on to get away from them.

I felt my lips moving. I began to pray, dumbly, without sound, without thought. For the first time since I was a little child, I prayed with my whole life poured into my prayer.

I blundered into something and caught hold of it. It was a sticky bole, the trunk of some sea-weedy growth, a slim, oily thing. I put my arms round it, and clung to it. I thought I could feel a heart beating in it—beating strongly. Then I knew that it was the echo of the beating of my own heart coming back to me from it. I laid my head against it.

The storm that had shaken me was passing. Peace was coming back to me, but I was weary—dreadfully weary. I slid to the bottom of the tree and lay with my head close against it.

CHAPTER SEVENTEEN

Phantasms

WHEN I AWOKE, it was no longer pitch dark. A pale, dim light was coming from above. I looked round me. I was on sloping ground covered with trailing growths. I stood up. I was stiff, and my body ached, but I was refreshed by my sleep. On my right hand, lower down, I saw something that looked like the Central Sea. On my left, the slope on which I was standing seemed to mount gradually, but the light was too dim for me to see far.

I felt hungry. I had eaten nothing since I left the city. I took the food they had packed for me out of my knapsack, and began to eat. It was slabs of snake-flesh, prepared with some sort of seasoning to preserve it. They had also put a large skin bottle of some sort of liquor into my knapsack. I took a drink. It was a thin, sharp liquor, like rather sour wine, but it satisfied me. I put the rest of the food and drink back into my sack and strode up the slope towards the left.

Thus began my second day's quest in the darkness.

The light was not so dim that I could not walk fairly quickly. The ground was slimy under my feet and clogged my steps somewhat, but not sufficiently really to hamper my going. My mind was cold and steady. Its hysteria of the previous day had arisen from the loss of its foolish illusions. As I plodded on now, I surveyed the new situation calmly.

The salient facts were that, while I had the freedom of the barren lands, and the darkness and dimness that lay over them alternately, I had no other freedom or access to any other place. There was only one thing that I could attempt in these lands. I could search for an exit from them into regions beyond the territory of this people. Search for my father was out of the question. He could hardly be in these lands, unless he were an outlaw; and, if he were, I should not be likely to come across him except by accident. This narrowed the radius of my plans.

The lands on which I found myself ran northward, between the Central Sea to the east and the barrier of mountains to the west. Behind me, the city and the southern mountains barred all progress. My possible action was, therefore, narrowed down to a northward journey, and a search of the mountains that ran northward on the western boundary. Somewhere in these mountains there must be a gap through which I might escape into regions outside the range of that people, perhaps even into higher lands, through which I might get back to the earth.

I decided, therefore, to strike westward towards the mountains, and search them for gaps or paths leading upward.

The chief obstacle in putting such a plan into operation was, of course, the darkness. If there had been sufficient light to show me the outlines of the mountains, that I knew to lie to the westward, I could have made for them, and worked systematically along them, returning to the settlements along the sea only when my food-supplies fell short. The difficulty was to keep direction, so that I might not find myself going round in circles. For this purpose it was important to get to the mountains while the light lasted, and I put that before me as my immediate object.

As I could not see any outlines of mountains, and the Central Sea was also dark, I had to rely for direction largely on the upward trend of the land. I kept upwards, therefore, as far as possible.

It would be tedious to describe in detail the journey I made on that second day, since it consisted of a dreary series of ascents and descents of foothills that began near the settlement that had refused me admittance.

Luckily for me, the light held, and enabled me at least to see whether, through the ascents and the descents, there was a steady upward movement. I felt quite confident that there was, and, though the ground for the most part was barren and stony, with no food-supply and no sign of life except an occasional snake, I climbed on with steady courage.

I had a sufficient food-supply for several days. There were streamlets coming from the mountains, and, as long as I had food and water, I did not see that I was running any serious risk.

On the other hand, I was under no illusions as to the nature of my task, or the slightness of my chances of success. I had no doubt that I should be able to reach the mountain barrier, unless there was an impassable gulf running along the whole of the western boundary, but, when I had reached the mountains, I knew that I should probably find bleak slopes of rock, on which no man could live long without food-supplies. If that were not so—if the mountains in fact led to fertile regions either beyond them or on their own higher slopes —the Masters of Knowledge would not have given me an opportunity to attempt to climb them. They did so only because they knew that I should be tied to their settlements by the need to return to them regularly for provisions.

However, I had no way out of that difficulty. If I could not get over the western mountains or through them, I should have to get through or over a similar mountain barrier or cliff barrier in the north, if I were to regain my freedom.

These were the thoughts that filled my mind as I plodded upwards over stony slopes and hollows, in the dim light of that second day.

Below, the light showed little but the nearest slopes up which

I had come. Around me, it lit up dimly stony foldings, without trees or vegetation or life of any sort. In front, it showed a series of similar foldings rising gradually. Then suddenly it flared up. A cloud of spears of the Aurora sprang back and forward, and there, straight in front of me, seemingly not more than a couple of miles away, a mountain range towered upwards to the light.

I stood and stared at it. It was barren rock, steep almost as a cliff. No vegetation grew on it. No passes pierced it. Here and there there were breaks in the precipitous walls. No wonder the Masters of Knowledge had left me free to wander!

I did not wait to brood over the problem. I had not yet reached the mountains. When I got to them, I might find them more accessible than they seemed to be at this distance. Now that I had good light I must use it. I started again at an increased pace.

I had kept my watch going, and, when I started, I had looked at it. According to it I had already been travelling nine hours and three-quarters since my sleep. It took me four and a half hours more to get to the real foot of the mountain barrier, but long before I had reached it I knew that there was no exit that way. It was a sloping cliff of rough rock that towered upwards thousands of feet, and presented neither gap nor foothold.

I slept that second night in a ravine at the foot of the cliff-wall. The light had begun to fade before I reached it, but was still bright enough to show me that I might as well rest, since there was no further progress possible towards the west.

Next day I turned my face to the northward along the cliff barrier.

I will not burden this narrative with the details of that third day, or the days that followed it. These were days in which my mind and body were being broken into their new task, deepened and heightened in some things, lowered and emptied in others.

If I had any illusions left as to my chances of escape before I began my search along the mountains, those days dispelled them.

When I started my journey northward on the third day there was a little light. After four or five hours it petered out, and I tried to blunder on through the darkness, with the help of my phosphorus balls.

It was the same on the fourth day. The darkness was complete, and I made little progress. On that day my supply of liquid ran out and I could not replenish it. I had got into a district where there were no streams. My food-supply was also running short, and I realised that I should have to get back to the lower lands as quickly as possible.

On the fifth day I turned my back on the mountains and groped my way down the slopes again towards the Central Sea.

So ended my first expedition to the mountains—the first of a series of such journeys.

Sometimes the light from above shone dimly or strongly. More often I journeyed in darkness. I no longer kept any account of time, since such account would be useless, meaningless. The only times that had any meaning for me were those marked out by the fitful coming and going of the magnetic sky-lights. These latter became of extreme importance. When they shone, they showed me the landscape, sometimes dimly, sometimes with a clarity like that of full moonlight, and it was during the periods when they revealed the country to me that I discovered, bit by bit, the nature of the western boundary of that land. It was sheer cliff, or mountain-sides, so steep and slippery that no man could possibly have climbed them even in broad daylight. Every slope that I climbed, every barren upland valley, led me to the same impassable barrier, flung me back defeated to the lower lands to get food and drink.

It might be thought that the gradual realisation of the hope-lessness of such a quest would have broken my nerves and my courage. I know now that it was doing so in a fundamental way, but, at that stage, I did not notice it. I had braced myself up for my task, tried to concentrate my mind into a single thought aimed at a single purpose.

If they had allowed me to stay for even the briefest period in their settlements, when I visited them for supplies, it is possible that I might not have centred my whole life on this one purpose, but they never allowed me to stay beyond the few minutes needed to provide me with food, so that these visits had for me no human value, even such as they could give.

I made them, therefore, as seldom as possible, so as not to waste my strength on journeys between the sea and the mountains. I ate sparingly, slept little while the light was available, husbanded all my resources, and kept doggedly to my search.

As I moved northward, the mountains began to fold into valleys that ended in *culs-de-sac*. I worked up each of them, and, at the end of each, I turned back and went north again along the foot of the barrier, seeking for the next possible way up or out. My hands and knees were torn, my clothes in rags, but I kept myself clean—I even kept myself shaved, though my stock of razor-blades got so blunt in the end that they tore my face. I did this, not deliberately, but automatically—because I had always done it, and it was a link with my life on earth.

For the same reason I made plans, resolutions, created for myself a mask of stoical courage and resolve, to buttress up my will. All my powers and qualities and feelings that were not necessary for my purpose must fall back into the lower regions of my subconsciousness. All the qualities and resources that I could use for that one purpose must be drawn upward, heightened, deepened, made dominant. I must become a ma-

chine, such as the men of this lower land had become, a creature with a single aim, a single idea, a mind and character
pruned, stripped, cleared of all the thoughts, feelings, tendencies, and habits that were not necessary for that purpose.

Such were my plans during those earlier days.

In those days they remained only plans. I had not yet
reached the depths in which they were to become realities.
They were then only brave thoughts, make-believe schemes
manufactured to keep up my courage. I was still too near the
normal, too human to be able to put them into effect. I had
not yet got rid of the ordinary human needs. I hungered for
human fellowship, even the fellowship of the automatons. I felt
starving for contact, for all the irrelevant things.

Lest I should be misunderstood, I want to make it clear
that I am not a gregarious man, not the type of man who needs
to be always in contact with his fellows. I can do without the
crowds and the clubs and the varied contacts that are the life
of so many men on earth. Before my descent, I had lived a
lonely, self-sufficing life. I had, as I thought, proved to myself
that a lonely life can be at least as deeply happy and eventful
as a gregarious one.

It was not, therefore, a mere superficial desire for company,
resulting from a habit, that was gnawing at my mind during
those early days. Nor was it even the physical darkness, nor
the lack of the light of the sun or the rain or the greenness of
grass that afflicted me most, though these were dreadful deprivations. It was the inner darkness, of which the Master had
told me, that was beginning to come upon me from the depths
of my own mind, and from which I was endeavouring to escape
to man's normal refuge—the comfort of other life around me.

If I had known that there was any animal, however low in
the scale of life, that would have accepted me, I believe that,
in the mood in which I was then, I would have tramped every
mile of the darkness to find it.

There was no living creature to be seen, however, in those earlier days, except the snakes that came up from the swamps to feed, and that fled the moment they caught sight of me.

I struggled on, and, though there were times in that early part of my wanderings when my stoical mask fell from my resolve, leaving me weak and hysterical or numbed, it served my need, and with its help I kept myself braced to my task in spite of the despair that assailed me.

Gradually that first stage passed. My mind began to get accustomed to facing its own darkness, alone. Its needs grew less and less, as it stripped itself for the struggle. It needed its heroic mask no longer. I was beginning to be in reality the man that I had planned.

The hunger for the help and the comfort of other life seemed to have passed.

I had closed with the inner enemy, as well as with the outer one, and, in the struggle, my mind gradually dropped every shred of individuality, personality, feeling, tendency, thought, that blunted or weakened it for its purpose, so that it became a clear unity.

If it had been rewarded for its singleness of purpose, and concentration of effort and endurance, by even the slightest shred of outward success or the faintest encouragement for its hopes, it might have remained a unity. But no such encouragement came to it.

In no single place did the great mountain barrier open upwards or downwards, except into valleys and ravines that were more ghastly than the peaks that towered over them. Everywhere there was death—not the death that struggles with life, but death completely in possession, very still in its potency in the darkness. Every valley closed in sheer black walls that barred the way to life. From each my will turned my body back to grope along the cliff valley until it reached the next wall and the next defeat and my will drove it back again to begin once more the futile quest.

What I would do when I had found the exit I don't think occupied my thoughts. Whether I would escape alone and abandon my father, or go back and try to rescue him—all that had become irrelevant.

There remained only one question, one problem: the discovery of a way out. My mind had canalled itself into that one channel of action, and it pursued its purpose with a concentration of attention that not only left no room for anything else, but produced a most remarkable degree of efficiency in that one task.

Not only was there a firm will to execute the purpose; there was also a remarkable power to deal with the material obstacles. The climbing of almost unclimbable cliffs, the fording of dangerous torrents, the passage of treacherous swamps—all these things were carried out with a sureness that would, I believe, have been almost impossible to a man in his normal state.

It was the same in dealing with the dangerous creatures I met. In the southern parts of the barren lands they had been rare, but, as I worked northward and the land got swampier and more possible for reptile life, I began to meet large serpents and big lizards with much greater frequency.

In the far recesses of the swamps and mountains, where they were distant from the lake settlements, these brutes had not seen man or got the terror of his powers that was so noticeable in the lands along the lake, and they attempted to seize me on several occasions. I was so concentrated on my single external purpose that it might be imagined that I would prove an easy victim. Exactly the opposite was the case. I was so alert to all external danger that I had an almost superhuman capacity for foreseeing the attempts of these creatures and circumventing them, or, in the last resort, facing them with an emanation of will and emotion that cowed them like a physical blow.

I felt at the time that my self-hypnotism had freed in my

subliminal life some source of power that is never realised in normal men, but, when I look back now on that period, it seems to me more likely that the unusual power of will and intuition that I possessed was the result of incipient madness, caused by the suppressed struggle with fear that was being carried on below the surface of my mind.

That this latter was the source of my abnormal acuteness of observation and power of will is, I think, clear from the fact that, a short time afterwards, my mind had begun to seek a different exit from the physical one that my body was seeking.

The first form of this flight of my mind, from the prison in which I had caged it, was, I believe, an hallucination in which I thought that it was my soul and not my body that was wandering in darkness in search for God and light and love.

The next avenue of escape was the creation of visions of the things that I had lost—the brightness and beauty of earth's growths, the rush of the wind, the swing of the sea, the waving of branches, the faces of men under the sunlight.

I began to imagine that I had died and gone back to earth as a disembodied spirit, or that I had been rapt up there alive in my body.

It was as if, after a prolonged period of bare monomaniac existence, my mind could bear it no longer, and had to bring back the old cluster of thoughts and emotions and habits, but in a different way.

When these visions first began, they were fitful and spasmodic, like fever fits, and, when I came out of them, they left me weak and desolate, like a man that wakes from a fever. As time went on, however, they grew more constant and permanent. I had reached the third stage of my development, in which I kept what sanity remained to me through the delusion that I was back on earth again, engaged in all the common little joyous things of daily life, with which I had formerly occupied myself, without knowing how precious and beautiful they were.

There can hardly be any doubt that this third stage lasted for quite a long period, before I struck the great cliff barrier that bounds the north of that land from east to west; and that, during that time, I was living in a state of deliberate self-delusion, in which I was trying to produce a simulacrum of the ordinary course of life on the upper earth.

I would find myself in the process of buying clothes, newspapers, or other necessaries of life on earth, holding elaborate conversations over an imaginary counter, while I waited for change from a luminous fungus or a sea-weedy tree that represented living people.

I have found myself sitting in a snake-swamp, discussing politics with the reptiles, or some book that I thought I had read, listening for their replies, answering them point by point, and then getting up and ending the visit with the usual social interchanges. I engaged taxis, took trains, wrote and posted letters, ate meals in hotels and restaurants, and carried through all the necessary contacts for these operations. I even went to church and worshipped with my fellows, who were either snakes or fungi or the sea-weedy growths, and took part lustily in the singing.

I don't think I ever did this without some other form of life being present to enable me to reproduce the scene, but any form of life seemed to suffice. A tree or a large fungoid growth did as well as a snake or a lizard, in order to enable my mind to go through the series of actions that supplied contact.

It will be supposed that, by this time, I had gone completely over the brink and was insane, at least while performing these acts. In fact, I do not believe that this was so. The acts certainly did not arise from the same sources in the mind as those that arise from the delusions of the ordinary lunatic.

They were, of course, accompanied and made possible by a definite form of hallucination, but, when I look back on them, in so far as I can recall the dim confusion that was my life during that period, I see them rather as a set of automatisms—automatic reproductions of former acts, a mimicry of human life above, instinctively carried out by my mind with the unconscious purpose of filling the emptiness that would otherwise have annihilated it.

I do not say that these transactions were purely memories of acts actually done in my life and re-enacted below in the darkness. I do not think that this was so. They were rather like dreams than faithful mimicry, in that they were a piecing together, oftentimes in a fantastic and improbable way, of bits of experience.

Some of the people, for instance, with whom I dealt or lived in these re-creations, were people that I had known on earth. Others were imaginary people, but, as in dreams, it is worth noting that I cannot remember in a single instance getting the face of the person in any clear line, or even an impressionist picture. I would know, for instance, that the man who was selling me matches had red hair and little blue eyes set closely on each side of a narrow nose like a fish-bone, but I never actually saw the narrow nose like a fish-bone, or the redness of the hair, or the blue of the eyes. That always evaded me, as did the answers to questions of which I did not myself know the answer.

The most inanimate form of life had now become for me what the presence of a human being is to ordinary men. It stood between me and nothingness, and protected my mind with a roof or wall of life, under the cover of which it could revive itself by remembrances when it was approaching too closely to annihilation by the cold interstellar vacuum where it moved.

It was as if, when it felt itself freezing to death in the icy emptiness of infinity and eternity, it instinctively created a warmth by collecting a heap of little human memories and making of them a fire, over which it crouched.

One of the peculiar things about this shadow life, in which my mind took refuge when in danger, was that it included not merely a mimicry of ordinary acts, but a mimicry of the minor illusions that often accompany a human act, when the act produces a more than usual passion of interest in the person.

I don't know whether other people have the same experience, but I often find that, when I am engaged very intently on some achievement, whether it be the making of a scientific discovery or the learning of a language, or even the perfecting of my command over a physical performance such as golf, a certain illusion tends to surround the particular thing, making it, for the moment, much more urgent than it really is, setting a time-limit in which it must be done, and, in general, concentrating on its completion with a passionate interest which seems inexplicable to me at a later stage, when my enthusiasm for the particular piece of work or play has died down.

Now, one of the peculiar things about the little fires of memory that I built in the darkness was that they reproduced these minor illusions of real life as to the pressing and urgent importance of the more intense and prolonged actions.

There were long periods of time when I went through the darkness of those mountains intent on some project that I was carrying through on the upper earth—an invention, an industrial reconstruction, a business deal; even, at times, the passionate search on the Roman Wall for the entrance to the world below—and this intentness was accompanied by all the manifestations that have accompanied it in real life—the sleeplessness, the pains under the right ear, the throbbing in the temples, the quick, irritable reactions to imaginary intrusions or interferences of other matters.

The most extraordinary thing, perhaps, of all was that, when my mind played in this way with phantasms of upper life, it often dealt with them with a clarity of thought that was not dimmed or enfeebled by the phantasmal nature of its operations. I remember, for instance, in my supposed rôle as a Midland industrialist, thinking out the problem of how to prevent the money capital that is used in industry from deserting the other type of capital, called "real" capital, that is its fellow and colleague in supporting industry, and saving its own skin alone in times of crisis. The problem is a difficult one, but I remember tackling it with amazing lucidity in some barren valley of a land in which no such problem had ever been allowed to present itself, and I can recall distinctly the letter I wrote to *The Times* embodying the conclusion my mind reached for the solution of the problem, namely, that such a desertion and betrayal by one form of capital of another, which was nailed to the field of battle and could not leave, should be met by the same penalty that meets a soldier who deserts on the battlefield: deprival of existence.

But, though I remember tackling the question and writing and posting the letter, I have no remembrance whatever of the real place or time in which I carried out this phantasmal act, beyond my deduction that it must have been some time in the later stages of my quest, when I was nearing the northern cliff barrier.

There can hardly be any doubt that the lucidity with which I worked it out was one of the most serious of the symptoms of growing mental disorder, and that, if my isolation lasted much longer, I should have become definitely insane.

One proof of this is that my consciousness of external things during that later period was so submerged in the dreams with which I was drugging myself that I can remember only in the dimmest fashion the details of real life.

The earlier part of my wanderings I remember vividly enough—the heavy darkness of the lower lands, the clinging slime underneath, the occasional dim light, the glimmering trail that was the movement of a snake, the stony earth that broke my feet on the upland slopes as I stumbled along through the darkness, the green and blue lights of the settlements on the rare occasions when I was allowed to come to them to replenish my supply of food.

The memories of the same things in the second stage, when I had concentrated fiercely for action, are even more vivid, particularly those of the pits of darkness that were ravines between the peaks of the great western range.

Then gradually my memories of the real life became dim— a spectral background for the much more vivid memories of the phantasmal acts I performed in my delusions. Real consciousness was leaving me. The result was not yet that which the Master of Knowledge had hoped to produce when he was sending me out alone to face the darkness, but that result was approaching. The process of disintegration had set in.

CHAPTER EIGHTEEN

Escape and Recapture

I DO NOT KNOW how long this strange condition lasted, before I reached the cliff barrier that blocked further access to the north. When I reached it, a curious thing happened. I felt suddenly as men feel at the end of the old year. I felt that something had ended, something new was going to begin.

I seemed to wake up to life, for I remember thinking, in a confused way, that, if the information that I had gathered in the city was correct, the cliff ran almost due east towards the great water. This is the first definite thought that I can recall about real things in the third stage of my wanderings.

I turned my face to the east and began to work eastward along the base of the cliff.

One would have said that this change of direction could mean little or nothing to a man in my desperate need. Yet, for some reason or other, it had a profound effect on my mind, so that my consciousness of real things began to come alive again from the torpor into which it had fallen. I know that, since I can remember quite clearly all my actions from the time when I turned eastward, whereas my memory of the period that went before that is merely a dream memory of acts, drowned in a phantasmagoria of illusions.

Perhaps it was because I had turned my face towards the sea! Perhaps some shadow of coming events cast themselves before me.

However it be, there is no question that the turning of my

face eastwards to the sea marked the point at which my personality began to pull itself together again and to take over unified control of my actions.

If my conjecture was right, the cliff along which I was now moving to the eastward was the face of the great mountain barrier under which I had come, on the ocean stream that had carried me through the swamps and the tunnel into the Central Sea. If this was so, I should presently be brought to a stop by the waters of the sea. If I asked for transport across it, it would not be given to me. I should be driven back again from the shores and the settlements to retrace my steps in the barren highlands that I had traversed in my northward journey. I had no intention of suffering this, if I could prevent or evade it.

Up to now I had not used any violence or deceit, but I had no intention of allowing these men to drive me back to the darkness that I now believed held no exit. I would search along the base of the cliff, however I did it. If a tunnel appeared, I would try it. If I could not penetrate into the cliff through any tunnel, or climb its face by any steps, then I would get across to the opposite shore by hook or by crook, by fair means or foul, and pursue my search on that side.

It was in this mood that I started to coast along the cliff base.

I had little food, but the ground was swampy and there were snakes and crabs and edible growths. From that point of view, the way presented less difficulty than the search of the barren heights. It also presented less difficulty from the point of view of visibility. If the swamps proved at all passable, they would in fact be easier from every point of view. They were phosphorescent in patches, so that there was always some light, and they contained a supply of food, if I could get at it.

I soon discovered, however, that these advantages were counterbalanced by the serious disadvantage that the going was extremely difficult. There were bits of rock and firm land here and there, but generally the land was a slough, and, as it got softer and more treacherous, I was constantly forced to retrace my steps and to follow a new line, where the rocks and tufts of firm land were near enough to allow me to spring from one to the other.

After some time, however, of this effort, I was brought to a complete stop. The waters of the sea were near, and had flooded the swampy lands so heavily that all footing ceased. It was neither swamp nor sea, but a mire of shaking ground that gave beneath the feet and sucked them under.

I spent no time in regrets. I never wasted any time now in regrets or repinings. I was inured to defeats, and took them as the normal ending to effort, all the more calmly as I had made up my mind fully not to accept defeat.

I turned back, and retraced my steps with difficulty to the outer edge of the swamp. Twice I went under to the knees, once almost to the hips. It seemed to me on that occasion that I could not pull myself out of the slime that was sucking me under, and, undoubtedly, if I had been in my normal mind and got fussed and nervy, I should not have been able to do so. But I was as cool as if I were engaged in digging in my own garden, and, in some way, by efforts that must have been almost superhuman, I drew myself out of that hungry slime and, after resting on a tussock and cleaning myself as well as I could, continued my journey.

When I came to the outer edge of the swamp, I sprang ashore and found myself standing on a water-snake that had the misfortune to be lying just where I alighted. It heaved and wriggled under my feet, nearly knocking me over, but I recovered and held it down long enough to enable me to draw my knife and cut its head off. I then sat down on the bank of the firm land and made a meal off the raw flesh and blood. This is the first meal that I can remember definitely over a long period of the later part of my journey in the barren lands.

When I had finished, I began a detour, round the edge of the swamp, towards the shores of the lake.

There was one thing for me to do now—to get a boat. To do this, I should have to get near a settlement—not so near that I should be seen, but near enough to watch for a chance to take a boat with oars.

How long I took to get round the swamp I do not know.

I slept once during the journey, and had two meals of edible fungi and seaweed, along with the remains of the snake I had killed near the cliff.

When I came near the sea, I realised that I must be nearing a settlement, for in the distance there was a luminous glow in the darkness, as well as the lights on the sea.

I had been carrying a phosphorus ball in my hand, as a torch, and I put this back in my knapsack and began to go slowly and watchfully.

It was unlikely that any of these people could see me before I saw them, since I was moving in darkness, whereas they were unlikely to be without lights, especially whenever they came off their phosphorescent paths, but I could never tell what might happen, and I knew that, if I were discovered in their neighbourhood, I should not be allowed to stay there. I should be provided with food and driven back to the barren lands.

There was one thing that I had never discovered—whether, when they drove me out of their settlements, they watched me to see that I did not hang round their neighbourhood. It was very probable that they did so, however, and this made it imperative that they should not discover me now. If they once got suspicious of my movements, they would take steps to ensure that I should follow the course mapped out for me by their Masters.

On the other hand, it was necessary that I should be able

to stay near them unseen, in order to seize a boat at the first
opportunity. The worst of it was that they worked as a communal mass. If they had been individual men living apart,
their homes and their boats would be strung out along the
lake, and it would be much easier to get hold of one, but here
their boats were kept together in the harbours and their habit
of working during the whole twenty-four hours, in alternating
shifts of eight hours for each third of the community, gave no
off-periods in which a boat could be taken during a common
sleeping-time, such as night affords on earth.

However, I had no choice but to wait and watch, and it
troubled me little. Time meant nothing to me. I felt no impa-
tience when I was baulked or held up. I had ceased to have
surface nerves. The trouble was gone too deep for that.

So I lurked in the darkness, watching, waiting. I saw boats
come in, go out, and come in again. I had nothing to eat except
the fungi, that I could gather in the darkness behind the town,
and some trailing plants that I had found refreshing and stim-
ulating when I was thirsty. No snakes dared to stay so near a
settlement, but I didn't trouble about this. With one side of
my mind I waited and watched like a timeless, inhuman thing.
With the other, I busied myself wandering along the Roman
Wall, talking to the farmers and their wives, getting meals in
"out-by" farms, watching the sunset over the Solway Firth.
None of their automatons could have been so completely intent
on his work or so completely detached from it, and from all
others around him, as I was. I had come by a different road
to be like them.

Suddenly the chance that I had been waiting for came, and
I was on to it like a wolf leaping on a stag after a long watch.

One of their people had, for some reason or other, not done
the usual thing, but had run his boat up on the shore near me
and passed into the settlement, leaving the oars in the boat.
Even then I didn't rush or fuss. I made sure that he was out

of sight of the boat before I ran to it. But, when I got to it, I made no delay. It was a light boat, like a wooden canoe with two oars, and I had it down on the water in a flash, had taken off the balls of phosphorescence that lit up its bow and its stern, thrown them into the boat, and begun to row, like a man possessed—as indeed I was—out towards the centre of the sea. Luckily there were no boats in sight, and I was able to put on all speed.

Then I saw that the current was carrying me past the settlement. The lights of the harbour were looming up behind me, and at any moment I might be discovered.

There was nothing to do but get past the harbour as quickly as I could. I let the boat go with the current instead of struggling against it.

My luck held. After all my failures I did not expect it to hold, but it did. Presently the lights of the town were left behind and I was in darkness, except for the flashing of the water. It was the first success I had had since I began my wanderings in the darkness.

When I had passed the harbour lights, I began to row against the current again, so as to try to get across at a tangent. It was not too strong here near the shore, but it exercised a steady pressure, and I wondered how far I was being swept down to the southward, away from the cliffs. I didn't want to go far from the cliffs. I had a feeling that the only exit possible to me would be through or around them.

However, I did not exhaust myself with drastic efforts. Here again I made no fuss. I pulled quietly, accustoming myself gradually to an exercise that had become unusual. I had always been fond of rowing, and had been in good training for it when I came down below. That was a long time ago—so long that I could not try to think back on it—but the personality that lived in the upper world now coincided with the personality that lived below. They were both performing the same

act, and, strange to say, this accidental fusion seems to have
been the thing that put an end finally to the division of my
personality. Suddenly I was a complete person again, no less
intent on my purpose, but no longer a creature with two selves.
I had a strange sense of having awakened, a sudden happiness
of regaining something profound that I had lost. I kept opening my eyes wide, as if the world of darkness had vanished
and I was back again completely in myself, a human being
struggling with abnormal circumstances but equal to them;
not dismembered or maimed under their impact.

I felt a conviction that the tide had turned. I wanted to
sing, to shout, to laugh. I had not sung or laughed or shouted
for years—no, not for years, I felt; not for many years. But I
didn't sing or shout. I was still cool and cautious. I laughed
to myself—chuckling happily—crowing, rather, like a baby.
I felt reborn, renewed, at the beginning of happiness.

I looked round me in the boat. The phosphorescent balls
lit it up, and I could see a fishing-line in the bottom of it and
two baskets at the stern. I stopped rowing and pulled the
baskets over to me. One of them contained some sort of worms,
obviously for bait. The other was full of food—cooked fish, a
hunk of a reddish bread they made from flour got from some
sort of dried roots, a little bowl of stewed fungi, and a seaweed
skin of liquor.

It was while I was looking at them that I heard the sound
of distant oars. I lifted my head and listened intently. There
could be no doubt about it. There was the sound of the movement of many oars, coming from a long way behind me. The
sound was curiously dull, as if the oars were partly muffled,
but my hearing had grown abnormally acute during my wanderings in the darkness, and it came to me quite clearly. There
were a great number of oars in action somewhere behind me,
in the direction of the settlement from which I had taken the
boat.

I looked intently towards the sound. There were no lights to be seen, and their boats always carried lights. Yet a great number of men were rowing out there, behind me, in the darkness, and the sound was coming nearer, a line of sound that seemed to stretch out from south to north, as if a line of boats were following me.

It might be some sort of fleet carrying cargo from the western side to the eastern, but it might also be a fleet of pursuers. The people in the settlement might have seen my boat when it crossed the lights of the town in front of the harbour, and, when the man who had left the boat on the shore had discovered his loss, they might have sent a flotilla of boats in pursuit of me.

The fact that the boats carried no lights made the second explanation seem more likely. A fleet on its ordinary business would certainly have carried lights. These boats had shipped their balls of phosphorescence, just as I myself had done, because they wanted to remain invisible. It was for the same reason that they had muffled their oars, or partly done so. They were pursuing something, and did not want to warn the quarry.

I had little doubt now that I was the person they were following. As I sat there listening to them, I thought the situation out calmly. If I began to row again, I should merely advertise my presence to them and I could not escape, as their speed would be much greater than that of a single oarsman.

On the other hand, if I let myself drift, the current would carry me southward, and they might perhaps pass to the northward of me, without noticing me. The darkness was profound, and, unless the glimmer of the phosphorescent balls in the bottom of my boat drew up some light over me, there would be no sign of my presence.

I drew the basket of food towards me and arranged it so that I could get everything easily.

Then I took off the garment that had once been my sports coat and put it over the balls.

I listened again.

It seemed to me that the line of sound behind was now somewhat more to the northward. The rush of the central current was beginning to sweep me out of their path.

I groped for the food and began to eat it. I could do nothing to help myself, and I realised that I was hungry. It was a long time ago, I thought, since I had consciously remembered that I was hungry. I had eaten when I needed food—otherwise I should not have continued to live—but I had performed the act automatically, as very low forms of life probably perform their animal functions. Certainly I had no remembrance of eating for a long time before the meal that I had made from the raw flesh of the serpent I had killed in the swamp at the foot of the great cliff. Even then, I had not consciously felt hunger.

Now I was hungry, as I used to be when I needed food before the darkness had seized me. Strange to say, the joy that came to me from this return of that old familiar experience gave me a feeling that, in spite of this pursuit that was coming after me, my luck had turned.

I lifted the skin of liquor and took a deep draught. The feeling of the warm, thick liquid was delightful. I put it to my head again. Then, as I tilted it up, I saw the glimmer of light in the dome above me. The sky-lights were beginning. Unless the thing was a momentary flicker, there would soon be a light over the waters. If the light grew, I should be visible, if the boats were near enough.

I watched the glimmer intently. It seemed to be flickering out. Then another sprang out beyond it. The first light brightened again. The two lights seemed to rush together, and a crown of crimson light glowed in the space where they had been.

I looked to the northward. The sea was now visible, but

only dimly. Even the near distance was still shrouded in a sort of mist of darkness. I listened. I could no longer hear any sound. The rowing had stopped. For a moment I thought that the boats had passed my course and were now so far away that I could no longer hear their oars.

Then I thought that this was unlikely. They had come too near me to have got out of range of hearing so soon. No. They had stopped rowing. They must have suspected that I was near them and they were listening for the sound of my oars.

I looked up. The crown of light had turned a brilliant rose-colour and was beginning to send streamers out on all sides.

Northward the sea was becoming clearly visible, and, in the dimness, I could see dark objects low down on the water. I thought that I could count eight distinct and separate smudges of darkness close together, on the line where the light melted into darkness.

There was no doubt of it. They were getting clearer, emerging as distinct objects, as the sea got brighter. They were lying quiet, looking, listening, as I was looking and listening.

My luck had turned again. Unless their sight was worse than mine, they would soon discover me, and all my experience of them showed that their eyes were not weaker, but much stronger, than ours for seeing in the dark.

I took up the fish and a chunk of the bread and began to eat them. As I did so, the sound of oars came to me again. I looked towards the boats. Yes, they were now spreading out in a line from east to west. The reason that they had seemed to me to be in a clump when I first saw them was that their line had been facing east, so that I only saw the boats that were straggling behind or in front of it. Now that they had swung their line in my direction, I saw that there were a dozen boats, and that they were making for me in a fan formation.

I went on with my meal. The dice had fallen against me. What was going to happen was fairly clear. I should be flung back once again on to the barren lands and the darkness. I should almost certainly die there. The vigilance of this people was too great—so great that I should never be able to escape across the sea to the other shore. Even if I had been able to do so, it was highly unlikely that I should have been able to discover a way out, but I felt certain now that, whatever exit existed, it was on that other side to which they would not let me cross.

It may seem strange, but I think that I have hardly ever enjoyed a meal as much as the fish and seaweed bread that I ate while I thought these things. It was partly, perhaps, because it had been so long since I had eaten a civilised meal, but I think that the sweetness of the food that day rose even more from the thought that before long I should probably be dead.

The boats had come very near now, and I saw that there were a dozen of them—large boats with six or eight oars apiece.

As they came up, those on the wings moved ahead of the others, so that in a few minutes I was surrounded.

I had finished my meal. I put the skin of liquor to my head and took a final draught. Then I sat still and waited.

One of the central boats was now alongside of me, and I could see a commander sitting in the stern. The others were automatons. The commander made a sign for me to step into his boat. I got up and did so. Then one of the men took my place in the small boat and pushed her off. The men in our vessel swung her head round and rowed to the northward.

So ended my attempt to escape across their Central Sea.

I had been put in the seat facing the commander, but he paid no attention to me, staring past me with the vacuous, concentrated stare of a hawk or an eagle. I made no attempt to get into touch with him. I thought that I knew what was going to happen to me. My tension had completely ceased, and with it, for the moment, all hope and fear and expectation had become dormant.

After my long wandering I was at least momentarily at rest. It was the first time that I had been allowed to remain in the company of human beings, and, for all their isolation and lack of contact, the feeling that they were round me had a soothing effect—that and the knowledge that, for the present, all decision and initiative had been taken out of my hands.

I must have fallen into a sort of dose, for it was with a start of surprise that I saw the shores of an island rise up on our left hand. I sat up and looked round me. The lights above were shining clearly on the sea in front of us and on a great cliff than ran across our path.

They had not brought me back to the settlement from which I had taken the boat. They were bringing me to the great cliff. At once I was all on the alert.

We were passing the headland of an island on our left. I looked behind me. There were no other boats in sight. We were alone on the waters. Then our boat passed the headland, and I saw the lights of a big ship lying off the island.

Immediately I recognised the scene. The island was the one on which I had first landed. The ship was the guardship that watched the entrance of the sea. I was back again where I had begun when I first entered that land.

Our boat turned and made for the ship. In a few minutes I was climbing up the hanging ladder, as I had done on that other "day" or "night" an eternity before. I felt as if I were repeating step by step an experience that I had gone through in a former life—a very distant one. The actions were indeed all the same, and carried out in the same order, except that this time I was not brought before the commander. I was taken to the bathroom, given a meal at the common table within the guard-room, and, after the meal, brought to a little cabin with a couch in it, like the one in which I had slept before.

CHAPTER NINETEEN

The Great Wall

I REMEMBER no more until I was awakened to be put ashore. I must have slept a long time, for, when I came up on deck, I found that we were running into the harbour of the city.

As the Central Sea is, according to my calculations, at least three hundred miles in length between the northern cliffs and the city, I must have made up during the voyage for a good deal of the sleep and rest that I could not get during my wanderings in the barren lands.

In any case I felt immensely refreshed and invigorated—completely renewed, in fact—and in a condition to face whatever awaited me, not merely with a stout heart, but with a strong body and a strong mind to carry out the resolves of my will.

It was a good thing that it was so, for I was soon to be put to a test that needed all my powers of resolve and endurance.

However, I had better narrate events in the order of their happening.

Before I left the ship, I got a meal in the common room. Then when I had finished I was brought to the commander.

Whether this man, or indeed the ship, was the same as the commander, or the ship, that had first brought me to the city, I don't know, but, when I was brought before him, the commander showed no sign of recognition. Nor did he send me any message with his mind.

The presentation of me to him was obviously some formality

that had to be gone through before I left the ship, for, after
he had looked at me for a moment with his intense concentration of vision, I was taken ashore.

During the time I had been on the ship or on the boat that
first captured me, I had not had any communication with
anybody, beyond the gestures with which they beckoned to
me to do what they wanted.

From the "silence" of both the commander who captured
me and the commander of the guardship I took it that my
outlawry still held, and that whatever was going to happen to
me in the city was to be a continuance of the same sort of
treatment that I had been receiving since I left the city, or a
sequel of the same type. I was confirmed in this opinion by the
fact that though, while I slept, they had cleaned and actually
mended my clothes for me, they had not again given me their
clothes, but had left me to dress in what remained of my own.
Their cleaning and mending of them was due, I realised, not
to any desire to make things better for me, but to their inherent
objection to lack of cleanliness or order.

I knew pretty clearly, therefore, when I was going ashore,
that I would almost certainly be called upon to endure some
severe struggle, yet, owing to the fact that my mind and my
will had emerged without a fundamental defeat from the
dreadful journey in the darkness, I now faced this coming
ordeal with a good heart.

If I had been in the hands of some human captors on the
upper earth, I should have been dealt with in such a way that
my physical nerves would not have been strengthened to meet
any subsequent ordeal, but, just as in the cleaning and
mending of my clothes, so in the treatment of my body this
people always acted, as long as I was actually in their custody,
after the fashion of the highest type of community.

Indeed, the contrast between their respect for the living
body, and all the things pertaining to it, and their total lack

of respect for the privacies and rights of the mind, was the thing that astounded me most during the whole period in which I was in contact with their civilisation.

Hitherto they had, after the first attempt of the ship's commander on my mind, refrained from invading it, except in so far as I allowed them to read my thoughts. It seemed unlikely that they could any longer continue to do so, unless they intended once more to banish me to the darkness. The latter seemed unlikely, since, if such had been their intention, it would not have been necessary to bring me back to the city. It was probable, therefore, that I was now to undergo an ordeal worse than any that I had experienced—one that would possibly leave my mind in such a condition that, whether they absorbed me or failed to do so, the experience would either kill me or leave me an imbecile or a lunatic.

These were the thoughts that crossed my mind as I went up the gangway and followed a guide along the quay.

We went by the same route that I had taken on my first visit to the city, and we ended at the same place—the enclosure of the Master of Knowledge.

When I was brought into the inner enclosure, he was sitting with his back to two globe-lights, that shone in my face as I stood before him.

As his eyes dwelt on me with their intense, passionless fixity, I felt that that timeless, motionless gaze could numb me to its will if the mind behind it decided to do so.

He was at the moment not exerting any power over me beyond that necessary to read my thoughts. Finally his message came:

"I see that, though you know our powers, you are still determined to resist becoming one of us."

"That is so," I answered. "I will not, and cannot, give myself up to you."

"Yes," came the message. "You believe that if you go back

to the darkness you will die, yet you are willing to die rather than be absorbed. You know that we can shatter your mind and what you regard as your individuality; nevertheless, in spite of all that you have gone through in the darkness, you are determined, if we shatter your mind, that it shall remain shattered, rather than that we should be allowed to remake and heal it."

"That is true," I answered. "You have read my mind fully, and nothing will ever change it. You will gain nothing by keeping me here. You may kill me, but you cannot absorb me. Unless you intend to kill me, or make me an imbecile or a lunatic, you should let me go free."

"You mean," came the message, "that we should let you leave our land, so that you may try to find the road by which you came here, or the road by which our fathers came here, and so return to your own country."

"Yes," I said. "That is what I mean."

"And then?" came the query.

I went silent. For the moment I had forgotten my father. Now I knew that I should have to return for him, if they set me free and I found a way to the upper earth. What was more, I knew that I should have to return for him with as great a strength as I could gather, in order to rescue him from this people. That would mean invasion for them and the break-up of everything. They could not set me free on such terms, and I could accept no others.

"Your mind has grasped the position clearly," came his message. "If you must come back for the man that was your father, you cannot be allowed to go, since it might mean great trouble for our people."

"It would probably mean complete destruction for your State," I answered, "since our people are many times more numerous than yours, and their weapons of war are much more destructive. It is possible that, if I were to tell the story to the

Government of my own people, they would think me mad and do nothing to help me; but I might be able to gather together a band of daring men who would come with me, and, with our deadly weapons, would destroy your State unless you surrendered my father."

"You believe all that you are saying," came back his message, "though it seems strange. The man you call your father would resist your attack on us with all his powers, yet you would come and take him away by force."

He stopped and watched me fixedly.

"I see," he said, "that you are in doubt. If you could be sure that the man you seek would resist your attack on this State, and, if necessary, die to defend it, you would not come back."

"No," I said. "If I could only be assured of that I certainly would not come back; but how can I be certain, unless you let me meet my father, and, even if you did let me meet him, perhaps even then I should not be certain."

He stared past me with his clear vacuous stare.

I stood watching him, hardly daring to breathe. Could it be possible that he was considering letting me meet my father?

His gaze came back to my eyes, and stared through them into my mind.

"Yes," came his message, "I have decided to let you meet the man that you still think of as your father. When you have met him, you will at least know how foolish are your plans about him. Perhaps, even, when you have met him, you will consent to be absorbed."

My heart bounded with joy. I could hardly believe that I had got his message aright.

"Tell me!" I cried. "Tell me! Have I got your message aright? Will you let me meet my father?"

"I will send you to where he is now," came the message. "The guardship will bring you."

"You mean now? At once?" I pressed. "You mean that you will now—immediately—send me to my father?"

The message came back this time with extraordinary force and clearness.

"Yes. Now. Immediately. I will send you, not to your father, since there is no longer such a person, but to the man that has taken the place of the person who was your father."

The emphasis of the distinction between the man I wanted to see and the man I was to see was so great that it imprinted itself on my mind. Yet my subconscious self refused to grasp it. I was in a whirl of joy that made it impossible indeed for me to assimilate anything.

The Master had beckoned to one of the men, and was giving him orders silently. Then he willed me to follow him.

I went, hardly knowing whether I was walking or flying. The sudden change from the tension of fear and the resolve to endure, with which I had entered the enclosure, to this state of ecstasy was so great that my mind was almost unhinged by it.

As I walked beside my guide back to the vessel, I kept talking to him, to myself, to everybody I met. I made the most fantastic gestures. In our world of upper earth I should have excited smiles and ridicule. Here I didn't attract the slightest attention. My guide didn't seem to hear me or notice my excitement. I didn't care. I went on talking and gesticulating to him and to myself.

Already I saw my father and myself on the high mountain down which I had first come, nearing the heap of ashes through which I had tumbled, when I fell through the trapdoor in the Roman Wall. I saw my father's face gradually growing more and more conscious under the influence of my voice and the nearness of upper earth.

I saw the two of us emerging into the sunlight and shading our eyes from its incredible brightness. Then I would look at him and see the sudden return of knowledge to his eyes, hear him call me by name, hear us laughing and shouting and running over the green grass.

It will be clear from this specimen of my imaginings that I was not in my right senses when I got to the ship. Nor did I recover them during the whole of her voyage northward.

I had no idea where the ship was bringing me, and at first I pestered everybody with questions as to how long it would take us to get there. Needless to say, nobody answered me. If I caught a man by the arm, he detached himself, as if he were detaching his coat from a thorn that had caught it, without violence, but without according me the slightest recognition.

When I tried to get to the commander of the vessel, I couldn't find him.

As we were now working up against the stream, the ship was going much more slowly than she had done on the other two journeys, which were downstream. If I had been able to eat or sleep, I shouldn't have felt the journey so long, but I could do neither, and the result was that the journey, which probably did not take quite two days, seemed to me to last a week.

One thing became clear to me after a while—that we were making for the great cliff barrier, or the land that lay under it. Otherwise the journey could not, I calculated, have lasted such a dreadful length.

I drew one bit of consolation from this—that when I had got my father we should have less distance to travel to get to the road that would lead us home.

It was in this mood that I first saw the great Wall.

I had been tramping the deck impatiently, trying to stare into the darkness ahead, when I saw, away on the right, a row of dim lights up on a height. Then the vessel turned gradually and made towards them at a slower pace.

My heart began to beat wildly. I had never seen one of their settlements so high. They were always on the flat, but this one looked like a fortress. Now the lights of a harbour were beginning to show in front of us, down on the flat, but, up above it, the ring of lights was getting clearer, as if there was a real town on a hill. There were certainly lights, one above another, along a line that stretched from west to east.

Then I saw a dark mass showing up between the lights.

I was looking at a cliff wall with lights shining through openings in it. Lower down, there were the lights of a settlement on a plateau over the harbour.

The words of a pupil in the school flashed into my memory: "The great Wall in the gap through which our fathers came down here!" This was the great Wall—the cliff with the lights in it was a wall!

Already, as we came nearer, it seemed to me that it was not a cliff. I thought I could see masses of masonry on its surface around the lights.

I had reached the frontier! Perhaps my father had never got past it.

If he had come down by that way, he might have remained there, perhaps in a sort of imprisonment, perhaps as a hostage, perhaps because he had been a soldier and they were using his former experience for the garrisoning and defence of the Wall. That was probably it. They were using his special aptitudes. They used each person's aptitudes. He was probably one of the commanders in charge of the defence of the Murus. He would naturally take up such a task, if he accepted their State, and, if he had accepted it and taken up that task, he might not be willing to come with me.

Still it was hardly credible that he could wish to remain in this darkness.

These people were not the Romans he had dreamt of. They were a monstrous, almost incredible distortion of the great idea that was Rome. It was not possible that he could wish to stay with them, if he were awakened from the trance into which they would have thrown him, and it was hardly possible that the shock of meeting me would not rouse him, even if he were in some hypnotic state.

He could not be like the others. He had been handled too late, and the effect on him could not be like that on people who had been changed when they were in the plastic stage. Perhaps he was hardly changed at all. These people could not understand a person like my father. They would have had no experience of the effect of their hypnotic rearrangements on the mind and personality of matured adults. They might be completely mistaken in their calculations.

As these thoughts poured through my mind, the ship was running into the harbour—a circular one, with good quays, like the harbour in the other city, though it was much smaller.

We were turning so as to come alongside the quay on the right hand. The place was well lighted by globes on pillars.

I went over to the starboard side of the vessel forward, and began to scan the quays eagerly. . . .

The vessel was now being brought alongside. I hurried back to the stern deck, to the cabin of the commander. He would need to see me before I left the vessel, and I wanted to be as near him as possible, so that there would be no delay.

At the same time I kept watching the quay for any sign of a tall figure. There was still nobody there, however, except the automatons who were waiting to moor the ship. Then a man with a commander's face passed me, going along the quay to the right.

I stared at him for a moment. It was probably our commander who had gone up the gangway amidships and gone ashore.

I cried out to him: "Commander! Commander!" He turned and looked at me. Then a man behind me took me by the arm and led me away from the side of the vessel, down the hatch-

way, and into the guardroom. There he put me on a couch,
and made me understand in some way that I must stay there.

I sat as patiently as I could on that couch, waiting; but I
couldn't keep my body quiet. I was trembling with excitement,
and I kept crossing and uncrossing my legs and arms, and
moving my body from side to side. Even my teeth kept up a
tattoo, the lower ones against the upper, in the effort of my
body to get into action.

All the time I watched the door.

Nothing happened, however. Men came and went, and I
thought that each was the messenger for me. Then, as nobody
paid attention to me, I decided that they had forgotten me, or
that this was not the place, after all, where my father was.

Hardly had I come to one conclusion when I jumped to
another. They were persuading my father to refuse to see me.
They were working on him with their hypnotic tricks, to make
sure that, even if he did see me, he would be completely under
their control, and would ignore or repulse me.

When at length the messenger did come for me, he had to
come up to me to attract my attention. I had my eyes fixed
on the floor, brooding over plans as to what I would do to
baulk their attempts to keep us apart.

At the sight of him, all my doubts fled. I had now only one
idea again. I would see my father in a few minutes.

I passed the man going out of the room, rushed up the stairs
and across the deck to the gangway. Two men intercepted me,
and took me by the arm. I tried to shake them off, but they
held me firmly. Then I saw that I was being brought to the
deck-cabin of the commander. I began to hurry. Perhaps my
father was waiting there for me. The curtains parted. There
was only the commander sitting in his chair.

"Are you going to take me to my father?" I cried out to
him.

"There is no such person," came the answering message,

"but you are now to be brought to the person that you have been sent here to see."

He looked steadily at me for a moment with his staring gaze. Then the men led me away to the gangway.

A man was waiting for me on the quay, and, when I came out, he beckoned to me and walked away to the right. I followed him.

The fixed gaze of the commander had somehow steadied me, and I no longer rushed along impatiently. It was not that the eagerness in my mind was any the less—it was, on the contrary, now at fever heat—but that it had got so great that it had fixed my body into a sort of frozen calm. This had happened to me under the stare of the commander, as if his will had fixed and set the tension of my body.

CHAPTER TWENTY

The Face of a Stranger

MY GUIDE passed along the quay with the swift, even pace of these people, then turned to the left and mounted a flight of steps that led up the wall of the quay.

At the top we found ourselves on a narrow platform of rock, from which more flights of steps led upward towards the lights of the settlement. Above that, again, I could see a great mass of masonry towering from west to east, with lights showing through a great number of openings that rose in tiers over one another, as if there were dwellings, storey above storey.

We had now reached the top of the plateau, and the enclosures of the settlement stood in front of us.

Somewhere in these enclosures my father was waiting for me. A broad road led through the enclosures towards the great Wall. We followed this. It was well lighted with globes on pillars.

I stared ahead eagerly. At every moment I thought I might see him coming to meet me.

From the main road other paths ran to right and left, but we kept on straight towards the wall. The road was mounting upwards, first in a slope, then by broad shallow flights of steps. At the top of one of these flights we came upon an armed man. I stared at him. It was the first soldier that I had seen in this country. He was armed, like a Roman legionary, with short sword in a belt and a spear in his hand, but he wore no armour—not even a helmet. He was an automaton, and paid no attention to us.

The great Wall was now looming high over us, a magnificent piece of rough masonry at least a hundred feet in height.

Two soldiers appeared from the right. My guide handed me over to them. They turned back to the right, then to the Wall again, and, after a few more paces, stopped.

We were at the door of a sort of porch that stood out from the Wall. A man came forward and beckoned me to follow him. My knees were trembling so that they hardly supported my body. I heard my teeth clicking against one another with a sound so loud in that silence that it almost deafened me, or was it the pounding of my heart that was beating on my ears with such a roaring?

We were passing along a stone corridor, with rooms opening off it to the right. Then the corridor turned a little to the left, and a door opened in front of us. My guide passed through it. I followed him. We were in a long, low room. There were four armed men in the room, one at each side of the door we had entered and one at each side of a door at the far end on the right. We went towards this. At the door my guide stopped for a moment, and motioned me to stop. Then he passed through the door. In a moment he came back and beckoned me to follow him in. I did so.

I was in a long hall, with a table at the far end. At the table three men were sitting—two men of the normal size of these people; the third man, who sat between them, was a head and shoulders over them. It was my father.

Even at the distance of the length of the hall I could see his face—not very distinctly, owing to the confused lighting, but quite enough to know that it was he.

I began to run. The guide caught me by the arm. Immediately a soldier caught me by the other arm. I pulled my arms away from them violently and hurried up the hall.

Then, as I came clear into the ring of lights that fell from the globes on to the faces of the men at the table, I stopped. The man in the centre was not my father! The outline of the face was the same as his, but there the resemblance stopped.

I was looking at the face of a stranger—not merely of a stranger as men are strange on earth, but of a creature entirely alien. The eyes stared at me with a dead fixity and were completely empty. But it was not only the eyes. The rest of the face was as blank and vacant as the eyes—empty of all the little detailed features that made the face I knew, empty of all humanity, all associations, all memory and experience.

I stood staring in dismay. Then, as I looked, a change began.

A thrill ran through me. The eyes were beginning to come alive with expression. But what was happening? The expression that was coming into them was an expression of hatred.

I stood staring, transfixed by the change that was coming over the face. It was no longer empty. The eyes were alive. They were now glaring with life, a life that seized and held me with hatred.

I stared back with a sickening feeling. All the time that I had been coming to meet him I had been so sure that, even if he had become an isolated automaton, I would, the moment I met him, rush over to him, put my arms round him, call him all the dear names we had for him, and so seize him back again from them. I had been dreaming that, if only I could meet him, no barrier that they could have put between us could withstand the force of the impact of my love for him.

Now I stood dumbly staring at him. I made no attempt to call or approach him. I would as soon have called out to the mask that was the face of the brute spiders as to that face in front of me. Compared with it, the faces of even the most isolated automatons were kindly. They at least were not malevolent, but those eyes that were staring at me out of my father's face were full of hatred.

It was not merely a message that was coming to me from him. It was a torrent of loathing for everything I stood for—my loves and hopes and fears, my memories of him and of my mother and of our life together, all the associations that went to make up my personality; those staring eyes expressed such hatred of it all that I felt myself trembling under their impact.

I instinctively tried to back away from him, but I could not move. His loathing of me was seizing me, pouring over my mind, burning it, searing it.

I tried to put up my hands to ward off the horror. I could not. I was paralysed, gripped in a vice. I made a convulsive effort, like the effort of a man in a dream to escape from some dreadful thing. Then I felt myself falling—falling—through gulfs——

CHAPTER TWENTY-ONE

Conflict

THE PERIOD that followed the meeting with the man that had taken possession of the body of my father is for me one of horror.

I have no clear memory of it in the upper regions of my consciousness, since I was held down in a deep coma for most of the time, but my whole being remembers it as if it were some pre-natal experience that was sensed with every nerve. I can give no continuous account of it, however, that could convey a coherent impression to any human being, beyond the fact that I felt like a creature whose mind and will were being dismembered by forces that were physical in their impact.

There are fragments of memories that drift through my mind; memories of an overpowering hail of blows that seemed to rain on my will; shadows like great dark wings that were battering and blinding me; a snarling horror that was tearing at my mind with beak and talons—but these can only have been phantoms of my own mind, scattered debris of some great mental suffering that I endured for a time that seemed an eternity, but that, for all I know, may have been short by human reckoning.

Another memory that remains with me from that suffering is a conviction that, if I gave myself up to the thing that was attacking me, I could have great peace.

This memory takes the form of a glimmer of rays that seemed to keep coming to me from above—a beating of bright power, as if from a great light that would descend upon me and destroy the horror, and envelop me in peace and perfect joy, if I would only surrender myself to it.

For moments even, the horror would cease. I would get a glimpse of perfect happiness. Then, with my refusal, there would come the swift searing impact again. For I always refused.

That was the marvellous thing. I refused to give myself up.

It was not that I was heroic. I feel that I cried out in my suffering, and cringed and whined. I have no conscious memory of that, but my body still seems to remember, in every nerve, pitiful whining cries that must have been wrung from it— cries, perhaps without sound, with which I must have answered the pressure on my mind when it became so unbearable that I must yield in some thing or die.

I did not intend to die, unless I could find no other way of escape from surrender to the thing that was violating me, and I did not intend to surrender, even if death were the final penalty that I must pay for not giving myself up.

I know why I did not give in. It was because, through the very torture that was being inflicted on it, my mind grasped fully the nature of the thing that encompassed it.

Until then the darkness had been only hovering over me. It had been hovering like a vulture whose wings shut out the world, but it had not closed with me. It had not come close enough for me to know it, as I learned to know it now, and this deep comprehension that I was obtaining of it made it impossible for me to accept it as long as my mind held. My emotion had been too profoundly aroused to allow of my will yielding.

If they had had sufficient understanding of me to invade me through the love I bore my father, they might have got me. Only through my father could they have worked on my emotion, but they had killed him, and put into his body this thing that hated me and could only arouse in me a corresponding hatred. Now they could never get me while I was alive and sane.

They may not have had any choice in the matter. Possibly my father could have been resynthesised only by deepening his monomania of hatred for the "Hun," the barbarian that had destroyed Rome. He had come to them late, and it is possible that they could have handled him in no other way but through his hatreds, which could not then be disentangled from his passionate love for Rome. If they had got him as a child, they could probably have eradicated in him all the seeds of hatred, as of all other feelings, except love of the State, but he had developed on his own lines in another world in which love of country, for most men, means a potential hatred of all other countries that might attack her. Now that his body was emptied of all knowledge and memory and emotion, except its love for the Roman State, the mind that possessed it could have only one feeling towards me when we met—a hatred of this thing that was not absorbed.

The creature that remained of what had been my father, instead of meeting me with love, met me with outrage. The result was that my emotions were roused to the fiercest opposition, and my mind was not alone left clear for resistance, but was driven on to it with every power it possessed.

One result was that, while my will bent all its forces to defend my personality, even if necessary at the cost of my life, my subconscious mind soared above the conflict, surveying and directing my energies to the fullest use of every power of endurance of which I was capable.

In this survey it left nothing unexamined, nothing untouched. It saw this underworld State clearly as the monstrous machine that it was—a blind thing, with no vision, no pity, no understanding, not even an understanding of that human need to love that it used to enslave its victims.

It saw that I was the only human being left in that world outside the machine; that, under that dome, which was the land of England, I must make a stand for humanity against the Frankenstein's monster that, having devoured the highest as well as the lowest, now functioned mechanically in a world in which man, as we know him, had ceased to exist.

It saw that, if this machine that had come alive could obtain knowledge—not wisdom or real knowledge, for of that it was incapable, but the technical knowledge that I had stored in my brains—if it could force this knowledge into its possession, with me as the controlling and directing robot, and add our scientific powers to its own tremendous discoveries, then a new and ghastly era might open up for mankind.

As I have said, I did not know all this consciously at the time, since my consciousness was only the spasmodic one of a man in a deep fever; but I must have known it with deep subconscious knowledge, for, when I awoke from the fever, I knew it all fully, clearly, as I have often on waking known clearly things that I did not know when falling asleep.

I also knew that now there was a danger to mankind from this people that had not existed before. I knew that the man who had displaced my father was seizing my mind, not because he wanted me to be absorbed in the Roman State, as the others did, but because the remnant of memory in his mind had sensed the value of the scientific resources in mine, and was determined to subserve them to his fixed and ruling passion—the crazy determination to seize back again the lands of the upper earth from the barbarians.

I have called his ruling passion crazy, but I do not mean that his idea was entirely impossible. It is true that, even if he were able to seize my mind and use it to equip the under-earth State with modern armaments, that people could scarcely have accomplished his dream.

Even with the extraordinary combination of powers that our

knowledge combined with theirs would have given them, their State could not have stood any real chance of a successful invasion of England in normal circumstances.

But normal circumstances are not always to be counted on even in England. If she were in death-grips with a very powerful enemy, if part of her population were in revolt, as the population in Russia revolted after the Great War, if a Fascist or Nazi section of her own citizens made common cause with the underearth invaders, because of the similarity of their doctrines, nobody could tell what might happen.

The danger would be greater because nobody could suspect that, under the green earth of England, an outcast offspring of its own people, that had bred inward in the fearsome human swamp into which it had been driven, was gathering itself for a spring into the upper world again, under the urge of a madman who combined the evil of the light and the darkness.

It was as if some monstrous reptile bred in the festering swamps were about to launch itself over the kindly chaotic world of men for which my heart was longing.

If that happened, then the sun could matter no more nor the rain nor the green of grass that was the thirst of my soul.

And it could only happen through me—if I gave in. That conviction was, I believe, one of the chief things that saved me.

As I have said, I did not consciously think of all this, at the time, with the surface of my mind. I could not have done so, since for the greater part of the time, I was dark on the surface of my mind to external things. But I knew it deeply, and this knowledge that there were possibly deeper things at stake than even the existence of my own individual soul did, I believe, nerve me to the endurance that carried me through to the end. However it happened, I did endure, and I did win through.

I won through because that people, although it is pitiless, is also passionless. When they realised clearly that I would

die before I gave myself up to them, they ceased their efforts
to absorb me.

Unlike many peoples on earth, they do not desire the death
of anyone merely because he will not yield to them. They bore
me no ill-will. Punishment for its own sake is not part of their
code. My death was not necessary to the State; therefore they
did not will it.

Their respect for the living human body is indeed an essential result of their doctrine of the irreparable waste and loss
that is death, according to their understanding of it. It is
to postpone this doom as far as possible that they have sacrificed all the things that seem to us worth living for; but they
are logical in their doctrine, and they, who so calmly kill the
individual lives of their people, will not, if they can at all
avoid it, murder a human body.

They certainly never do so deliberately, under the cover
of fine catch-words such as "atonement" or "punishment" or
"justice," much less under battle-cries like "the duty of the
State." They liberated me when they saw that, if they continued to work on me, the only result could be my death.

When I say "they," I do not include amongst them the man
who had been substituted for my father. The capacity for
hatred that my father had brought from our world, had, as I
have already said, not only not been eliminated with the destruction of his personality, but had been intensified in the
being that had taken his place, and, if the final decision as to
my fate had lain with him, I should now be dead. I had proof
of this later, but, even before the proof came to me, I needed
no evidence stronger than the hatred that had poured itself
through the eyes that looked at me from my father's face,
and the hatred of me that the mind which now possessed his
body implanted on my subconscious life during the period of
hypnotic trance or coma, when my body was lying helpless
under its power.

One other effect produced by my conflict with him was that I comprehended at last the truth of their statement that there was no such person here below as the father I had known.

I could no longer have the slightest doubt. My father was dead. They had killed him and put something else in his place —a creature whose only knowledge of me was the knowledge of hatred; a being entirely incapable of anything so complicated as the life of even the simplest person on earth, though endowed with an almost superhuman will-power, generated through the liberation of its monomania from all qualifying knowledge and circumstance.

CHAPTER TWENTY-TWO

Free

I LAY STARING UPWARDS. A quiver of nausea began to shake me. I tried to hold myself, but couldn't. My body was moving in convulsive waves of flesh that ran round it, but, as the waves ran over me, the sense of nausea was lessening. Something was passing off me. I was feeling freer, not in the mind, but in the body, as if some cramp that had seized my frame was losing its grip.

Gradually my body became relaxed. I lay quiet. My mind was now beginning to grasp things. A blackness was lying over it, a feeling of deep anguish and dread.

Then suddenly there came a sense of a great liberation. I had escaped! The darkness was behind me—not on top of me, all round me. I was free of it.

I felt myself breathing in deep gasps, like a man who has just escaped from drowning. But I *had* escaped. The horror had almost got me, but I had escaped. Then I remembered. It was my father!

I lay for a moment stiffened with the knowledge.

The convulsive waves seized me again. They wrung my body. At the same time an upheaval of emotion was shaking my mind. The creature that had tried to seize me was my father.

Gradually my mind eased to normal grief. My father was dead. He had left us a long time ago. Now he would never come back to us. It was not he that loathed me and had tried to strangle my life.

248

There was nothing left now in this world below—nothing that remained for me to do but to go back to the upper earth, if they would let me, and if I could get back. My mother was waiting for me there and the normal life of men. I could now promise that, if they would let me go free, I would not come back to this darkness. Why should I come back? There was nothing to come back for. They had been right all the time. Now I could go home. That would be the best thing—if I could. If I stayed, I should have to kill my father's body. I could not go on living and seeing it in the possession of that creature.

No! I must go, as soon as they would let me, or I should be forced to deprive that body of life.

A man came towards me with a vessel and put it to my mouth. I pushed it away. He put it to my lips again. This time I did not struggle. It didn't seem to matter whether I drank its contents or not. Arms lifted me up from behind and a hand tilted my head back slightly. The liquid was trickling into my mouth, and I gulped it down with an effort.

At once a feeling of quietness began to creep over me. The man put the vessel to my mouth again. This time I took a deep drink. Then I was laid back on my couch.

I woke to the rhythmic beat of oars. I did not open my eyes, but lay there, letting the rhythm of the oars run through me. I was at peace—the complete peace of complete loss. My life as I had known it had come to an end. The motive-force that had given the chief meaning to my life since I could first remember—all that was gone. I could now go back to the ordinary life of men, that I had never fully lived.

The world that I had lived in was shattered, buried under the debris of its own wreckage. The new world I was to live in would be a poor, ordinary thing to put in its place, even if I could get back to it. The chances were that I could not.

If I did, I should see the green grass again, and feel the

sunlight and the rain, and marry and settle down and have children—children who would not have any dreams, such as I and my father had until he died.

My mind shifted back to him. Had he died before he came down—died, in part, during the war? Was the man who came back to us in 1919—the man without joy or laughter or life, apart from his obsession—was he the man that my mother had married, the father I had loved so intensely? Do men die while alive even on the upper earth, and give way to wandering spirits that seize their bodies? Was the man who had been robbed of his personal life here below—was he my father, or only an intruder who had already ousted my father from his body during the dreadful struggle when thousands were hurled from their bodies at every moment?

The face of the man who had come back to us had never been the face of the man I had known—the subtle, charming face, full of delicate suggestions and laughter and intimacies. I thought of that other rigid face of the soldier that had returned—stern, hungry, simple, with an austere, pitiless simplicity. Could that have been the face of the father who had made the house ring in the old days with his joyous, fantastic mirth—that isolated man with no joy and no laughter? Surely not. Either my father's personality had died in part in his body, or else his soul had been driven out in some great stress or shock and a stranger had taken its place—a stranger that had taken over his obsession with his body but little else of him. Could such things be?

At the mere thought of him my body quivered with hatred. He had infected me with his, and I returned loathing for loathing. As I thought of him now, I felt a tide of rage and hatred pouring over me. If I stayed here below, I must seek him out and tear from him the body which he had polluted, even if I had to destroy that body to reach him.

For a while, as I lay there, my mind was trembling, quivering with hatred. I would get him yet, tear him asunder, give my father's body decent burial—Christian rest—not leave it as a slave to this thing that had seized and polluted it.

I sat up. I would go to him now.

Then I remembered. I was on the ship. He was away up to the northward—planning, scheming his invasion of the upper earth, a sediment of memory of the Great War still in his mind, working it like a poisonous yeast. He wanted to go back and kill and kill, and seize and confiscate.

I lay back on the couch. He had been foiled. In the shock of my emotion at the sudden knowledge of the loss of my father he had had his only chance to seize me. As I lay under that shock, he had flung himself upon me and failed. I would go away from him. It was his nature to hate and to seize. I was becoming like him.

The thought sprang at me that perhaps he had partly got me. He had infected me—this hatred that shook me even now. No! I must get away. To avenge my father's death would be useless. The thought could have come only from him to torment me. How could it be done? Only by murdering my father's body. Perhaps some shred of his personality still remained. If there were even the tiniest deposit left in the bottom of the vessel, once so filled with his personality, I could not smash the vessel.

No! I must go! I must go at once—away from the sight of that hateful face.

The movement of the oars had stopped. The vessel must be running into harbour. Where had they brought me? Back to the city, probably, to the Master of Knowledge. The door was sliding back. A man was beckoning. I must have been a long time asleep or unconscious on the ship, if we were now back in the city.

I got up and followed the man. My body seemed to have lost all strength. My legs were hardly able to hold it up, and it sagged forward, as if the trunk could not support the head and shoulders. My knees were knocking together with weakness. It was as if I had just begun to recover from a long fever.

The man brought me to the bathroom. I got my clothes off and dropped into the bath. It was warm, and thick with salt, and my nerves began to lie quietly. Restfulness was again coming over me, and a sort of peace. The strong, briny smell of the water came to me, like a whiff of the upper world to which I belonged, warm and thick and stirring. I rolled round in it and felt it soak through me, and, as it soaked into my pores, strength came back to me, and resolution, and the will to live. I would begin a new life, if I got to the earth—a real one this time, not the life of a dream, so mad that it came true from its own intensity.

The new life would never have that intensity which drove the old one on the rocks. It would be a calm, happy life, with men and women and children in it—not like shadows, as they had been before, but in the middle of my life, if ever I could get back to it—my mother, too.

Suddenly I was burning to get away, to get back to the upper world, the sun, the sea, the laughter of men. I got out of the bath and dressed hurriedly.

When I slid the door back, a man was waiting outside to bring me to the guardroom. Here they gave me a meal. I didn't want to eat. Then I remembered that, in order to succeed, I must eat. My physical strength must not fail my will. When I tasted the food, I found that I was hungry, and ate a good meal. Then I was brought out of the ship, along the quay, and through the enclosures to the Master of Knowledge.

I felt that it was the last time that I would see him. Soon I must either be dead or mad or gone from this land. I should surely never see him after this time—not I, the person who was now coming to him.

He sat, in the same place under the globes, as if his body

never moved. I could hardly believe that it ever did move, so motionless, so eternal did it seem, as it sat there, poised, staring into space and eternity.

A message was coming to me from his mind.

"You no longer misunderstand. You know there is no such person as the man that was your father. You will never come back here, if we let you go."

It was not a question. It was an affirmation. Still, I wanted to make things so clear that there could be no misunderstanding.

"No," I answered aloud, "I will never come back again. There would be nothing to come back for."

I stopped. I found myself trembling. I was in the presence of my father's murderer—one of those who had shaped the creature that had entered into possession of my father's body —yet it was not anger that was shaking me. All that was gone. I felt myself in the presence merely of a machine. Could it be possible that it would let me escape? That other would have violated me, murdered me, rather than let me escape. Could it be possible that this being would let me go free?

He was sitting impassively reading my thoughts. Now his message was coming. He was ordering me to go, to leave their land and not to return.

I was free! Free! In spite of my father's hatred and determination to hold me until he had wrung my powers from me, they were setting me free!

I could hardly believe it. I must get away at once, before they had time for reflection, before my father had time to come to the Master of Knowledge and imbue him with his plans.

Then I realised that, as I thought those thoughts, the being in front of me was reading them. I was revealing all my plans, hopes, my father's plans, my thoughts of them, to the mind that was watching me. At any moment now, with his knowledge of my thoughts, he might recall his order.

I turned and ran out of the enclosure. At every moment I expected to be seized and brought back.

A man was coming after me. I began to run down the path towards the harbour. I knew it well by now, that path.

I dashed towards the passage on the quay. Would the ship be still there?

She *was* there, a little farther down. I dashed towards her. There was a gangway from the quay to her second deck. I rushed up the gangway. At the top a man pushed me back. I looked round me wildly. Two men were coming along the quays. Were they coming to seize me?

I stood staring towards them. As they came near, I saw that one of them was a commander. He was sending me a message. What was it? What was it? I was to go into the ship. I stopped, held by a new fear.

"Where?" I shouted aloud. "Where are you bringing me?"

"To the northern pass, to send you off our land," came back the message.

I went up the gangway. I wanted to get out of sight into the recesses of the ship.

The Master of Knowledge had ignored my thoughts and the revelations that they had brought to him. Possibly he had despised them. That he had powers that could enable him to force me to yield up my knowledge, or even to resynthesise my mind, I could hardly doubt. The forces that I had felt in his eyes were of quite a different range from those that I had already resisted successfully. If he were to become obsessed, like the other man, with the dreams of hatred and reconquest, that the latter had brought with him from the upper earth, or if, under the influence of the memories and ambitions brought by the other man from above, he should decide to seize my body and brain with all its modern knowledge, I did not doubt that he could do so. I had been saved, so far, by the fact that he was too far removed from human ambitions, or from the memory of human knowledge and the grasp of modern scientific powers, to desire to take from me any of my equipment of material science.

Probably he had no conception of it, even such a dim conception as remained like a residue of memory in the mind of the man who had come from the earth. If he had any conception of it, it was clear that he did not, at present, value it sufficiently to think it worth while using me to obtain possession of it. But this state of mind might not last. If the conception of my powers dawned on him, what would be more natural than that he should decide to seize my brain, with the scientific wealth of ages stored in it? And, if he did so, what would the future hold in store for me?

They had brought me to the guardroom and left me sitting on a couch there. I sat watching the door, waiting with every nerve of my body for the movement of the oars that would send the ship away from the man that sat, under the globes of light, in the enclosure so near me.

If it should once get the idea of emerging from its lair! If its mind should conceive the idea that the creature at the Wall possessed!

I have no greater fear than other men. I had already shown in my wanderings in the darkness fortitude and endurance that were at least up to the average. I had met the man that had seized my father's life and had not given way, but I confess that I was afraid—pitifully afraid—of the being that was sitting in the enclosure so near me. I did not feel that I could meet him, if he attacked me. I had only one thought—flight to the uttermost bounds, away from his power.

When at length the ship started, I relaxed. Only then I realised that all the time I had been sitting rigid with fear.

During the whole of the voyage north I did not sleep, until the last section of the journey. In the beginning I could not have slept, even if I had wanted to do so. Then, as lack of

sleep began to wear me down, I tried to keep awake. It was
the most foolish thing I could have done, since a person is
most subject to hypnotic influence under deep fatigue or
deep emotion, and the lack of sleep would have been one of
the most effective factors against me, if anyone had tried to
dominate me in that way during the voyage. I knew all this,
and yet so great was my panic that I could not let myself fall
asleep, until, finally, somewhat before the end of the journey,
nature had her way and forced me to sleep.

CHAPTER TWENTY-THREE

Pursuit

I DO NOT SUPPOSE that any stretch of water on the upper earth will ever be so profoundly associated in my mind with deep emotions as that Central Sea. Certainly there is not likely to be any stretch of water that will again be the scene for me of such sharp longing and panic as I felt during the two journeys that I made in the guardship from the city, northward to the Wall.

It is probable that, by this time, the cumulative effect of all I had gone through was beginning to undermine my nervous system and my balance in a deeper way, perhaps, than even my ordeal in the darkness. But it is also possible that the panic which I felt during that second voyage northward was the result of a deep reaction from the intense tension that I must have endured while I was struggling in my trance with the forces that were trying to overpower me.

My reserves of nerve-power must have been drawn on deeply during that struggle, and I may not have felt their depletion until I had rested sufficiently for the tension to die down.

It is when the tautness has finally left the nerves, and they collapse on to one another, that losses become effective, and the extent to which the reserves have been depleted begins to tell on the whole organism.

Now I was filled with the wildest panics and suspicions. Even when the boat was moving into the harbour, I still kept looking back at the sea, in the fear that a ship might be pursuing us with a countermanding order.

They were bringing me to the gangway. The commander himself was now coming with me. He did not communicate with me, beyond ordering me to follow him.

I hoped desperately I should not meet the man that was in my father's body. If I met him, I didn't know what would happen. I wanted to be clear of all that now, if they would let me go. I would go forwards, upwards, back to the earth, if they would only let me. If I got back to the sunlight, I would always go forwards, not against the movement of days and years, but with them—with the sunlight, forward, not back into the darkness.

I hadn't let anybody fill my father's place, when he had left it to go to the war and hadn't come back. I would fill it now, if only I could get away without meeting this man who hated me.

We were mounting the terraced steps, and a commander was coming to meet us—not my father; another.

My hands kept clenching at the thought of him. That room in there was the room where he had hurled himself on me.

The two commanders had gone forward a little together, probably talking silently.

Now a man was taking my knapsack. I held on to it. His message was coming to me. They wanted to store it with food. I gave it up. It was an old knapsack of my father's which had been bought in Germany before the war. If that other man saw it, he might recognise it, begin to remember perhaps, but it was too late to think of things like that now.

I sat on the stone bench that ran along the bottom of the great Wall. I was on the wrong side of it still—the inner side.

In front of me, the enclosures sloped down to the terraces. Below that the Central Sea lay, running into the darkness. At the farther end of that sea, the Master of Life, who could have held me, was sitting. I could see him clearly. He was letting me go, with all my knowledge. I felt that he himself was doing it through these men here, who were only his hands.

Should I really get free? Could it be possible?

Now they were bringing the knapsack back to me, and with it a big bow and a quiver of arrows. They were bringing me in, through the Wall.

It was very deep, that Wall—twenty feet at least. At any moment my father might come out of a side-door and stop me.

I was through the Wall, on the other side, a big space lit with globes, and, beyond the lighted space, a narrow wood in front, to the left; to the right, cliff walls.

The two commanders were standing at the door of the Wall, watching me with their fixed stare. Did they wonder what I was going up to?

I looked back at them—waved my hand. They made no movement. They were back in the tunnel behind the door. It closed.

I was outside—outside the Wall, outside my father's life, outside everything. All that had given intensity to my life was behind me. I was free—free to go upwards and forwards into an empty world of bright sunlight, if I could find it. My fears had been groundless. They were gone now.

I fixed the knapsack more firmly on my shoulders and turned my face to the wood.

I knew now how much of my life had been lived in my father's life. He had filled me. I had lived in him. Now he was gone, behind that Wall. His body was lost to him and to me. His spirit gone. Until now I hadn't known how much I had possessed both, in hope and memory.

During that quest in the darkness I had lived through that possession. But he had deserted himself. Now I also was leaving him—taking flight from him.

When I came back to my mother, could I tell her that I had left him below—that she could put away the clothes she had been keeping ready for him?

Then I remembered the eyes. There was no use dwelling on things like that.

I began to hurry. Now I felt cold about it all—quite cold. The man I knew was dead, had been dead a long time—dislodged, flung into space. The thing that I was leaving had no association—it was merely a body I had known, worn now by a stranger.

This man held himself differently from my father. My father had always walked with a slight forward droop of the neck, but this man held his head rigid and upright. There was no use going over all that again. My business was to get away, to escape, to get back to the upper earth.

The cliff walls were falling away from me on the right, the light from the Wall almost gone. No light came from above either, but down below, to the left, there were dim scattered lights here and there. If I went down there, I could get to the great river, perhaps, by keeping to the north-west—not straight down. But, if I kept on upwards, as I was going, there might be a higher road along the mountain, where brutes would not be lurking. They would be more likely to be down below, where the food was.

If only some light would begin from above, there might be a clear way. Perhaps I might even find a road going up the mountain, that would lead to some exit—the road by which the man I was leaving behind intended to come back to seize the upper earth, when his time came.

It would certainly be strange to see these automatons up between the English hedges, hiding away from the light in the shadow of the bushes, as they crept along to the attack. But of course they would move by night—they would have to move by night. The day would be far too bright for them. They would be like owls.

What would they make of the colours of the flowers, those eyes that never saw colour? They would not understand the beauty of the earth. To them it would be hateful—dreadful as the light is to bats or badgers, unnatural, a thing to be destroyed.

A blackbird's song rang in my ears, as clearly as if I were listening to it, and I could see the faces of the automatons when they heard it. I could see them clearly, and hear the cries of the newspaper boys in London:

"Invasion of England from Below"—"Attack of Underground Robots"—"Fascists gone over to the Invaders."

I dragged my mind back. I must concentrate on my task, not let it wander. I should need all my will and mind, if I was to escape.

The way beneath me was no longer a path. It was a series of rocks and clefts. I could see nothing. At any moment I might break a leg, fall down a cleft, if I didn't take care.

They had put a phosphorus ball in my hand and others in my knapsack, but their balls were so dim. They showed so little light. I must be careful. I couldn't afford to let my mind drift.

I remembered that they had put other lights into my bag besides the phosphorus balls—candles with big phosphorus heads. I wondered whether I should risk lighting one of these. It might draw the attention of creatures from afar, who would see it, though they couldn't see the phosphorus ball. This was not like the inner lands round the Central Sea, where all brutes went in fear of the automatons—except far away up in the barren heights. Here I was back in the jungle. At any moment something might attack me. I decided not to light a candle—not yet, at least.

I stopped. There was something coming. A stone had fallen behind me. I could hear it now—a slight movement, but clear. I was being trailed. The ball of phosphorus that I was carrying in my hand had drawn some lurking creature from its den, and it was coming after me.

I put the phosphorus ball back in my pocket and stood listening intently. The thing had stopped. Not the slightest sound broke the stillness. Perhaps it was crouching for a spring. The sound had seemed too far away for that, unless

the creature was an enormous one. It hadn't sounded very big
—a lithe movement, like a leopard or a hunter.

I stood staring back. If I moved, it would follow me. In
the darkness I couldn't move without using the phosphorus
ball—not over such ground. Yet, if I used the ball again, I
should be visible to it. It could come at me in any way it liked,
while remaining itself in the darkness.

I must go forward. I could not remain there, standing. I
must risk a light, but, if I were to use one now, it had better
be a big candle. That would, at least, throw a bigger circle of
light—clearer light too.

There was not the slightest sound now.

I felt in my knapsack for the candles, then remembered that
they weren't there. They were in the bag of serpent-skin they
had hung over my left shoulder. I took one out. My mind was
getting clear and concentrated now. The confusion that had
been hanging over it, since I had met my father, was going.

The creature behind was remaining perfectly still. Probably
it could see me in the darkness, but there was no gleam of
eyes. Perhaps it was only a snake that had slithered into a
hole, after it had been disturbed by my passage.

I began to breathe more freely. I stooped down and struck
the head of the candle against the rock. It flashed, burst into
flame.

I lifted it. I was on the side of a rocky slope with clefts between the flags. Below, to the left, it was flatter, as if there
had once been a road. I had wandered off the road in the darkness. I had been thinking of other things, instead of concentrating on my task.

There was still no sound behind me. It was almost certainly
a snake. What could a hunting creature be doing up in this
rocky slope?

I scrambled down the slope. Yes, that was the path again,
or something that looked like a path, as if men had once come

and gone a great deal over the rock. If I could follow it and keep my mind clear, it looked as if I might get to some exit. It must lead somewhere. But my mind was not yet clear, not as clear as I had thought. It was strange that it should be so clouded now, the first time that I was free and knew everything, with nothing to confuse me—everything settled, the upward road in front of me, and a sort of path to follow. Before, I had been going nowhere. Now, two or three days might bring me home, out to where there *were* days. If only I could keep my mind clear. . . . The confusion that was clinging to it was not coming from excitement. It couldn't be.

I was quite calm in other ways, much calmer than I had been before. Strange that I should be getting so confused in my mind.

I stopped dead. That was certainly a sound behind me, like a man falling and recovering himself. There could be no doubt.

I lifted the torch high over my head and stared back into the darkness. It must be a man. No beast would have fallen like that, or got up with that sound of a man recovering himself.

A man! It could be only a man, and, if it was a man, it could be only one man.

I stood tense. *HE* was following me!

He had been pulled off me by the others. Now he was following me. If it was that man, he was coming to wring my knowledge out of me, without anyone to hold him back this time—trailing me, to spring on me in the darkness. . . .

I stood waiting. I was an easy mark for an arrow, standing there with my flaming candle, but that would not suit him. It wasn't my death he wanted—not till he had used me.

I had no doubts now. The bleak, rocky slopes were alive with him. I felt the air pulsating with him. But he wasn't coming on. . . . He was lurking, waiting. He would follow me until I dropped. Then he would be on top of me, with nobody to pull him off, until he got me or I died.

I mustn't fall. I must go on very slowly and steadily, and not fall or wear myself out. He might fall first, if his hatred didn't make him stronger. He meant to get back to the sunlight. I was necessary to him for that. Not necessary in the way I had intended to be, but the other way.

He could not come back to the earth, if he could not bring the others with him. Return would be meaningless to him, unless he brought Rome back to the sunlight. I was necessary to him for that. He could not afford to kill me. What he wanted was to tear my will out, seize me, then make his spring back to upper earth from my knowledge.

He wasn't like those others, willing to stay below, knowing nothing of their loss. He knew of it—of the robbery of their heritage by the barbarians. That was why he was disobeying them, breaking away from their intentions. He knew, better than they did, that I alone could enable them to get back.

After his recovery from the fall he had made no sound. If he had, I should have heard it. But his hatred of me and his greed for me were betraying him. They were coming in waves to me.

I turned and went forward. I had been so sure, a short time before, that I was free. After all my experience, I should have known that it couldn't be true. No day could come out of that night. If he got me, he would absorb me this time. He knew that. He had broken something in me that had been standing upright until I saw him, using my father's eyes to look at me with hatred. My will had held then, but now it would not hold. It had fallen apart, collapsed. If I fell now, he would get me.

I went on slowly, cautiously. I could rush back at him, toss the candle up into the air and then shoot as he stood revealed. He would not be expecting that. Then he would never get up again to the world above.

No. That wasn't what I was thinking. My mind was getting

confused again. Was he working on it, sending out waves of hypnotic suggestion to cloud and blindfold it?

I cleared my mind with an effort. It was probable that he was working on it. I must keep it clear. There was no use thinking of shooting at him. I couldn't get myself to do that. Not now. Later on, perhaps, I might have to do it, if he drove me to it. He would not attack me for the present. He would merely trail me, try to hypnotise me, wait for a fall to lame me, for fatigue to wear me down. I must hurry upwards, but carefully.

The path was beginning to trend downwards to the left. Down there, dim sparse lights like fungus-gleams were showing. It was getting clear beyond the light of the candle.

The magnetic rays were beginning above me.

I looked back. He wasn't visible yet, but he would soon be. Should I give him the choice of going back or being shot at? When the lights above were full, it might be safer to do that and force him to take his choice. Otherwise, if an accident happened to me, he would get me.

The path was going down. I stood staring at it. I did not want to go down. It was dangerous to leave the path, but I felt that I couldn't get myself to go downward again. It would be almost a physical impossibility. Besides, I didn't know where the path led to. Already I had climbed a good distance upwards. I hadn't noticed that I had got so high, I had been so occupied thinking; but now, with the light showing, I could see how high I had got. Down below, quite far below, I could see the lands I had left. We must have been climbing hard, he and I. We must be miles nearer home. I could not go down again.

The landscape round me was now quite clear. Those lights that the path led towards—that was a wooded valley with fungus-trees. In front of me, the rock-slopes had trailing vegetation. They led upwards towards dark masses, with lights that must be woods of phosphorescent trees.

I must be back in the forest-land that went high up, beyond

the other great cliff, the first one down which I had come. If I kept on, I might come to that cliff.

But where was the big river, the salt river that came from the sea on the earth and made the Central Sea below? It must be somewhere down there on the left, or perhaps under the mountains over which I was travelling. It had brought me through a tunnel under the mountains, and they had been wooded like these. But I could not make use of it now, as I did on my journey downwards. It was going in the wrong direction. No use going down towards it, even if I were sure that it was there. I should merely get into swamps infested by snakes. I must keep to the heights.

I looked round. He was not visible.

I turned my face to the mountain-slopes and went upwards.

My mind swung back to him again. What should I do? I could not afford to go on with pretence any longer. I should have to face the situation sooner or later. Should I, or should I not, kill my father? No use going on with any self-deception about its not being my father. It was useful in the beginning, to put between me and that first shock—when he struck at me— cotton-wool-lint, to keep the wound from hurting too much. I couldn't have stood it then, without that pretence that it was another man that hated me, struck me down. But it was no use now. I couldn't get any more good out of it. It was too highly dangerous. I should have to make my choice soon between killing him or allowing him to seize me. The man was mad, but he was my father. The person who was following me had always been there, inside my father's skin. He had always been there, making him different from himself at times, even in the old days—a double personality, not like my mother.

What was that they had said below? That their fathers had thought that a bundle of intimacies was a personality—a heap of differences and little intimacies. That was the man I had known—the bundle of intimacies stuck round the surface. The other man had been inside all the time, hard and merciless and empty, except for one idea. Now they had stripped away the bundle of little charming ways that was the other, and the inner man was there alone, bare and merciless and empty. Not like my mother. When she had been stripped of all the outer things, that were often such a worry to us, she had been deep and full.

My mind was wandering again; not confused perhaps, but wandering away from the work in hand. What I wanted to get clear was that it *was* my father who was there all the time, only now he was stripped bare. The man that was pursuing me was my father—not any other. I couldn't offer him the choice between going back or being killed. I could not bluff him with that threat. I had known it myself all the time, while I was pretending that I could give him that choice. I had better give up such thoughts now. He would know it, and *he* was not pretending, not any longer. No little intimacies or weaknesses about him now. He was stripped to the bone, naked and empty, except for his one idea.

He couldn't kill me, any more than I could kill him, not only because he couldn't get my knowledge if he killed me— there was that too—but he wouldn't kill me in any case. What he wanted was to drag me down to where he was—to justify himself for his betrayal of everybody and everything. Because of that he wouldn't let me get back, when he had robbed me of my knowledge. That was coming to me from him, coming clearly to me from behind. He was threatening me, bullying me, trying to frighten me into confusion, as I had thought of frightening him.

The rock-slopes were gone, hidden away under the ground vegetation. I was working through undergrowth now, up a wooded slope. It would not be so easy to follow me, now that I had no light in my hand, but *he* would be able to do it. He would be sure, like a dog or a leopard.

There was a steady drip from the trees. Queer! A drip from above!

I turned my face up. Yes, a drizzle of rain! Rain! Where
had I got to? I couldn't have got out above—not yet—not
for a long time yet, though I was very high up already. Yet it
was rain—a drizzle.

That was why there was so much vegetation up here on the
heights . . . because it rained. But there couldn't be rain without clouds.

Then I knew. By the time the leakage through the earth
reached this depth in its fall it had become a spray, a mist.
But we were getting up.

"We" were getting up. Yes, I had accepted him. He would
remain with me until he got me. Then "we" would go back.
I would go back obediently. He was sure of that . . . sure that
he could get me, because he had always got me, from the time
I was a small child . . . got me with his lovely little intimacies, that
had withered so early . . . most of them long before "they"
had taken the rest from him. He didn't know how much he
had changed, how much I had changed.

What a fool I had been!

The whole pattern of my life had been shaped by these little
intimacies. My mother, who had cared for him and me, she
had been left outside . . . my own life, that had been left outside too.

But they hadn't absorbed *him* here below. If they had, he
would not be here now, against their orders. . . . They couldn't
absorb *him*. It was *he*, always, who absorbed others . . . my
mother . . . myself. It was not his fault. We had wanted to be
absorbed by him . . . everybody wanted it. He would have
invaded those men below, too, if they had had anything to
give him, but they hadn't. I had—now.

He would preserve me, and bring me back, preserved. Not
absorbed, but preserved, like something in spirits, something
precious taken out of a living thing. He had always owned
me, and I was necessary to him now.

It was curious to think that he could always have done without me until now. If I had been drowned that day in the mill-race, he would have been sorry, but he would have gone on with his Roman Wall. He hadn't needed me then, but now I was precious.

Before, up on the Wall, I had carried things for him—only that—run messages. Intimacies were sometimes necessary to him also. . . .

Could I let him take me back with him? Incredible. . . . I couldn't do that . . . I might have to kill him in the end.

It was well that I was making no more pretences about a son's not being able to kill his father. I would kill him, if I had to do it.

The light above was holding well, and the going was almost as good as on the bare rock. I was getting very high up. Behind me the valley seemed a great distance below, and the ridge I was standing on very high.

Down in front of me was a small valley, then the higher ridge beyond. No hunting brutes either, except the man behind, though there had been moving shapes in the distance under the trees, like shadows. . . .

He wasn't visible, but he would be somewhere behind me, amongst the trees. He would climb presently to the ridge I was standing on, when I had left it. If I climbed into a tree, below in the valley, he might pass on. He could hardly come up the tree after me without my noticing him, and I wanted to sleep.

I wanted badly to sleep . . . not to eat, but to sleep. I must have been a long time climbing . . . a long row of dark times, in between the times that I had been thinking of him——

No. I must not sleep. I couldn't risk it. Suppose *he* was sending me to sleep, using hypnotic suggestion even at that distance! I didn't know his powers. I must push on . . . keep awake.

CHAPTER TWENTY-FOUR

The Man Behind

I WENT DOWN the slope into the valley. It was a shallow one. I should soon be on the other slope.

When I had gone down a little, I slipped behind a tree and waited. He would have to appear on the sky-line, on the ridge. Yes. There he was, creeping over it on his belly, tracking me down. He must still think that I had not seen him. I could send an arrow through him easily.

I turned and went on.

Yes, he had always been a thin soul, empty, bloodless, under all the little charming ways that had made you feel him so warm . . . not like my mother. He had needed sacrifices to keep him warm—my mother—myself—— like all thin souls, he had to fill his emptiness with something, some idea, some stuffing for the emptiness . . . like the people below, the thin people of the darkness. They were right. They couldn't have lived in that emptiness without some big thing stuffed into their souls.

Sacrifices, too. It was strange how these thin, bloodless people were always rushing after sacrifices . . . blood-sacrifices, any sacrifices, of themselves, of others; mimicking the greatest, whose emotion for the sufferings of others was so great that they couldn't endure it—so great that they must end it by the sacrifice, if necessary, of themselves and others to save all.

But these little men had no emotion, except for themselves

and the idea they had blown themselves out with, like the frog, to make themselves big. They wanted sacrifices only to justify themselves.

Now he wanted a blood bath above on the earth, where men were still full of life, chaotic with the sunlight.

Even John Sackett was thick with life, like my mother . . . even Edward, that silent man. John didn't need to fill an emptiness with dreams and megalomanias and blood. If he had gone to the war, it wouldn't have emptied him. It mightn't even have deepened him, any more than it could deepen my mother. But the war hadn't taken him away. He was too useful at home. And he was glad enough to stay at home. He didn't want a war to fill his thick stupid soul.

But there wouldn't be any more sacrifices to fill the man behind me; no more pretences either. I knew it now. If necessary, I would kill him . . . rather than let him lead his monstrous crew back to the upper earth . . . better that one of us should come back to my mother than neither.

Catchwords and sentimentalities were more of the stuffing that little men padded themselves out with. They wouldn't fool me any longer. There was no confusion in my mind now. I had shaken him off my back at last. His waves of hatred could come after me, but they would find no resting-place, nor would his hypnotic tricks . . . neither the new ones he had got now, nor the old ones he had lost in the war.

I was not going to be like that thrush I had seen on the rectory lawn one day—the first of May too—a busy speckled thrush, hopping about on the grass. There had been the stooping shadow and a cry. . . . Only one cry. Then hawk and thrush were resting quietly together for a moment on the lawn, the hawk's talons through the back of the thrush. It was waiting under them, quietly, without any sound, flattened a little to the ground. My shout and my futile stone, that seemed to be weighted with slowness, had broken the tableau.

They had gone up together, quietly and swiftly, the thrush still making no sound, so completely did the sharp talons possess her.

That was the way he intended to bring me back, with talons completely through, this time—curved inside, hooking—and the wings beating above me. He would feed me to his megalomaniac dreams that were born of no pity for the people that lived and died in the darkness. Much he cared for them! No. He would not bring me back that way; dead perhaps, but not alive and hooked.

I had come out on the other side of the valley, and was going up quickly, in spite of the trailers on the ground. The light from above was bright, and the fungus trees more frequent now. The mountain-side was as clear again as in brilliant moonlight.

I switched round rapidly. Yes. He was there, running from one trunk to the other, imagining himself an Indian hunter. He had always played at things, and even now when he wasn't playing, not playing in the slightest, the forms, in which he did things, remained.

But there were other things, too, that weren't playing. What was that shape following him, keeping behind trees too? It wasn't a man or a shadow. A lassoing brute!

The drizzling mist had stopped, and the air was hot—hot and clammy. I still felt sleepy, heavy with sleep, but I was fighting it off.

He wouldn't find it as easy as he had thought, especially now that there were three of us.

Yes. The lassoer was stalking him. Should I shout back and warn him?

My mouth was dry, so dry that I could hardly make a sound. I stopped and pointed backward.

The man had stopped too. At least, I couldn't see him. He was probably behind a tree, watching me, or perhaps watching the great spider. The latter had stopped too, partly hidden behind a tree. We had all stopped.

Ah! That was the whizz of an arrow! I ducked behind a tree, but it was not meant for me. An arrow was quivering in the tree behind which the lassoer had been standing. But he was there no longer, vanished——

A shadow was sweeping through the trees away to the left. . . . Now it was gone. . . .

My father was evidently armed too. That made it easier. I had forgotten that he would be armed. He could shoot as well as I could. Better. . . . It was he who had trained me to shoot with the bow in the old days.

I was thirsty, very thirsty. There was no water, though the ground was damp, but I could chew the pulpy trailers of that ground growth I used to chew so much, when I was looking for my father out in the barren lands. I never thought, then, that he would be looking for me and I trying to get away from him.

The trailing stuff was good—a little sticky but good . . . food as well as drink . . . perhaps some sort of stimulant too. It was rich and juicy, almost like a soft plum, but without any sweetness.

I didn't want to sleep now. The movement of my feet was freer. It eased me, liberated me, to swing upwards with that free easy movement.

I felt more confident in every way. He was armed. So was I. We could deal with each other on equal terms, when it came to that. If he had been trying to send me to sleep, he had failed. I was fresher and stronger now than when I started. He would have to follow me up to the upper earth, if he continued to trail me. Either that or fight.

The steamy heat had gone. It was cooler up here. The air was clean, coming down from above too . . . a little stream of air coming down, making the trees whisper.

Ah! Another lassoer, rather near this time. If I hadn't been climbing with such a swing, like a man that knows his own business, it might have tried to stop me, but, when it saw me so sure and paying no heed, it had let me pass—as a wicked dog does, bluffed, impressed by the confidence of the other animal. If I had felt defeated, it would have come on. . . .

Yes. He was behind still. That patch of open ground had given him away, as I thought it would. Perhaps the lassoer had seen him hunting me down and was tracking us both.

I was not circumscribed by him now. He was only behind me, a line, not a sphere encompassing me, as he had always been before. The line was still dragging at me to come back, but it was getting thin, frayed. The drag was feeble. My reach had gone a long way beyond him. . . .

They had said, below, that rhythms were bad for people when one man's rhythm was forcing the pace of another. They had stopped that. There were some good things they had done. My rhythm had gone wrong, because his rhythm had forced itself on me, during all that long time when he had mattered.

He used to make the paper-boats for me, and sail them, first on the tub we had sunk in the ground for the ducklings, afterwards on the puddles in the road. That was the time when he mattered—when his paper-boats raced down the rocky little streamlet on the side of the road, racketing along, while I ran after them, yelling and shouting. But his face was alive then . . . with little currents in it, and bits of breezes and spots of sunlight, when he was in a merry mood.

It was a pity—this thing that had happened to him . . . all the living things dead in him, even before he came down. It was heart-breaking almost, if you allowed yourself to think about it, even though he wasn't worth so much, inside it all.

If he had suffered anything when he was young—been hurt or left there alone—he might have grown something inside him. But that charm of his never gave him a chance. If it hadn't ended in madness, it would have ended in worse—futility, more charm, a fading away in the end.

I was beginning to get tired again. A giddiness was coming into my head—a dizziness that was making me stagger. If this went on, I should have to kill him after all—to put aside the prejudices men are shaped by, and kill him. Anything else would be madness—suicide, and worse.

When I came home to my mother, and told her that I had killed him, what would she say? I wouldn't tell the others. "Man sentenced to be hanged for the murder of his father." "Parricide under the earth." "Murderer confesses." I could hear the cries.

No, they wouldn't have that. Nobody would know but she and I, and she would understand. I couldn't conceal it from her. She would know that I had done it, if I tried to hide it. But she would understand.

Better that one of us should come back to her than neither. Better that one of us should come back than both, the way he intended us to come! She and all those others seized and murdered in their sleep . . . murdered in their minds or in their bodies.

This dizziness was getting worse. I was almost blinded with it. If it got much worse, I should be at his mercy.

It was time to end this. Yes. He was there, behind that big fungus tree, waiting. Well, I was coming back to him. He wouldn't have to wait long. . . .

Ah! He was running back—running quickly, too! No way out that way.

Now he had stopped, and was watching me standing looking at him.

Yes. Even shooting him down wouldn't be so easy, unless I could hide from him and lie in ambush. But it had to be done somehow. I must get back to a world where there were familiar people, normal people like John Sackett and the

foreman at the works, Carter—yes, that was the name, Ned
Carter—and the parson up at Julian's Pond, who had come
to tell us that my father was gone, and that girl that John
Sackett wanted me to marry, the girl with the short nose and
nice, thick, yellow hair and blue eyes—very blue and bright.

She had given me tea once, alone, and the face had looked
so warm. She had life in her, though she hadn't got through
to me then. She hadn't tried to make me love her, like other
girls who wanted to catch me with my own feelings, tangling
my feet up in a net of them. She had seemed concerned with
her own—a most stable sort of person.

They had all been sure that her love had centred on me,
from the first day I came to Sackett's, long ago during the
war, when I was only a boy at school—as far ago as that. I
was blind then to everybody but this man who was behind me.

If I could go to her now. Perhaps she was having afternoon
tea. It was strange to think that. Tea with hot scones, like
those she had made for me, that day, because the others made
them heavy. If that could only repeat itself—in a few days, a
week, up above these walls that shut me down for eternity ...
me who had been born up there above, not down below, like
those others.

My mind was wandering. I must pull myself together, get
back to the upper earth. How could I ever have left the sunlight, no matter what he dreamed? One "out-by" farmhouse—
"Hope-Alone" or "Seldom-Seen" or "Back-o'-the-Sunset"—
was worth all his kingdoms. One gable, with its life inside it,
warm and thick, or a sail on the sea, or the smell of tar, or the
first green finger of the larch that grew over the Pond. ...

Perhaps it was winter now, and the firelight would be
glancing over the walls of the breakfast-room. The circle of
days and months was still there.

I would be willing to come back to the darkness to die, if
I could get a day up there ... one day from morning till night

—with firelight and the sound of voices. I hadn't said "good-bye" when I was leaving. I hadn't understood anything. If I could say "good-bye," especially if the nests were in the trees . . . the little rookery at the back of the house. . . . I could say "good-bye" in the evening, when the rooks were saying "good-bye" to the day. I could say it with them.

I would come down into the darkness again, if I must, into this ebb without any flow. I would not appeal to God against the darkness, nor to men. This trap of anguish would be bearable for a while afterwards. I could live with Eternity, if I could say "good-bye" to Time.

Even an hour, if I couldn't have a day—an hour in the early morning, or before sunset—it could matter little to anyone to give me that. Then Time could remain in the distance, up above, for ever.

Ah! I was walking with my hands stretched out—out and upwards. I pulled them down with an effort. They felt as if they were nailed above me. I was giving way.

I must deal with the man behind before I gave way.

There were rocks now appearing through the trees. The mountain-side was coming through. At the turning of that rock I should be out of sight for a few minutes. I could hide . . . wait for him there.

I sprang behind it. I was completely out of sight. That tree with its thick heavy leaves . . . that was the place for me. He wouldn't suspect that I was up there.

CHAPTER TWENTY-FIVE

I Find My Father

When I got into the tree above the rock, I saw him at once. He was creeping stealthily from tree to tree, dropping on to the ground where there was no cover, slinking from trunk to trunk. I was giddy—my head reeling. Still I should be able to drop him with an arrow, when he came near enough. I could hardly miss him in the open spaces near me.

I put an arrow to the string. My hand was trembling. I tried to hold it firm. No, I could not do it. I would let him pass and take another road. If he didn't see me, I might stay on in the tree—sleep off this dizziness. . . .

Suddenly I was wide awake, clear in my head. Right under me a lassoer was standing, watching him . . . not merely standing watching . . . drawing back behind a rock. It was waiting.

When the man came, I knew what would happen. The lasso would shoot out like the arms of a polyp. The man would be down before he could draw a weapon. His arms would be pinned to his body . . . his body dragged along the ground at a gallop. He would disappear into a cave in the rock, and there be murdered slowly—his blood sucked out, until he died. Perhaps, a painless death . . . but certainly death. I should be freed of him. I should have some chance of reaching the upper earth, seeing the light, hearing the voices of men. Then I heard myself shouting—yelling out to him to beware. He stopped, staring towards me. At the same moment the lasso came through the air. He sprang aside. It was round his body, but his arm was free. I could see him feeling for a weapon. Then I was climbing down the tree, falling, tumbling down to his rescue. As I sprang down, I kept yelling out, to scare the lassoer.

The man was down. He was being dragged off.

As I reached the ground I heard a loud snarling. It was he. He was up again—a knife in his hands. He had cut the lasso and was rushing at the lassoer. It was standing waiting for him, whirling another lasso. His snarling seemed to be affecting it. For a moment it hesitated, as if held back by the man's rage. The next moment its lasso flew. But it was too late. The pace of the man was too quick. As the lasso fell, the man sprang aside. Then he was upon the creature, plunging his knife into its chest, its head, its body, with snarls of rage. The lassoer fell, screaming.

I turned and ran. The man was a maniac. The thwarting of his plans had driven him completely insane.

As I ran, I could hear the screams of the lassoer dying away into a gurgle. From all sides, whistling cries began in answer.

I stopped. Things were galloping all round me, towards the mêlée. Above their cries, the yells of the man rose in answer. I looked back. He was the centre of a ring of lassoers . . . closing in on him. Now he was rushing at them.

I found myself running back towards them, yelling wildly. As I ran, I loosed an arrow from the string to which I had been holding it taut. Some of the lassoers had turned round to face this new enemy. One of these, struck by my arrow, began to scream and rear up. For a moment, a row of monstrous faces was staring at me. Then, just as I was on them, they broke and fled.

I stopped. The brutes were flying in a mass in front of me. Others were rushing towards the sides. The man was running after the lassoers in front. As I looked, he stood for a moment, loosed his bow from his shoulder, and flung it on the ground. Then he rushed forward after the main body.

He was silent now. So were they. Presently they had all vanished in the dimness of distance.

I stood staring at the place where they had disappeared. Then I turned and hurried away in the opposite direction. I had no doubt now about the man. What little was left of his mind was unhinged. Whether that was caused by the shock of his conflict with me, or of his rage at the thwarting of his plans by the lassoers, the remnant of his reason was certainly gone. No sane man could have acted as he did towards the brutes that had attacked him. His hatred of me had been converted, by their sudden attack, into an insane hatred of them, that had frightened even their ferocious minds, when it was loosed upon them. That storm of hatred had demoralised them. That was the reason of their flight. I had now some vision of the torrent of hatred that would be let loose on me if he came back and caught me.

I hurried on. Suddenly, behind me, the silence was torn by a yell that rose and fell and rose again in a long howling crescendo. Then it was drowned by a tumult of hooting and whistling.

I stopped. The yell rose again, over the din of the other sounds. I began to run in the direction of the cries. The man's voice died away. The hooting ceased. They had closed with him.

I found myself running back through the darkness as fast as I could, crying out to him as I ran. There was no answering cry. Again everything had gone silent.

I stopped, staring forward.

Before me, in the dim light, a ring of lassoers was visible, standing in a sort of half-moon, watching me. What had happened?

I drew my bow, put an arrow to the string, and went towards them.

Then I saw what they were staring at.

In front of them, two of their fellows were crouched over

something. I ran forward, shouting, until I was within bow-shot.

They never moved. I stood and sent a shaft at one of the crouching brutes. He fell, got up again, and rushed aside. The other had lifted his head, and, staring at me, began to swing a lasso. I shot again. He fell.

I rushed forward. The second lassoer rose again, then fell, flailing with his legs. The others gave back.

I ran on. On the ground, the body of a man was lying motionless. The second brute, that had been on top of him, was rolling and screaming beside him. The line of the others was falling back a little. I ran to the man. His throat was cut. A glance showed me that he was dead, but it was my father that was lying there dead—not that other.

I threw myself down beside him. His arms were pinned to his body with lassos. Under his neck a pool of blood was growing.

Yes; it was my father's face, not the face of that other. I was looking into the face I knew so well of old. The eyes were staring back at me with an expression of utter astonishment. It was hard to believe that he was dead.

The line of lassoers had halted about fifty yards away, and now stood facing me in the dim twilight, as if they were trying to understand my actions. The movements of the brute that I had shot were dying away in spasmodic convulsions.

I looked round me. I could see nothing at the sides or the rear.

I had no doubt what would happen. The lassoers were only waiting to see what I would do. If I went forward, they would lasso me at once. If I tried to retreat, they would follow me and lasso me also. Now they were merely waiting for me to show what I was going to do. They had been made cautious by the fate of their comrades, but they would not let me off. In a short time I should be dead.

I looked at the dead man. He had brought me and himself

to this, and now he was beyond all trouble. Those staring eyes
had such an expression of astonishment, and they were my
father's eyes. If I had come up in time, or stayed with him,
I might have saved him.

Had he wakened before he died? If he had, it was dreadful
that the last thing he had seen was those hideous masks. I
might have spoken to him, if I had followed him instead of
running away . . . he might have spoken to me. I had failed
him in the end.

Perhaps even now I could save the body from being dese-
crated by these brutes. I had still a little time left.

I looked at the line of lassoers. No. I had no time left. They
were beginning to close in on me slowly.

There was a fallen tree just in front—a sea-weedy thing
that sprawled across the way between them and me. I went
over and crouched behind it. Then I put an arrow to the
string. The line had stopped its movements again. They were
waiting to see what I was going to do behind the tree.

I was striving to think what I could do with the body
before they got me. Then I remembered my match-candles. I
felt in the bag of serpent-skin. There were some still left, two
at least, if I could get time to use them. The creatures were
still standing. Now one of them was moving forward.

I took careful aim, and loosed the arrow. It struck him in
the middle of the breast. He fell over, screaming. The others
fell back hurriedly. I had two more arrows, and the one that
was stuck in the second brute I had shot. With these I could
keep them off, perhaps, for long enough to do what I wanted
to do.

I took one of the match-candles out of the bag. I needed a
little heap of sticks and dead leaves. They were easy to get,
for they were on the tree—sticks and leaves, withered but
oily. The next thing was to find a stone to strike the candle
on. I couldn't see one near me, the light was so dim. The

line of lassoers had halted again. They were now about eighty
yards away, bunching together, preparing for a rush.

At my back a little air began to move, as if there were an
air-current from above. Then I saw the stone behind me, protruding from the ground. A rock of some sort, nearly covered.
I got up, and moved back to it.

The brutes were coming on again. They thought I was
retreating.

I hurried to the rock, and struck the phosphorus head. It
hung fire, as if it had got damp. They were coming on. I struck
again. It caught. I ran back, shading the flame with my hand.
They stopped. I raced to the tree, and put the flame to the
little heap of sticks and leaves I had made under it. It caught,
and spurted up into a tongue of fire. Then I put an arrow to
my bow and waited.

They were now about thirty yards away, and pushing out
their line into a semicircle, as if to surround me. Suddenly the
flame leaped up. The oily branches of the tree were beginning to burn like candles. The flame was running along the
tree.

As the tongues of fire darted up, the brutes stopped again.
A little wind from behind me was fanning the flames.

I ran back to the body, and began to drag it towards the
tree.

The lassoers stood motionless, watching the flame . . . it
was mounting now, running along the tree, crackling and lick-
ing upwards.

I laid the body across the tree, right in its path. As the
flames lit the eyes, they seemed to stare back at me with that
intense surprise. I had not time to close them.

I drew back. The fire was now beginning to run along the
ground beyond the tree, fanned by the wind. The line of
lassoers began to give way. They stood out clearly in the
light of the flames, that were tossing upward and forward now.

Their line was halting, bunching. They were moving towards the flames, slowly. . . .

Ah! A bunch of them was running towards the fire, with a wave of lassos whirling over them. I stared at the advancing line, an arrow ready on the string.

Were they going to rush through the flames to get me? If they did, I should have no chance against them.

The first line of them was in the flames—springing up, falling, dashing back against the others, screaming. At that moment my father's body began to flame upon its pyre. As the flames tossed upward from it, the screams of the lassoers seemed to make a fitting keening for the body that had bred such dreams.

I thought of that first funeral that my mother and I had given him on the Roman Wall, in the quiet of an English dusk, the pressure of her arm on mine, as the light faded, and the day that had ended one part of our lives died into darkness. Was she still waiting for him, and me, up there above the darkness?

I could scarcely believe that there *could* be such a person, waiting above in the starlight or the sunlight, while here below my father's body burned on its pyre, to the accompaniment of the screams of a horde of creatures more fantastic than those that made the nightmares of my childhood so terrible.

I felt dizzy and sick. My head seemed to be whirling round. The heat was choking me.

I drew farther back from the fire. The current of air was blowing it away from me, but it was now rising into a wave of flame that was rushing to right and left. The heat was getting unbearable. My head was burning.

I turned back. If at any moment the air-current shifted and set in my direction, I should be caught. I began to run—stumbling, panting.

I had escaped. I knew that I ought to be glad of that but I could feel nothing.

The cries of the lassoers were drowned in the roaring of the flames.

The trees were fewer now. The air was fresher. I was gasping, and had to stop running.

I looked back. Down below me the valley seemed to be all catching fire. Beyond, bare mountain peaks began to show in the light. I looked ahead. The trees were very sparse in that direction. I could see that the mountain I was on ran steeply upwards. I started again through the trees. Then they ceased, and I was on bare slopes, with thin trailing vegetation.

My head was still throbbing, but, here above, the air was clearer. Behind me, the country through which I had been travelling showed as a broad wooded valley between the mountain I was climbing and another that rose over against it. I could not see the summit of either. Somewhere, up above there, was the earth roof through which I must penetrate, but there was no way of knowing if any of the peaks joined it, or, even if they did, whether there was an opening through it.

The shock of the fight between my father and the lassoers had cleared my mind for a while, but the confusion was falling on it again.

All those scores of barren peaks that were being revealed in the light of the lake of fire below me, how could I know if any of them led up to the earth surface? . . . Scores and hundreds of peaks, crowding in on me, like vast sums, great rows of figures in gigantic sums of addition or subtraction.

I tried to pull myself together. My mind was wandering. I had escaped from him and from the lassoers. I mustn't let myself die in the darkness. I must keep my mind pulled tightly together.

It was clearer now. I looked round me at the world that the flames were revealing—tumbled barren peaks, deep valleys in between them, on the lower ranges. Here and there a waterfall gleaming in the light of the flames. The sea of flame was rushing downwards and spreading to left and right, so that at every moment new peaks and valleys and waterfalls stood revealed.

I was clear in my mind now . . . I must keep on thinking clearly. There was probably no exit in all that wilderness, and, even if there were, my chances of finding it were not good. But if I kept my mind clear, I might have some chance.

I went on. . . .

Even if the fire were to remain, to light all these barren slopes for me, I should have little chance . . . but it wouldn't remain. Presently the flames would die away. I should be once more in darkness. The thought steadied me, like the touch of a cold finger.

I had been in the darkness before, but now I was going upwards. If I could keep my senses together, I might have a chance. I should probably die, but better die going upwards.

A few minutes ago I had been sure that I should be dead or dying by now, but that danger was past. All the dangers that I had been so much afraid of—the Master of Knowledge, my father, the creatures that had killed him—all these dangers were gone, put behind me. There were no more fearsome things, nothing but the emptiness and the darkness—not even the sea-weedy trees, nor any fear under them.

With the fears, all the hopes were gone too. Emptiness was without, and emptiness inside me . . . and it was getting cold.

The emptiness inside me and the emptiness outside—they were cold. A few minutes ago I had been hot—roasting. Now I was shivering. Too hot still at the top of my head, where the beating pulse was going on—and on. . . .

I must get upward. Now that I had passed the trees, everything was so empty and clear. The mountain peaks looked hard—clear and hard. They were not blurred, like all the things I had been seeing. Things were sharp and clear now once again.

I was quite clear too. I felt no fear, no emotion of any sort. I had exhausted all that. Everything was very clear again, the mountain peaks and my own life . . . all that I had done and left undone. I was not troubled about it. It had been so. That was all. I saw it very clearly, in a great calm.

Perhaps I was mad, like the man that was burning below me. He would be burnt up by now, the eyes and the hatred, or was it astonishment?

There was no more fear. Everything was clear, all barriers down . . . all states the same in my mind. . . .

I might have lived a different life, or I might have given myself up to them below—or stayed with the Sacketts, living with machinery. . . .

Suddenly I began to laugh.

I stopped, then went on again. The face of John Sackett was floating in front of me. But why should I laugh at it? He had always kept rubbing his hands one over the other, when he was trying to get me to marry and settle down beside him and live for the motor-business.

I remembered the first day I had heard John Sackett speak disparagingly of my father. It was in the days before the war, and I had come into the room, unseen, where he and my mother were talking. I had trembled with rage at the outrage, and had gone out to my father, where he was mending a fishing-rod, seated on an upturned box. I had put my arm round his neck—the neck that had been cut across, below, in the burning wood—and he had looked over his shoulder and laughed at me.

I could still feel the roughness of his cheek where I had touched it, and the softness of his neck. His neck had always been soft and full, not like my mother's neck, that had been once. All that meant little to me now. I just remembered it. Perhaps it was he that had followed me up from the Wall, perhaps not. It didn't matter at all . . . not much anyway.

What mattered was to keep my mind clear—keep off this dizziness.

Below, the fire was distant now. Its noises had died away. Silence had come back, like the silence of those men below, who were so fixed and isolated, waiting for death in an eternal calm, without thought or waste, safe, completely safe. . . .

I burst into laughter again. I stood there, laughing, while the tears rolled down my cheeks. John Sackett's balance sheets, his yearly statement of accounts, with the hidden reserves for caution, the hidden reserves—safe too!

I stopped laughing. What was that noise rolling round the rocks, breaking the silence, like loud laughter? Now it was dying away in a series of chuckles. . . .

It was the echo of my own laughter at the thought of John Sackett's hidden reserves in the balance sheet. But there was nothing to laugh at. They were very useful, those hidden reserves. Better be over-cautious, like the men below—the automatons that were saved from all trouble by the Masters of Knowledge.

My father . . . now he was safe too, his madness gone, burnt up . . . everybody was safe.

There was that sound again, up on the heights to my left. I was not making it. It was not an echo, but a sound that was making me feel thirsty. It was water, water that was coming down from the top of the earth.

I was very thirsty. . . .

CHAPTER TWENTY-SIX

And See Green Grass in Fields Again

WHEN I AWOKE from my sleep beside the waterfall, I had no feeling of being refreshed. It was as if I had been in a drugged state rather than asleep, but I was not so dizzy.

The way up from the waterfall was smoother. There were no trees nor any growths under my feet, but I found it heavy on my body to drag my feet upwards. An extraordinary fatigue was clogging my movements.

The air was colder now, much colder . . . a breeze from above. It should have refreshed me, but my body was heavy.

Morsels of thought or memories of my father kept coming to me, as if from the wind that was now coming streaming down—the cold wind from the earth that I had often shared with him, up on the Wall, in those January days . . . the days, even in May sometimes, cold as January . . . before the war.

That May evening when we found the kestrel dead on the Wall, with its ash-coloured plumage and its fixed beautiful eyes . . . he was telling me his dreams. His dreams had come true—dreams vacuous like the eyes of the kestrel . . . but true.

That evening, after we had shown my mother the hawk, he had burned it in a fire in the garden, so that it would not decay and be eaten by the worms. . . . That was the sort of thing he did before the war, though my mother and the Sacketts thought, then, that he was full of faults.

That day that I had first heard her talking about him to

John Sackett . . . but I had thoughts of that before. Afterwards she knew. They had said, that day, that he was a creature of impulses, she and John Sackett—that he was unstable. Life was not a thing of impulses, and it was time that he learned that. I remembered their words.

That evening, when a speck of froth was floating in my soup, I had thought of their words, and looked across the table at my father and smiled. My father hadn't known why I had smiled that evening, but he had smiled back, and we had shut out the Sacketts, who were talking, my mother, and her brother John. Mother had said to me, "You're not eating anything, Anthony," and I had burst out laughing—the unity between my father and myself had been so clear. No use telling John Sackett or my mother.

Afterwards we had gone out to the orchard where the apples and pears were ripening.

Perhaps they were ripening up there again. . . . Or was it too late or too early? The wind from above was very cold. It couldn't be summer up there—unless it was May again, and cold in the evenings. . . .

Up on the Wall the air had always a lovely sharpness, even on the hot summer days. But, when the lights come out in the farmhouses below, it often died down, the sharpness. My father used to say that it was always warmer in the darkness.

Down below, in the darkness, it was warm. But up here, near where the light was, it was shiveringly cold. . . .

I stood looking down. Far below there were red glimmerings, but the peaks had all vanished. But for this dim light above me, all the light was gone.

The way was dim—shelves of rock, with the cold wind coming down along them.

I shouldn't waste the light standing there looking down. I had no time to waste. Up above, not so far up now, men were living . . . very near me now, if I could get up to them. It couldn't be far . . . if I didn't waste time before I got too exhausted. . . .

Up above, the wheels were turning in John Sackett's workshops. He had always said that there was no reason to waste time, and that I shouldn't stay up so late at night when I could work at my inventions, just as well, in the daytime. But he had sometimes come in very late at night himself, and it was not inventions that had kept him up. He said, then, that a man had to give way to a man's needs or he would die of it. It would be better for me, too, if I lived the life of an ordinary man—got drunk and other things—not been like my father, who was only a shadow. John Sackett said that. *He* did not move in a mist of unrealities.

A wave of knowledge came over me, an awareness of all that life. Before now it had only been memory—that house where the Sacketts lived, with its square, three-storeyed front and the stucco over the door, it was as real as the Wall; and the people in the streets—men with bowler hats . . . John Sackett's phrases that my father made such fun of: "I must confess——"; and, "How he could get himself to——"; and, "I may be wrong, but——"

He was so certain of everything, John Sackett, and so clear. I could see his pale blue eyes in front of me, and his blue suit—bright blue, with a tie of the same colour, only a little brighter—and his voice saying: "I must confess——"

That was my father's voice, now, mimicking him: "I must confess——" And my mother's voice protesting. She had always protested before the war . . . not after he came back. She had loved him deeply. Her scoldings were her way of showing it, but now she was patient, waiting above. . . .

"Don't mind me," she had said to me that night—the night he had gone. "Don't mind me. I'm not suffering. He had to do it. I might have been with him more then, as I'm with him now."

It was a strange new knowledge of my mother, that night. She had been the strong one, like a deep sea—not an intelligence nor any of these things.

In one way it had been death to her—real death—but she had passed into another world, out of the surges of the little waves that had troubled her.

The way was getting difficult—very difficult—now that the dim light above was going and the fires below had died down. It was difficult, and it hurt a good deal—some of the falls . . .

If the path hadn't been there—the queer unexpected path from the waterfall—it would be very hard to find a way up this hill, so steep and slippery now, and with the hard edges.

If I could light one of the big candle-matches, I should be able to see.

I was panting, and my heart was bursting, the way was so steep. If I could go on steadily, thinking of other things instead of the black dome of rock overhead that would not let me through when I reached it. . . . It was when I began to think of it that I knew that I was afraid.

I pulled myself together. There was a buzzing in my ears. I could hear something calling out to me. I drew myself up. It could not be possible that anything was calling to me. Perhaps it was only the buzzing in my own head, like the buzzing of a bee. Perhaps it was the stone ledges that were so hard in the dark, and so steep and echoing. My steps were loud on them. I could hear them now, and the echoes of them, though I hadn't heard them before. They seemed to be exaggerated— yes, that was the word, "exaggerated"—the word my father was so fond of using when my mother came in with some story, any story about anything, even the day when I myself had nearly been drowned in the mill-race below the bridge, and for the first time I had seen my mother face my father as an equal.

I felt my mother's hand still as she pressed mine to her

breast that day. She had a rose pinned to her dress—a yellow rose—and she had pressed my hand against its thorns, not knowing.

That was the first day that I had seen her strength—that she was the strong one; that she could work miracles. Now if she were thinking of me, willing me to come back to her . . .

I felt that the power lay with her now, if she were alive . . . and, even if she were dead, she would have strength, not like my father.

She had endured agonies for both of us, while we had gone our way. There was nothing now between her and me that she couldn't break through . . . only a skin of earth.

We had left the trouble to her, but now I was coming back to her. It was she who was calling to me. It must be she.

I was so confused! If she was near me—if I could reach her —I would go down into the depths with her. She wouldn't be alone there, as she had always been. . . .

The wind was very cold, and I was shivering. I was so hot, too, burning . . . and the wind was cold.

I had been down there where it was warm, but I couldn't stay there because their politics were so strange . . . but it was warm there, and they had a peace that was not to be found up above—a suffocating peace. They made their lives to fit them there, like a suit of clothes to measure, not a heap of stuff and patches. . . .

I must stop this wandering thought, pull my thoughts together. . . .

The calling had ceased, but, up above, there were fantastic shapes, as if there were men—men waving lights down at me. . . . I must be raving . . . but I was awake.

If I could hurry on and shake off the raving. . . .

That noise was coming again—the noise of men calling. That was the noise of my own voice answering, calling back to them.

If I could run, I might be able to stop calling out to these phantoms that were calling back to me, coming down at me from above. If there were only light, I shouldn't be afraid. . . . If I could light one of the match-candles that they had given me, but it was on my back, over the knapsack.

Above me, lights were shining . . . lights in the hands of the phantom men in my path.

If I could get past them, up into the earth. . . .

I made a great effort, breaking the things that held me. My heart was bursting . . . flashes piercing the darkness round me . . . everything crashing, bursting. . . .

I was over a gulf . . . falling into the darkness.

.   .   .   .

A voice was saying, from a great distance:

"I didn't think you could do it, Mrs. Julian. He had gone so far. But you have. The fever is gone. Listen to his breathing, smooth, steady. You've done what we couldn't do."

I listened to the voice. It had the labour and the music of life, the coarse deep music of life. I was back in the dark lands again, where voices like that came to me.

How had I got back into the lowlands near the Central Sea? It was only there I had heard voices like that, since I left the earth.

And I was at peace, not taut or tense, but at peace—a soft ebb and flow, ebb and flow, full of sweetness—and there was my mother's voice now.

"I knew, when he came back to me, Doctor, that he wouldn't go away, so soon, again. He must have wanted terribly to come back. He was always like that——"

I knew that if I opened my eyes the voices would be gone. I lay very still, listening. It was strange that there was light above my eyelids. I could feel the light coming through them.

My mother's voice was speaking again:

"If they hadn't heard his cries, Doctor . . . the chances of the huntsman having to follow the dogs down into that old disused mine-pit were so small . . . if God hadn't willed that he should come back to me . . ."

Then the man's voice came again:

"It's not the first time that same fox has escaped through that cave. It's strange that you should call it a mine-pit, Mrs. Julian. You know the country people round here always maintain that it's not really a cave, but a mine—an old Roman mine. They say it goes on miles and miles down into the darkness, and certainly we've lost good hounds down there after that cursed fox. But this time it was a mighty fortunate thing he went to earth there, or else——"

"God answered my prayers, Doctor," came my mother's voice.

"How he got into the mine, or the cave, or whatever it is," came the man's voice, "it's that that beats me. Do you know, Mrs. Julian, that he was so far down that, when they heard the cries first, they didn't know they were the shouts of a man. They thought it was some wild beast crying away down there in the darkness. And you've seen what his kit is like— as if he had been wandering for months or years in a tropical jungle."

"I knew that he would come back, Doctor," came my mother's voice again.

"Those extraordinary candles he had in his knapsack, too," said the man's voice. "And the curious phosphorus balls, and the bag of serpent-skin. Where were these made? Not in England, I'd swear, nor anywhere else that I know of. The whole thing beats me. And how did he get down here to Yorkshire?"

A woman was laughing softly. It was my mother's laugh. I was dead, but my soul was with my mother.

"Anthony?" came her voice softly over my eyes. "Anthony, can you hear me?"

I opened my eyes slowly. She held them with her own, flooding me with the healing sweetness of her look. I thought of those other eyes, and suddenly I was shivering. Then her arms went round me, holding me in their warm security. She was speaking:

"God has brought you back to me, my son."

Her arms tightened round me.

"Yes, mother," I said.

THE END

Joseph O'Neill (1878–1952)

Joseph O'Neill was an Irish educationist and author. He worked as the Permanent Secretary to the Department of Education, Irish Free State, between 1923 and 1944. Although not strictly an SF writer, O'Neill used SF instruments to make cultural and political points with great eloquence. *Land Under England* (1935), about an underground world where citizens are controlled by telepathy, is a satire on Hitlerian totalitarianism.